One Week
to the
Wedding

ALSO BY OLIVIA MILES:

Mistletoe on Main Street

A Match Made on Main Street

Hope Springs on Main Street

Love Blooms on Main Street

Christmas Comes to Main Street

One Week
to the
Wedding

OLIVIA MILES

FOREVER

New York   Boston

Copyright © 2017 by Megan Leavell
Excerpt from *The Winter Wedding Plan* © 2017 by Megan Leavell

Cover design by Brian Lemus. Cover photography © Rebekah Westover. Cover copyright © 2017 by Hachette Book Group, Inc.

Forever
Hachette Book Group
1290 Avenue of the Americas, New York, NY 10104
forever-romance.com
twitter.com/foreverromance

First Edition: June 2017

Forever is an imprint of Grand Central Publishing. The Forever name and logo are trademarks of Hachette Book Group, Inc.

The publisher is not responsible for websites (or their content) that are not owned by the publisher.

The Hachette Speakers Bureau provides a wide range of authors for speaking events. To find out more, go to www.hachettespeakersbureau.com or call (866) 376-6591.

Library of Congress Cataloging-in-Publication Data

Names: Miles, Olivia, author.
Title: One week to the wedding : a women's fiction novel / Olivia Miles.
Description: First edition. | New York : Forever, 2017. | Series: Misty Point ; 1
Identifiers: LCCN 2017003011| ISBN 9781455567225 (softcover) | ISBN 9781455567218 (ebook)
Subjects: LCSH: Man-woman relationships--Fiction. | Weddings--Fiction. | BISAC: FICTION / Contemporary Women. | FICTION / Family Life. | FICTION / Romance / Contemporary. | FICTION / Romance / General. | FICTION / General. | GSAFD: Love stories.
Classification: LCC PS3613.I53223 O54 2017 | DDC 813/.6--dc23 LC record available at https://lccn.loc.gov/2017003011

ISBNs: 978-1-4555-6722-5 (trade pbk.), 978-1-4555-6721-8 (ebook)

Printed in the United States of America

LSC-C

10 9 8 7 6 5 4 3 2 1

To Avery

Acknowledgments

Thank you to my editor, Michele Bidelspach, for believing in my characters and storytelling and giving me the amazing opportunity to branch out into women's fiction.

To my agent, Paige Wheeler, thank you for the endless support and invaluable advice.

Thank you to my copyeditor, Lori Paximadis; my production editor, Carolyn Kurek; and everyone at Grand Central who has a hand in polishing my books and making them shine.

And thank you, as always, to my readers.

One Week
to the
Wedding

Chapter One

⁓⁓⁓⁓

If there was one part of her job that wedding planner Kate Daniels struggled with most these days, it was the dress fitting. She used to enjoy these appointments, finding it a true perk to sit in a beautiful, sun-filled boutique, surrounded by breathtaking gowns made of satin, lace, or tulle. What wasn't to love other than the occasional meltdown of a bride who hadn't had much success with that crash diet, or the long, patience-testing afternoon spent with a bride who tried on every dress in the store—twice—and still couldn't make a decision? The wedding dress was the focal point of the entire ceremony, a symbol of hope and happiness and dreams that had finally come true.

Except not all dreams come true, Kate thought as she wrestled with the overstuffed silk pillow wedged behind her back. Her stomach roiled with bad memories, and she tried to stay focused on the reason she was here at all. Her best friend was getting married. She could have a good cry about her own misfortune when she went home, and if recent history proved anything, she probably would. But right now she would hold herself together, show her support, and not let her self-pity taint what should be a very special moment.

"Do you need any help?" she called out. It would be easier to make herself useful, assist with a zipper or buttons or a train. Anything would be better than sitting on this too-stiff velvet love seat, trying not to let her gaze drift too far to the left, where another bride was trying on the very dress Kate had chosen for herself not so long ago, her girlfriends fawning over her selection.

"I'm fine. I just... Well, let's see what you think." Elizabeth stepped out from behind the pink satin curtain of the dressing room wearing the classic strapless ivory ball gown she'd selected months back when William first popped the question to her, and despite the ache in her chest, Kate couldn't help but smile.

"You look stunning," she whispered. She had known Elizabeth since they were five years old and placed next to each other in Ms. Richardson's kindergarten class, bonding over their love of Barbie dolls and their mutual affection for Ken. She had been there every step of the way that had led to this day. How many summer afternoons had been spent twirling in their mothers' lingerie, clutching dandelion bouquets, Elizabeth's reluctant younger brother bribed with candy into playing the groom, even though he always took off across the lawn before the vows were complete.

Elizabeth turned uncertainly in the gilded three-way mirror that anchored the small store. "I was planning on wearing my grandmother's pearls, but now I think a necklace might be too much."

Kate nodded her head in agreement. "They're too formal for a beach ceremony. Besides, the gown speaks for itself." And it did. Some ball gowns could be heavy or overly formal, but this one gave just enough of a nod to the bride's classic style while still feeling summery and light. With its low back and subtle details near the waistline, it was perfectly pretty; there was no other word for it.

"I think you're right." Elizabeth scrutinized herself in the mirror and released a nervous breath. "I just want everything to be perfect."

Kate smiled tightly. Every bride said the same thing. She'd said it herself at one time not so long ago.

She frowned. It felt like a lifetime ago. In fact, it felt like another person altogether. Some strange alternate reality where she was the blushing bride pondering menus and color schemes and the band list. Now she was back to doing it for other people.

"It *will* be perfect," Kate said, standing up to fluff the back of the dress. "I'm seeing to it myself."

"You know why I'm so nervous, don't you?" Elizabeth turned to face her properly, her eyes clouding over as her mouth thinned.

Kate squeezed her friend's shoulder, saying nothing. Elizabeth was still recovering from her first and only meeting with William's family, which hadn't gone very well. It had been a bit of a disaster, really, not that Kate would be saying that today. No need to bother with the wedding just a few days away!

"I'm sure it will be different this time," she assured her, even though she wasn't so sure about that. "They were probably just surprised is all. You and William hadn't dated very long," she pointed out, not that an engagement after six months was entirely unheard of, though it was quick. Six months to plan a wedding on the other hand . . . that was rushing it a bit, if anyone asked her.

"I'm just worried that they'll come to town and make trouble. Especially William's brother." Elizabeth gave her a long look.

Every wedding Kate planned had some element of familial tension, and in this case, the source was rooted with the best man. Oh, she'd dealt with her share of unruly wedding party members—groomsmen who hit the bar a little too hard during the cocktail hour, bridesmaids throwing hissy fits over their ugly dresses, mothers-in-law showing up in white—and Alec Montgomery was no different, really. Though she hadn't met him yet, she knew enough about him to know that he'd show up and play the role as dutiful brother. He and William were close, after all. And society weddings didn't leave room for public outburst or noticeable drama.

No, that was usually left behind the scenes, she thought, chuckling to herself when she considered all she heard and saw.

She checked the row of satin-covered buttons on the back of the gown, making sure none were loose. "You'll be so caught up in the excitement of the day, you won't even notice he's there," Kate assured her, knowing this was true. People claimed they barely remembered their wedding days, that it was all a blur. That it was too surreal to capture. Too overwhelming in its emotion.

Kate released a soft sigh. Not that she would know firsthand. "I emailed with him a few times about the rehearsal dinner. He was very laid-back about the whole thing."

"Probably because he was too busy to care," Elizabeth said. She shook her head as she stared at herself in the mirror. "I'm still amazed he even agreed to come to town for the bachelor party tonight, what with how glued to that office he is."

"Well, it's a Saturday," Kate said.

Elizabeth turned to face her. "So? That man works seven days a week. William used to, too." Elizabeth tutted as she took her veil from the sales associate and set it on her head. "I know I sound dramatic, or like some anxious bride, but I'm nervous, Kate. He really doesn't like me, I can tell. It's like I'm not good enough for him, or something. It's hard enough knowing your new family doesn't like you, but given how he disapproves of William marrying me or, should I say, marrying into my average American family, I wouldn't put anything past him."

If it were any other bride, she'd chalk it up to high emotions, but Elizabeth was levelheaded and not prone to exaggeration. When she'd come back from Boston, weeping into her Chardonnay and recounted the chilly reception she'd received from William's father and brother, Kate had known that there was no drama or enhanced details for the sake of telling a better story. Kate had seen the red flags then, braced herself for a time when William might call the whole thing off, but time moved forward and now she didn't see that happening. William adored Elizabeth and their life in Misty Point. There was no reason to project her own disappointment onto her friend's situation, even if there were some unsettling parallels.

"You've been watching too many of those reality shows again," Kate said now, and a sharp pain hit her at the thought of their beloved weekly tradition of wine and bad television and endless laughter. They'd been doing that in some shape or form all their lives, really. It was soap operas and pints of ice cream as teenagers—two spoons, no bowls—and later coffee and tabloid magazines. Once they hit their twenties, and even lived together for a brief time after college, it was wine and dating shows.

Would that tradition end now that Elizabeth was getting married? Maybe not right away, but eventually...Elizabeth and William would want to start a family. They'd find other couples to hang out with. And Kate was single. Again. Maybe indefinitely. After all, there'd only been one real boyfriend in her entire life, and the whole town knew how that had ended.

"If you're referring to the season where Tiana, who was kicked off in episode one and had to be removed by ambulance for her hysteria, returned for the final flower ceremony and hovered ominously in the background, hiding behind a rosebush, then, okay, maybe I have been a tiny bit swayed." Elizabeth laughed, but she soon frowned again. "I mean it, Kate. I'm worried. I can't stop thinking about the way Alec just stared at me through that entire dinner. He doesn't like me."

"Well, you're not going to be best friends. It's more common than you think." Kate laughed nervously, wishing she could better disguise her growing alarm. There was no way that anything or anyone could upset this wedding. If that happened, Elizabeth wouldn't be the only one in tears on Saturday. Kate would be crying all the way to the unemployment line. "It will be the happiest day of your life. I promise."

Elizabeth looked unconvinced. "If you say so."

"I do say so." If she had any control over it, at least one of them would have the wedding day that she deserved. Kate turned her friend's shoulders to face the mirror, admiring their reflection. "I still can't believe you're getting married," she said, feeling that tug in her chest again.

"Me neither," Elizabeth said, her tone laced with wonder. Kate recognized the sound of it—the disbelief that all your dreams could actually be coming true. That years of hoping and waiting were over. That you could be so lucky. That your entire future was decided, and bright.

It echoed the emotion Kate had felt once. She blinked quickly, then smoothed Elizabeth's veil, trying to not think about everything that had happened instead.

An hour later, Kate triumphantly scratched the final dress fitting from her to-do list and said goodbye to Elizabeth, waving cheerfully from her perch on the cobblestone steps outside the bridal salon. She held her smile until her friend was safely out of sight and then fell back against the wrought-iron railing with a frown. For months she had obsessed over every detail of this wedding—right down to spending an excruciating amount of time holding various invitation samples to the light to determine the closest shade of pink to the bridesmaid's gowns—but not everything, she knew, could be controlled. An inebriated guest, she could handle. A sniffling flower girl, sure. But a stubborn man who didn't support the wedding? He'd require a tight leash.

And that was why she, as best friend, maid of honor, and wedding planner extraordinaire, was going to personally greet him upon arrival.

But first, she had a haunted house to visit.

★ ★ ★

Bree was sitting behind the counter of Rose in Bloom when Kate reached the end of Harbor Street, the main drag in their small Rhode Island town. Even before her fingers could reach for the handle, she watched as her cousin shot up off her stool and darted to greet her.

"Thank God you could make it," Bree gushed, fumbling to turn the sign on the door to CLOSED.

"That's what cousins are for," Kate said with a smile.

"Well, I still can't thank you enough. The thought of going into that house. Alone." Bree shuddered as she turned the key on the shop door and dropped it back into the pocket of the denim jacket she wore every day from April through September. Even in the flower shop she owned and operated, she was rarely without it, claiming the refrigeration made her cold.

Now, though, the shivering had nothing to do with the warm summer afternoon temperature and everything to do with Bree's paternal grandmother's house.

"What are we checking on this time?" Kate asked as they walked down the block to Bree's station wagon, a modern one, but still a purchase solely made for the sake of her flower deliveries.

"It's not supposed to rain, at least not according to the five-day forecast," Bree explained.

Kate climbed into the passenger seat. She could only hope that the weather held up until at least next Saturday. A hurricane could hit Sunday for all she cared. But for Elizabeth's big day, the sun had to shine.

"I need to air the place out for a bit."

"Does that mean in a few days you'll be calling on me for a favor again?" Kate asked.

Bree gave her a pleading look. Even though she was older by a year, she had always looked up to Kate. And Kate had taken her under her wing, welcomed her into the fold, away from her brother and strictly boy cousins on Bree's other side of the family. A rowdy lot from which Bree clearly needed saving.

Kate laughed. "Fine. You know I'm always here for you when you need me."

Bree gave her a small smile. "And you know I'm always here for you, too."

Kate looked away before she turned emotional. Bree, like Elizabeth, had always been there for her. And that was why today, her first Saturday off in more than a month, Kate was choosing to help both of them out rather than grab her towel and hit the beach.

Rose Callahan's house was not far from the center of town, but too far to walk. Still, they arrived within minutes and, as usual, sat in the driveway with the talk radio that Bree preferred filling the car.

Finally, because time was a tickin', Kate said, "So, ready to go in?"

Bree drew a long breath. "I wish I didn't have to."

"But it's your house!" Kate exclaimed. She looked up at the beautiful Colonial, not quite old enough to be registered with the historical society, but full of history and charm all the same. Rose had kept the house impeccable, right up until the time of her death last fall.

Grumbling something under her breath, Bree released her seat belt and popped the handle on the car door. Kate hurried to catch up with her, knowing there was little sense in running in her heels, considering that Bree wouldn't cross that threshold on her own.

Her cousin took her time fishing around in her handbag for the key, still kept on a crocheted ring most likely made by Rose herself. They'd discussed the fact that she couldn't bear to put the key on her regular keychain just yet, back at the visit where they had to hurry over on a particular cold winter day to make sure no pipes had frozen and burst or anything else catastrophic that came with a mostly abandoned house.

"Have you thought any more about moving in?" Kate asked as she stared down at the half-dead perennials in the planters that anchored the front door.

"No. I can't do that!"

"Because it would upset your cousins?" It had been a sticky situation, of course, when Bree, the only granddaughter of a woman who had borne six sons and never a daughter, was given not just the flower shop but also this house.

Bree said you could hear a pin drop in the room. If ever the boys had managed to convince themselves that somehow Rose wasn't the favorite grandchild, the reading of the will was bitter confirmation of pecking order.

"Oh, they're over it now," Bree said tersely, leading Kate to think they were no closer than they'd been last Christmas, when apparently every Callahan had snubbed her vegetarian contribution of a butternut squash side dish.

Bree wrestled with the key and finally managed to jimmy open the door. "This thing is solid wood," she said, giving it a sound knock. "Swells in the heat!"

"They don't make them like that anymore," Kate agreed, wondering if her own door was solid wood. She hadn't considered it before—she'd simply fallen in love with the sunny front room and back stone patio—but now she had the sudden urge to check.

Maybe this was her problem. She didn't inspect things closely enough...at least not when it came to matters of the heart.

They wandered into the hall, which remained intact, exactly as it had been the morning of Rose's fatal stroke. Even her handbag still sat perched on the console, its zipper open, as if at any moment Rose herself would come around from the kitchen, wiping her hands on her apron, to riffle through it for a stick of gum.

Kate would never admit it to Rose, but she wasn't exactly comfortable in this house. Not when it was like this—frozen in time. No wonder Bree was too freaked out to deal with it herself.

Bree marched into the living room and wrestled with the window, finally managing to crack it a few inches. Without pausing, she marched back into the hall, brushed past Kate, and disappeared into the kitchen. From the sound of her grunting, the back windows were just as challenging.

"It really is a beautiful house," Kate said, admiring the built-in shelves that framed the fireplace. "But I understand it would be hard to move in, with all the memories..."

That handbag! She had to stop staring at it! Was it open on purpose? Was Rose coming or going?

Just stop thinking about it, Kate.

"I can't move in here," Bree said firmly as she appeared in the hall again. She turned into the dining room and threw back the curtains.

"Of course. It's hard to let go—"

"If I move in here, then what kind of message would that send to Simon?" Bree demanded, officially silencing Kate.

Kate stared at her cousin, hoping she wasn't hearing what she thought she was hearing. Did Bree actually think that she and Simon had...a future?

"I think that would send a message to him that you are a smart, independent woman," she said carefully.

But was that what Simon was looking for? Of course not! Simon was looking for a sweet, easygoing girl who went along with whatever he wanted, no questions asked. And unfortunately for her, Bree was currently that girl.

"I recently bought a house," Kate pointed out.

"Yes, but you've given up."

"I have not!" Kate blinked at the wall. Had she? Sure, she hadn't gone on any dates in a year, but that wasn't the same as giving up. She was busy. With other things.

Better things.

Christ. Maybe she had given up.

Bree shot her a pointed look. "He'll never propose if he thinks I've made commitments that don't include him."

Kate pressed a finger to her forehead. There was a lot she could say in response to that, but she decided to pick her battle. "But you own this house. Outright. Why continue to pay rent when you could live here for free?"

Bree hesitated, but only for a moment. She shook her head as she flicked the metal latch on the window and reached for the handles. "I don't think it sends the right message. Simon and I have been dating for almost a year. Now isn't the time to do anything that would mess up our plans."

"Oh." Kate hadn't realized that things had become serious with Bree and Simon. Last she knew, Simon had still refused to spend a Friday night with her cousin because that was "guys' night."

Bree set her hands on her hips. She was slightly out of breath. "I just . . . I just need to tread lightly."

Kate counted to three, willing herself not to overstep. She could tell Bree that it was obvious that Simon was not thinking of rings or white weddings, but then she'd just be accused of being bitter. And maybe she was. Maybe Simon was a wonderful, devoted, adoring boyfriend worthy of her cousin's affection.

And maybe the sun was blue.

"Are you seeing Simon tonight? Before the bachelorette party, I mean?" It was Saturday, but the festivities didn't start until seven thirty.

"It's his bowling league tonight," Bree said, frowning. "He's there all day."

Ah, right. His Saturday activity. Co-ed league. Bree wasn't invited. "Team only" was the excuse.

Kate opened her mouth to give a heavy dose of tough love and then shut it again. Some lessons just had to be learned the hard way. After all, hadn't she overlooked the warning signs with Jake? The wandering eye, the disapproving family, the way they had drifted further and further apart at a time when they should have been coming together, planning their wedding?

Right. No more thinking about that. It was time to focus on the present. Not the past. "Well, I'll help you with the upstairs windows, but then I have to get back to town. Elizabeth's future brother-in-law is arriving for the bachelor party tonight, and I want to go over a few things with him beforehand."

"The best man?" Bree's eyes lit up. "Is he cute?"

"Why? Are you thinking of breaking up with Simon?" Kate asked hopefully.

Bree frowned. "Of course not! I was thinking of you."

"Ha." Kate shook her head as she reached for the banister rail. "I have enough to worry about without romance complicating matters."

Chapter Two

It was a warm June day, and the downtown streets of Misty Point were filled with tourists milling around, browsing boutiques and antique shops and lining up at the ice cream parlor. Kate made a mental note to pick up a fresh mystery novel at the bookstore before heading home. These days they filled her spare time just fine—plenty of excitement but all the drama neatly resolved by the last page. And no romance. Definitely no romance.

A wave of salty sea air accompanied her as she tapped along the cobblestone road to the Beacon Inn. She'd personally seen to the out-of-town guest room reservations, and she knew the arrival times of the entire wedding party throughout the week. She couldn't fight the satisfied smile that played at her lips when she reflected on her diligence. It was because of her attention to detail that she knew the best man was arriving from Boston this afternoon for the bachelor party, checking out tomorrow, and returning Friday with William's father for the rehearsal dinner.

Take that, Meredith.

She knew what her boss thought of her these days. Meredith

Smith had a comment for everything Kate did wrong lately but never anything she did correctly. Not long ago, Kate was a rising star at Bride by Design, and she was determined to remind herself—and her boss—that she still had what it took to succeed in this business.

And this wedding was her chance to prove just that. After all, the Montgomery name was a big one in Boston. She planned to submit photos from the event to a bridal magazine.

The Beacon Inn was an icon in Misty Point and the perfect introduction to their quaint Rhode Island beach town. Kate was confident that guests traveling from all over the country would be impressed with the panoramic Atlantic views and the sweeping front porch dotted with white rocking chairs. Hotel guests relaxed on deck chairs looking out at the iconic Misty Point Lighthouse or played croquet on lush green grass that stretched to the sea, where the waves silently lapped at the white sand. Seeing it now, Kate felt her heart swell with hope in place of nerves. This was going to be the most beautiful wedding she had ever planned. There was absolutely nothing for her or Elizabeth to worry about.

Still... better safe than sorry. She pushed through the large front door and stepped into the expansive lobby, helping herself to a piece of saltwater taffy at the front desk. A quick conversation confirmed that Alec Montgomery had not yet checked in, and with a lingering glance around the room, Kate marched back out onto the veranda and settled into a rocking chair. It creaked beneath her on the sand-worn floorboards.

With any luck, Alec would have a few minutes to spare to go over some details for the rehearsal dinner. She'd use it as her reason for being here.

Kate checked her watch and bit down on her lip. She hadn't the faintest clue what Alec even looked like, having only his brother's dark looks and the less-than-flattering stories she'd heard from Elizabeth to go from.

Frowning, she knit her brow and riffled through her bag for her notebook. In large, loopy scroll she wrote Alec's name and propped it against her bare knees, feeling all at once silly and paranoid.

"Excuse me?"

Kate jumped in her chair and lifted her chin to face the owner of the voice. Her pulse began a slow and steady drum as she stared at the man before her. With rich brown hair that curled ever so slightly, Alec was a good two inches taller than his brother, but there was little doubt to their relation.

"Alec Montgomery?" As if that wasn't glaringly obvious.

Alec's dark eyes crinkled with confusion as he scanned her face. The corners of his mouth curved upward into a surprisingly friendly smile that made Kate feel nothing short of ridiculous for being so wary of his motives. "I'm afraid you have me at an advantage. You are?"

"I'm Kate Daniels," she said, realizing that probably wasn't enough explanation. "The wedding planner."

"Ah yes. We exchanged a few emails about the bachelor party." He gave her hand a firm, well-practiced shake. It was hot outside, and even the sea breeze did little to break the heat. She had the unnerving sensation that her hand was a little slick.

He pointed to the sign. "It's nice to know someone's thinking of me." And then, so quick she couldn't even be sure she caught it correctly, he winked.

Wait. Was he *flirting* with her?

No. Men didn't flirt with her. She was too serious, always had been. Even Jake had worked hard to break the ice that first time they'd met. Claimed she made him work for it. That he loved a challenge.

Her lips thinned. Red flag number one. The man loved the thrill of the chase.

She cleared her throat, eager to get back to business. He hadn't winked, she told herself firmly. He probably just had a tic. "I was passing by the hotel and I thought I'd stop by and see if you'd arrived. If the room suited you..." She trailed off with her excuse as she awkwardly thrust the makeshift sign into her bag. Really, she should have just bided her time, checked in occasionally at the front desk, and called up to his room. And she would have done, if she didn't have another hundred things to accomplish in the span of a matter of days, not to mention the bachelorette party that was only a few hours away, which she'd also taken over planning.

The paper crumpled under her awkward movement, and Kate had the uneasy feeling that Alec was watching it all. She pressed her lips together and forced herself to look up at him. Yep. There was a decided gleam in those deep-set eyes. She broke his stare, her eyes roaming over the black canvas backpack thrown over Alec's shoulder and down to the bulging briefcase at his feet. It was time to remember why she was here. "Have they already taken your luggage to your room?" she asked, tilting her head.

"Got everything I need right here." Alec smiled as he patted his backpack, and Kate felt that little pinch between her eyebrows deepen.

"That's all?" She blinked rapidly.

Alec shrugged. "I travel light."

"And it's just one night," she said, reminding herself of his intention to make the seventy-mile drive back to Boston the next evening, something he'd been very clear about in both his emails to her and in his communication with his brother. He'd be back in time for the wedding. That was all she needed to worry about.

"Actually, change of plans," Alec said. "I'm staying the week."

Kate twitched with panic. "I didn't know, or I would have made sure they kept your room available."

"Don't worry," Alec said easily. "I straightened it out."

"Good. Good." Kate nodded. So the best man was sticking around for the entire week, after all. Well, that would certainly put all of Elizabeth's concerns to rest. She was just about to mention that she'd be sure to drop off an itinerary of the week's wedding events when her eyes drifted to that backpack again. There was no way he could have stuffed a suit into that bag. Much less a pair of shoes. The wedding attire would be taken care of, but what was he planning on wearing for the rehearsal dinner?

Her mind raced with the implications of this problem as her eyes latched on to the briefcase sitting quietly at his feet. She could take him shopping, or direct him to a few appropriate stores...but if a man was this helpless when it came to proper clothing, chances were she'd have to guide him through it. If she switched around a few appointments the day after next, she could squeeze it in. She chewed on her thumbnail, trying to think through the tight schedule.

"I'm kidding!" his voice boomed, and Kate lifted her eyes to see Alec laughing and shaking his head. "The bellhop is taking my luggage upstairs. I checked in a couple of minutes ago and thought I'd come out here for a coffee." He gestured to his briefcase. "This is just full of files. Business stuff."

"Business?" This week was supposed to be about the bride and groom. "What do you mean, *business?*"

Alec shrugged. "I can't be expected to put my life on hold simply because my brother's getting hitched, can I?"

"It's only for a few days," Kate said archly. "And we have a lot of fun activities planned for the guests who are arriving early." She shifted on her feet and began to defensively cross her arms across her chest, stopping herself just in time. No need to catastrophize here.

"A few days too many," he continued with a sigh. "I'm a busy man. Too busy to spend my time driving back and forth from the city, so I'm here for the week."

Of course. His priorities were crystal clear. Honestly, one would think she would know better by now! *Been there. Done that. Never to be repeated.*

"If you have a few minutes, I thought we could quickly go over the plans for the rehearsal dinner."

Alec looked at her in surprise. "Right now?"

"Your father doesn't arrive until later in the week, and I need some last-minute input. Since your family is hosting, I thought you might have a few personal things to contribute."

Alec glanced at his watch with a look of impatience. "What time is the bachelor party tonight again?"

"Eight," she replied.

Sensing his hesitation, Kate took the opportunity to flash her biggest grin. Guilt was always a last resort, but one she fell back on all too often in heated situations like this. "I know it means so much to William that your family is hosting the rehearsal dinner." She didn't bother to add that it was also, typically, tradition.

Alec frowned at her. "And how do you know that? You're just—"

Kate interrupted before he could say something that would cement her displeasure with him. "I'm Elizabeth's best friend."

Alec's brow creased as he studied her. "I thought you were the wedding planner."

"I am. And I'm also Elizabeth's best friend. And the maid of honor," she added, maintaining her smile. "So, as best man, you should expect to be seeing a lot of me for the next few days."

And that, she realized, was something she didn't know what to make of anymore.

★ ★ ★

Elizabeth's best friend. He should have known there'd be a catch. It was no secret that he and the bride had gotten off to a rocky start. Seeing as his brother had sprung his engagement—and exit from the family business—on him completely unawares, he actually thought he handled it all pretty well, all things considered.

Still, did he really want his brother living in Misty Point, marrying this woman he hardly knew? If he was being honest, no.

Alec looked out to the ocean, suddenly feeling like an outsider during this wedding week. He'd have to muster up some level of enthusiasm to fit in. He didn't want to ruin this time for his brother; he just wanted to . . . stop it. William had gotten sidetracked, caught up in a pretty girl and a laid-back lifestyle, but Alec saw the situation objectively, and he knew that whatever happiness he'd found here was as fleeting as the tide coming in over the sand.

William belonged in Boston. And like it or not, Alec *needed* him back in Boston. More than anyone could ever know.

A warm breeze blew off the water, and Kate pushed a loose strand of light brown hair from her face, even though it was determined to flutter around her nose. Alec shifted the weight on his feet impatiently, refusing to give in to the lure of his surroundings the way his younger brother had done. Setting his heavy backpack next to the briefcase at his feet, he studied them both, frowning. He'd come outside to make a few important calls before the bachelor party tonight, but this wedding planner didn't show any signs of budging. With a sigh, he rubbed the back of his neck, wincing at the knots that tensed his muscles. "I thought we were doing the rehearsal here at the hotel," he said.

"Well, yes, everything for the wedding is going to be held here," Kate said, nodding quickly as her eyes flashed from the slight encouragement. He fought off a grin. Damn, she was sort of cute. Cute, but annoying. "But there are still a few details to go over."

"Such as?"

Kate tossed up her hands. "Where to start? The wine selection. The dessert tray. The seating arrangements."

"Seating arrangements?" He didn't even know half the people on the invitation list. William had always been the social one, and he'd clearly made himself at home in this little seaside town.

The wedding planner nodded firmly. "It's my experience that guests are more comfortable being assigned a seat. It cuts out confusion and needless drama."

Alec eyed her watchfully as she rattled off the mounting list of decisions that still needed to be made, wishing for the umpteenth time that he came from a normal family, where his parents stepped in and happily oversaw conventional traditions.

"How much time is this going to take?" he asked when she stopped to take a breath.

Kate's eyes drifted to the doors and then back out to the stretch of lawn. "Oh . . . maybe half an hour?"

"An hour." More like an hour from the shifty look in her gaze. Alec dragged a hand over his face, making a few quick calculations. Traffic out of the city had been hellish. The afternoon was already gone, and so were his plans for it. An entire day was lost, and with everything going on in the office right now, he wasn't in the position to be taking days off to plan seating arrangements or taste wine. No, he was here to make the most of his time in Misty Point—playground to the multimillionaires who needed an escape from urban life.

Things at the family's personal investment firm had been bad for months, and with no one else to blame, all fingers were pointed at him. It was a weight he couldn't shrug, despite his sleepless efforts. But this week sparked a chance to get things back on track. The way they used to be.

And his meeting Monday with commercial real estate mogul Mason Lambert was his ticket.

She gave him a reassuring smile. "How about we just go over the menu and some other smaller details, and I'll take care of the seating arrangements on my own?"

Okay, so maybe she wasn't going to be so bad. Still, he wasn't one to back off on a negotiation. "That the best offer you have for me?"

She tipped her head and offered a slow smile. "Well, you are the best man, after all. I can't take away *all* your responsibilities."

Best man. Was that really what he was? Once he would have said so, but more recently, he wasn't so sure. He and William had come a long way from their days spent working side by side at the Montgomery Group. If Elizabeth had never come along, he and his brother would still be strolling the office halls, relishing in the sweetness of their mutual success, and celebrating with drinks after work. Now Alec was left to eat alone in his office most nights, scrambling to try to drum up new business to make up for the lack of revenue. Going home to an empty apartment he'd bought for views he was never even there to enjoy. Starting the routine all over again the next day.

Once he'd had drinks at the bar on the corner to look forward to after a long, hard day. Saturday mornings on the golf course or an afternoon catching a game at Fenway. William was more than his brother. He was his best friend.

A lot had changed since William left. Too much.

Turning back to Kate, he attempted a half smile. "And is it the duty of the best man to oversee the rehearsal dinner?"

"Well, it is traditionally the responsibility of the groom's family, yes."

"My father won't be any help," he said tightly.

Kate sat a little straighter, blinking rapidly. "Yes, of course. William explained everything."

Everything? *Now this was interesting.* William was typically tight-lipped about their family dynamics—they both were. If he were a betting man, which he wasn't, he'd wager that William had stopped far short of explaining *everything*. Some stories were best untold. "So, you're friends with my brother, then?"

Kate looked at him in surprise. "Very good friends. He's marrying my best friend, after all."

Ah, there it was again. Best friend. Best man. "And how is Elizabeth?" he managed in a tone that was less sincere than he'd hoped, no doubt painting him as a less-than-ideal future brother-in-law, that much he was sure of.

"She's fine," Kate replied, careful to say nothing more. Silence stretched as she glanced up at him through hooded lids. She gave a soft sigh that made him realize he was testing her patience about as much as she was testing his.

Deciding it was time to admit defeat and deal with the inevitable, Alec offered her a slow smile. Business would have to wait until tomorrow—or tonight. He wasn't much for sleep these days. "Okay. You win. Consider me at your service."

Her gaze shot up to his as a relieved smile took over her face. "Oh, thank you," she gushed, and he felt his eyes narrow with curiosity.

"This really means a lot to you, doesn't it?"

Bristling, Kate tucked her shoulder-length hair behind her ears and hoisted a large binder to her chest. "Well, it's my job. Besides, we both want everything perfect for William and Elizabeth's big day, don't we?"

Alec gave a curt nod and picked up his backpack and briefcase, sweeping the grand front porch for a bellhop. In a place as serene and idyllic as this, one would think he could finally settle down and relax. But resting was the last thing on his mind at the moment. Kate might think he was here to play the doting best man, but what she didn't realize was that on Saturday,

Alec had every intention of standing by his brother's side back in their offices in Boston, not at the end of the aisle.

Dropping onto one of the white wooden rocking chairs that lined the porch, he tried his best to force an expression of interest while he listened to Kate describe the menu options for the rehearsal dinner, but it was becoming increasingly difficult to keep his heavy lids from drooping. He'd been up since four and hadn't gotten to bed until after midnight, and if the urgent emails that kept lighting up his phone screen didn't stop soon, he'd be pulling another all-nighter.

"Mind if we discuss this somewhere I can get some coffee?" he asked.

"Around the other side of the porch," Kate informed him. He followed her around the side of the wraparound porch, quickening his pace to match her brisk stride toward the café tables.

Alec threw his body weight back into a wicker chair, feeling the knots in his back loosen a bit. "Can I get you anything?" he asked, signaling a passing waiter. Kate shook her head in response, and he placed an order for a large coffee. Deciding he needed a break from talking about all these wedding details that Kate was so passionate about, he inquired, "So William's friend Eric is throwing the bachelor party tonight?"

Kate nodded. "At Nolan's Pub."

"A pub?" That wasn't William's style at all. William would want something sleek and modern. A high-end nightclub in Boston. A four-star restaurant. Not a pub. A wave of guilt washed over him. He should have planned the event himself. William was his brother, after all. Instead he'd spent his time picking up the pieces William had left when he quit the family business.

He shifted his eyes to Kate, holding her stare bluntly. Pinching her lips, she pulled her heavy bag onto her long, slender legs and sighed. "Yes, a pub. Is there a problem?"

Alec shook his head. "You do things pretty casually around here."

"You haven't even seen it. It's a very nice pub. Besides, this is a beach town. It's summer. You should try to relax a little more."

Something told him she could do with a little of her own advice. Rather than arguing, he bantered, "Who said I'm not relaxed?"

She glared pointedly at the cell phone he held in his hand. She uncrossed and recrossed her legs, giving him a full view of the length of a smooth thigh in the long slit in her skirt. "Let's get back to the menu for the rehearsal dinner."

"Funny you should tell me I need to relax. You're the one getting all bent out of shape over a dinner." He settled back into his chair and folded his hands behind his head. "Judging from this place, I'm sure anything on the menu will be just fine."

"Then it seems we have nothing more to discuss." Without another word, she stood and began retracing her steps toward the staircase, showing no signs of stopping.

Well, now he had done it.

He leaned forward as he watched her walk away. "Hey, Kate!" he hollered, watching with a smile he couldn't fight as she halted and then whipped around, her eyes blazing even from this distance. "How about we go with sushi?"

Kate's mouth gaped. "That's not an option."

"Why not?" Alec asked with sudden interest.

"You can't have sushi for the rehearsal dinner!" Kate scoffed. She returned to the table and sat down.

"Yes, I can," Alec said, leaning back to rest his head in his hands. He shifted his back a little, wincing at the tension that had built up near his tailbone.

Kate widened her eyes. "No, you can't. You saw the details I put into the décor. This is supposed to be rustic, casual...nautical."

Nautical. Alec bit down on the inside of his cheek. If she thought he was laughing at her, she'd just storm off again. And he wasn't laughing at her. He was just...amused. Intrigued, even. And damn it if he wasn't enjoying her company just a little. "I thought you wanted me to be involved in the planning of this event." He dropped his arms as the waiter delivered his coffee. He took a sip, drinking it black. Hot and strong.

Kate clutched her handbag to her chest. The waiter stepped back and then moved on to the next table. "That's true."

"So, now I'm planning it!" He would have thought she'd be relieved. Instead, she looked on the brink of tears. "My brother loves sushi."

"But it's all wrong for the occasion," Kate insisted. "What about crab cakes or seafood risotto? William loves the crab cakes here."

Alec took another sip of his coffee, hoping he could flag the waiter down for a refill. "Tell you what," he acquiesced. "Go ahead with the crab cakes for the appetizer and the seafood risotto for the main course. You obviously know what you're doing."

Kate eyed him warily but her expression had softened. "Well, if you're sure..." She frowned. "It's just that I know how much William loves the crab cakes here."

There it was again. He didn't need a stranger telling him what his brother did and did not like. His gut burned as he considered her words. When had he and William stopped being best friends and started becoming distant relatives? Growing up, he would have done anything for that kid—he still would, even if that meant making sure that William didn't go through with making the biggest mistake of his life.

"Back in Boston, William and I loved going to this sushi joint down the block from our office. Think they could maybe set up a raw bar on the buffet table?"

Kate nodded, looking more subdued. "I'll see what I can do," she said. After a slight pause she added, "But . . . it shouldn't be a problem."

Alec grinned. "Good!"

"Believe it or not, I have put a *lot* of planning into this event," she insisted.

As if that much wasn't obvious. Hoping to keep the conversation going until he'd at least finished his coffee, he said, "So you enjoy party planning?"

From across the table he watched her eyes simmer. "It's a little more than party planning."

"Well, it's a party. And you're planning it." He should stop now. Something told him this wasn't going to end well.

"Have you ever been married?" Kate asked, and the slight smile on her lips told him she knew the answer.

"Nope," Alec said. *And I don't intend to,* he didn't bother adding. "Have you?"

Kate's cheeks turned pink as she skirted her gaze to the left. "I'm asking only because if you *had* ever been married, then you would know how much goes into planning an event of this size. It isn't just about sending out invitations and picking out a pizza and some balloons. There are a lot of moving parts. Some people spend two years planning their wedding. It's more than just a party. It's...a memory."

Alec watched her shift in her chair and glance out to the sea. She was being decidedly evasive, and that intrigued him. A woman with something to hide was always more interesting than one who wore her every emotion on her sleeve.

His phone pinged again and he glanced down with a frown to see his father's name on the screen. His jaw tightened, and he fought back the urge to silence the ringer, maybe chuck the whole device out in the ocean.

"I should probably take this one," he said instead, starting to stand.

She pushed back her own chair, and he was suddenly aware of how close they were standing. She extended a hand, and he took it in his, lingering for a moment on the firm grip, wondering what it would be like to touch her in a different, softer way.

"I had scheduled your suit fitting for ten tomorrow, but I could try to shift it to later in the day now that you're not rushing back to Boston," she said.

"Ten will be fine," he said, vaguely recalling the appointment but assuming it was on his calendar.

"Till tomorrow, then," she said.

He said nothing as he connected his phone and held it to his ear. And even though he was standing on the porch of a beautiful country inn with a panoramic view of the Atlantic, suddenly he was right back in Boston. Back to reality.

Chapter Three

⎯⎯⎯ ⦕⦖⦕⦖⦕⦖ ⎯⎯⎯

She'd left her car at the bridal salon, and after driving it back to her regular parking spot behind the vintage building off Harbor Street that housed her office, it took ten minutes of sitting in her car with the engine running and the cool stream of forced air blowing on her face before Kate trusted herself to finally turn off the ignition and go inside. Appearing even remotely flustered was not an option right now with her boss watching her every move.

This was nonsense. So the man was good at eye contact. It wasn't like he was doing it on purpose. It was a sales tactic, no doubt, if not in business, then with women. And it was a red flag. Along with everything Elizabeth had said, of course.

And really, he was quite tiresome.

Turning off the car, Kate shook her muddled head clear and walked the three blocks to Bride by Design, the small wedding planning company owned and operated by Kate's old classmate, Meredith Smith, who was even more unbearable now than she'd been in high school, back when she was cheerleading queen and Kate was secretly working up the courage to try out for the team. The office was located at a busy corner in the center of town, and its bright green door and crisp white window boxes spilling with colorful flowers lent a cheerful ambience. But despite its outward appearance, there was nothing happy about the place. Oh, it used to be a fine enough place to come every day. Her boss had always been a bit of a pill, but Kate hadn't minded so much. It wasn't like they needed to be friends. They were both perfectionists, and they had a mutual appreciation and understanding of each other.

But once you were on Meredith's bad side, you stayed there—Kate had learned this sordid fact the hard way.

A familiar knot of dread mixed with fear twisted at her insides as Kate unlocked the door and stepped inside. Sweeping her eyes around the empty reception room, Kate held her breath and listened for her boss. It was a Saturday, and most of the planners had weddings this weekend.

The few other girls on the administrative staff were gone, of course, off enjoying their weekends with their boyfriends of the month or primping for a night down at Paddy's, where they might catch the eye of one of the summer people—the ones who just came to Misty Point on weekends to enjoy the salty air and slower pace. The room was strangely quiet. She moved silently over the soft wool rug in shades of warm neutrals. She used to adore the chic and classic décor—the elegant touches like crystal chandeliers illuminating the soft blue walls and enormous bouquets of fresh flowers brightening every turn—but those days were long gone. If there had been any other wedding planning company in the small town of Misty Point, Kate wouldn't even be sticking around.

Not like Meredith would be offering her a glowing reference anyway.

She flitted with her favorite nocturnal fantasy of late—the one where she coolly handed Meredith her resignation letter and a week later opened her own bigger and better company. But then, like always, she thought of all the things that could go wrong. The money that could be spent and wasted. The house that would have to be second-mortgaged or worse. The feeling of having tried. And failed.

She frowned at herself. She really needed to do something about this cynical attitude she was developing. It didn't bode well for a wedding planner. She was supposed to believe in the general goodness of people. She was supposed to believe in everlasting love.

She managed not to snort under her breath.

Closing the door to her small office behind her, Kate slipped her handbag onto the hook behind the door and tucked herself into her desk chair. She turned on her computer, and as she waited for it to power up, her eyes drifted to the space on her desk where she'd once kept a framed photograph of her and Jake. She had looked at it so many times over the duration of their two-year relationship that it was habit, and not one she wished to continue. Hastily, she slid her pencil jar to its place and made a mental note to bring in another, more suitable photograph instead. Like one of her dog.

She hadn't been in the office since yesterday afternoon, when she'd left to attend a menu tasting with a new client. Now she sorted through the handwritten stack of messages that Sara, the office receptionist, had left on her desk in her absence. She read them quickly, barely bothering to skim for anything other than a potential crisis, and then breathed a sigh of relief when she saw that nothing had gone wrong—no vendor conflicts, no flowers stuck in transit, nothing that could somehow be pinned on her, because that was what Meredith was hoping to do, of course. Next she scanned through her emails, happy to see that the photographer had sent a confirmation for next Saturday's events. One less thing to worry about, she thought, rubbing her forehead. Still, she'd go over the key poses and general schedule. Just to be sure.

She pulled the hefty Jones-Montgomery binder from her bag and flicked through the vendor contracts and itineraries, but she knew them by heart. There was nothing left to check or recheck.

Kate shut the binder and pushed it to the edge of her desk. She leaned forward and put her head in her hands—a brief indulgence she could permit herself only behind closed doors. Any further weakness right now would result in a pink slip. It didn't matter how hard her heart was breaking, or how nerve-wracking it was to know this was her last shot. She had to pull it together. It was that simple.

"Kate?" At the sound of Meredith's sharp, rapping tone, Kate startled and tipped over her coffee mug, which was thankfully empty.

"Yes?" she called out, and then cursed under her breath. She could have been in Boston now. Should have been in Boston. Living in Jake's town house. Working for that event planning company she'd had two interviews with right before—

Well. No sense in thinking about that.

Meredith appeared in the doorway. All five foot two of her. Her blond hair was still pulled into the bouncy ponytail she sported all through high school, but the brightness in her blue eyes had dulled over the years.

Kate would have been happy to commiserate. Thirty was a far cry from eighteen, when the world felt so full of promise. But something told her that Meredith wasn't interested in a little pity party over a bottle of rosé anytime soon. No, Meredith, as she loved to tell everyone, drank only French Champagne. And that wasn't exactly in Kate's budget at the moment.

Because yes, fine, she would admit it: sometimes she did still dare to dream. It was a brisk, fleeting, maybe even foolish moment when she stowed an extra twenty in her Future jar, as she'd fondly called it. Usually by the time she was screwing on the lid she was muttering under her breath, becoming angry at herself for even daring to think that things might turn around or something might actually work out. But every once in a while, when she passed the jar, her heart sped up and for a moment...

Meredith cleared her throat. A truly tedious habit that made her seem like an old schoolmarm, not a girl who deep down loved nothing more than flipping cartwheels while her cheerleading skirt flew up to her waist.

"Hello, Meredith," Kate said pleasantly. She was genuinely smiling, unable to shed the image of the former Meredith from her mind.

"I thought I heard you came in."

It amazed Kate that such a simple observation could be made into an accusation.

Meredith slipped into one of the two light blue velvet visitor chairs opposite Kate's antique ivory desk. Her petite frame was clothed in an expensive ivory suit. Her unreadable eyes stared through Kate until she began to squirm in her seat.

Rather than giving Kate credit for being at work on what was technically her day off, given that she had no event to oversee today, Meredith remarked, "It's always a surprise to see you here. Ever since that five-month vacation you took, I have to do a double take when I actually see you come through the door."

Kate silently counted to three. "It was *one* month, Meredith," she said evenly. "And it wasn't a vacation."

It was a leave of absence. A medical leave of absence. And Meredith knew it. And the reason behind it. Hell, the whole town knew the reason behind it, much to her horror. But while most were kind, if pitying, others, like Meredith, never ceased to find an opportunity to scratch that wound.

Meredith just shrugged. "If you say so."

A heavy knot formed in Kate's stomach. It was a sentiment she had become all too familiar with since returning to Bride by Design. It was the feeling of defeat. Silence fell over the room as Kate talked herself out of saying something she would regret. She loved being a wedding planner—even now, in spite of everything—and she wouldn't let anyone take that away from her. She'd lost enough already.

"How's the Jones-Montgomery planning going?" Meredith inquired.

"Good," Kate said with more conviction than she felt. Seeing this as an opportunity to exhibit her competence, she pulled the checklist to the front of her desk and skimmed it quickly. "The flowers are scheduled to arrive Friday. The cake will arrive two hours prior to the reception. Elizabeth had a dress fitting today, and I don't foresee any further alterations."

"What about the suits?" Meredith interjected.

Kate swallowed hard. She hadn't been questioned on such basic tasks since she first shifted over from assistant to planner more than five years ago. It was Meredith's way of trying to wear her down and push her out. She was no dummy. But until Kate had something else lined up, she would stand her ground.

"All the men have been fitted but one. The best man is scheduled to have a fitting tomorrow at ten," Kate replied, not bothering to elaborate on the fact that she was personally going to oversee the appointment. If she didn't, there was a strong chance Alec wouldn't bother to go. His mind was obviously elsewhere; he had openly admitted that he was in town to work, not partake in the wedding festivities. But Meredith didn't need to know about this issue—it would only alarm her. Besides, Kate had it under control.

Or, at least she hoped.

* * *

Two hours later, Kate unloaded the last gift basket from the trunk of her car. Balancing it with two others as best she could, she used her hip to force the passenger door closed. An older gentleman was kind enough to hold the hotel door for her, and always surprised lately to see that chivalry was not completely dead, she breezed into the cool, air-conditioned lobby of the Beacon Inn with a smile that could only be brought on by a warm heart.

"This should be the last of them," she told the woman behind the front desk. She slid her eyes down the hotel's reservation list one more time, taking care in cross-referencing it with the out-of-town guest list she had printed at the office. Most would be arriving on Thursday and Friday, but Kate already felt lighter knowing that the welcome baskets were dropped off at the hotel, ready and waiting as the guests filtered in. "One per room," she added, her pen poised over her list. "Not per guest."

A deep, gravelly voice purred into her ear, causing her to jump. "So you were the one behind the basket of treats in my room?"

Kate whipped around to face Alec square in the eye, and her heart skipped a beat when she took in his chiseled face and twinkling eyes. She soaked in the broad, muscular chest that was hidden behind a crisp button-down shirt he had casually rolled to the elbows, and okay, her knees went a little weak.

Eye candy, she reminded herself. She could look. But she could definitely not touch.

"It's a welcome basket." She felt a twinge of pride that he had noticed her effort. She'd stayed up way too late three nights last week compiling them. "All the wedding guests staying at the hotel receive one."

Alec's lips twitched into a smile. "And here I thought it was something special just for me. Mixed nuts are my favorite, you know."

Kate narrowed her gaze, flashes of her ex-fiancé blinking as bright as a fire alarm. The man was full of himself, and if he was looking for a girl to stroke his ego, he was looking in the wrong place. So he was cute. Lots of men were. And most of them, from her experience, were not worth falling for.

"The saltwater taffies are made locally, and I thought everyone would enjoy—" Kate began, and then faltered as she saw the sheen in Alec's eyes. Pinching her lips, she looked away and then said briskly, "I should get running along to meet the girls. And you should probably be leaving to meet William soon."

"Leaving so soon?" he asked, casually leaning a hip into the counter.

She raised an eyebrow at him. "You suddenly have time to spare?"

He looked her up and down, his lips curving slowly and—dare she say it—suggestively. "Honey, I always have time for a pretty woman."

Kate narrowed her eyes. Once, she would have basked in that kind of comment. Now...

She straightened her stance. "First, I'm not your honey. Second, you hardly had time for me this afternoon, and my looks haven't changed since then. In fact, neither has my outfit."

His gaze dropped to linger on her pencil skirt. A flattering purchase thanks to the Spanx she faithfully wore underneath, but one she suddenly regretted. The last thing she needed was for him to go getting any ideas.

She lifted her tote from the front desk counter and shrugged it onto her shoulder. "I'll see you tomorrow for the suit fitting," she said through a tight, professional smile, but Alec's firm grip on her upper arm halted her. Heart thumping, she shifted her eyes to meet his.

She hadn't been touched by a man other than her father since Jake. Hadn't wanted to. At first she didn't want the memory of his touch to be replaced or tainted. She wanted it to linger, to savor it, even when she knew she shouldn't, that she was just making it worse for herself. But she couldn't help it. Clinging to those feelings—the weight of his arm around her waist when they slept, the smooth, firm hold of his hand on hers—it was the only thing she had to remind herself that she wasn't crazy. That he'd loved her... once.

"Wasn't there something you needed to tell me?" Alec asked, waiting patiently for her response, but all she could do was stare at him blankly. "Are they going to be able to do the raw bar at the rehearsal dinner?"

Kate felt her face blanch. "Oh, that." She'd completely forgotten.

It was a small oversight, one she could have dealt with tomorrow, or maybe even Monday, but it would have been just enough to have Meredith sailing into her office, looking for trouble.

She vowed to add another twenty to the Future jar tonight.

Alec slowly loosened his hold on her arm. He shrugged as he jammed his hands into his pockets. "Don't worry. I called myself. We're all set."

Well, he could have told her that in the first place. "Thank you," she said. Eager to get back on better footing, she asked, "Did you see the itinerary in your basket?"

"Couldn't miss it," he remarked, and Kate felt her shoulders relax. She'd worked hard on that schedule, printing it on heavy cardstock and including a watercolor image of the Misty Point Lighthouse. It was all in the details, after all...

"Well, if you have any questions about other things to do in town, I'm happy to refer you to some of our hot spots."

"Hot spots." Alec looked at her warily. "What exactly do people do around here for fun?"

Kate shrugged and jammed her pen back into the pocket of her handbag to avoid eye contact. She could hardly admit to him that she spent most of her evenings at home these days or that she looked forward to her trash TV and wine night with Elizabeth more than was probably normal. She'd always been a homebody, and she didn't see anything wrong with it, but she doubted a man like Alec sat home alone each night. He was probably too busy dining in the best restaurants night after night, throwing around his money on his flavor of the week.

"I probably spend my evenings much the same way you do," she said simply.

"The same way I do?" Alec repeated. He leaned into the counter, folding his hands at his chest. She couldn't help it; she glanced. Hard and a little chiseled, and those shoulders... "I doubt that."

Kate tipped her head. "Why would you say that?"

"Because I spend most of my evenings in the office," he explained. "And the nights I'm not sitting behind a desk, I'm busy schmoozing at charity events and dinners."

Kate peered at him thoughtfully, trying to assess the validity of his statement. It seemed plausible enough—after all, Elizabeth had made it clear that he made no time for a personal life— but it was hard to believe with his good looks that he didn't have anything—or anyone—else in his life. "Surely there must be something you enjoy other than work."

Alec jutted his bottom lip. "Guess I haven't stopped to think about it."

"So all work and no play, then." She could be accused of the same these days.

Alec's lips curled into a mischievous smirk. "Well, now, I wouldn't say *no* play..."

Kate worked hard not to roll her eyes. For some reason she felt as disappointed as she did disgusted. It wasn't that Alec had women in his life. Heck, he could have a harem of women— and he probably did—and it wouldn't matter. What mattered was that his casual admittance to his nighttime activities only served as a fresh reminder that Kate was not so lucky these days. Romance didn't come easily to her—she couldn't embrace that same casual attitude about it that Alec possessed. And she wished she could. She wished desperately that she could.

If she could just move on . . . somehow. Then she might finally stand a chance at picking up the pieces of her broken heart.

She managed a smile as she hitched her handbag tighter. "Well, I should go."

He nodded, but showed no sign of moving. "Enjoy your wild night."

Kate laughed. It would hardly be a wild night, but dinner out with the girls was exactly what she needed right now. There was no room for a man in her life. Especially the one standing in front of her.

Chapter Four

⊶⊷

It wasn't until Kate had pulled to a stop on her gravel driveway that Meredith's voice had faded from her mind and she finally felt her shoulders relax. Somehow, it didn't matter what she knew to be true, her boss had a way of rattling her, homing in on all her little insecurities, making her question her past, her present, and more than anything, her future.

Despite everything that had happened in the past year, she still loved being a wedding planner. Loved thinking through each detail, making each event unique and special and beautiful. She never tired from seeing the months—or sometimes years—of planning come together for a few, fleeting, magical hours. She was forever inspired by new venue locations, food presentations, and flower trends. To lose that... She'd lost enough already.

She set a hand to her stomach, reminding herself as she always did that there was no use taking the office home with her, at least, not her boss's icy warnings and threats. Worrying would only make things worse.

She sighed and sat in the car after she'd turned off the ignition to admire the small white cottage that was now her home, a reminder that things were improving and that her life had moved forward . . . somehow. When Jake had called off the wedding—if you could call it that—she'd been unable to see even one day ahead, much less a month or a year. Yet here she was. Settled. Happy. Or at least content.

She hadn't thought it was possible at first. But it was Elizabeth who had been there, showing up at her then apartment door with wine and chocolate and those celebrity magazines they used to love so much. Elizabeth made an effort to point out all the divorces, especially the really messy ones, and Kate had loved her for it. And it did brighten her spirits to see that she wasn't alone, and that even though Elizabeth was falling in love with a guy who was in many ways a kinder, better, more loyal version of Jake, she understood.

Jake hadn't just been Kate's fiancé. He was the only guy she'd ever really loved. And she hadn't been good enough.

"Nonsense!" Elizabeth had scoffed when Kate ever voiced her deepest feelings. "You were *too* good!"

In time, Kate had come to know that Elizabeth was right. She'd stopped missing Jake before he'd even moved back to Boston. Her hurt was replaced by white-hot anger and a pain far deeper than losing your fiancé and all the dreams you'd built around him. He hadn't just let her down. He'd betrayed her.

She blinked, then forced her eyes on the house and the puffy peonies that were on their last bloom. She'd clip some tonight, before it was too late and their petals scattered in the wind. So there was no man around to give her flowers. She'd give herself flowers. At least then she could be sure she always received the variety she liked, not those orange tiger lilies Jake had been partial to sending her on her birthday.

She always felt better when she saw the three-bedroom Cape that she'd purchased just after Christmas—a new start for a new year, she'd told herself. Though small, it was cozy and far from cramped, and anything bigger would have only made her feel alone, like something was missing.

And something was missing, she knew, when she dared to admit it to herself. A few things, really. But in their place she had filled her life with new treasures, from a favorite book to the sweet little dog who was now staring at her out the window, his paws on the sill of the dining room windows, his ears alert, and no doubt his tail wagging.

At the sight of Henry, Kate felt her face break into a grin, and she thrust open the car door, eliciting a series of yelps that could be heard through the glass. She hurried to the front door, stopping only to pull her mail from the old-fashioned box that was nailed to the cedar siding, and bent down to pet her puppy as soon as she'd turned the key.

Henry licked her face excitedly and bounced on his hind legs as Kate reached for the leash she kept on a hook near the door. She knew she should probably crate him when she was gone, but she didn't have the heart to do it, not when he had so much fun playing with his toys and exploring the house. When Henry had first come into her life, she'd spent all day with him—they went everywhere together, even the grocery store until he'd been discovered in her handbag and they'd been asked to leave— and now that she was back at work, well, Henry hadn't adjusted well to that, if the chewed-up corner of her armchair said anything.

Kate clicked the collar around Henry's furry neck and patted his head. "I know, little guy. Change is hard. But if you can do it, I can do it."

Kate toed off her work shoes, slipped into flip-flops, and led Henry out the front door, where he happily lifted his leg to her beautiful hydrangea blooms, which had finally peaked last week. Still, she could only smile. Elizabeth had remarked more than once that Henry was spoiled rotten, to which Kate could only proudly agree, minus the rotten part, of course.

Henry deserved a life that was overflowing with love. Didn't everyone?

She felt that little pang in her chest that had a way of creeping in at inappropriate times. For a while, her mother had tried to cheer her up by saying that she would find love again, she was still young, but she didn't believe her mother, and under the circumstances, she didn't want to talk about it, and now, months later, she still didn't.

She flicked through the mail as she walked, shaking her head when she found not one but two letters for her neighbors tucked into her pile. The first was for old Mr. Sherman, who lived on the other side of Kate and who only appeared outside to mow his grass with an electric push mower that required an extension cord that Kate forever feared he would run over one of these days, and of course, to give Kate long, detailed reminders about the exact location of their property lines. Many an afternoon since moving into her home, Kate had stood next to her driveway, listening patiently as Mr. Sherman pointed to a random blade of grass on the completely indiscernible patch of green that separated their two homes from the front, while he motioned where this imaginary line divided the three-foot space. Kate mowed her own lawn with a bagless push mower she'd purchased at the hardware shop. She'd thought she was being neighborly by going all the way to his driveway, but then she realized that Mr. Sherman was territorial. The next time she'd taken great effort to stop halfway between her driveway and his, but the very next day, Mr. Sherman had mowed his lawn, leaving a pointed quarter-inch strip of tall blades between their homes. Clearly, sending a message.

Careful not to cross any more imaginary boundary lines, Kate tucked the envelope into his mailbox and darted in the opposite direction. The second envelope was for William. Perfect. Kate never minded an excuse to catch up with her friends, even if she'd be seeing Elizabeth in a short while anyway.

Their house was a Cape, like her own, but unlike hers, it had an addition on the back that allowed for a home office for Elizabeth's interior design business and an extra bedroom above that would no doubt house their future children.

She and Jake had never discussed children. Red flag number two.

Kate walked up the flagstone steps and knocked on the paned window of the slate-blue front door rather than ring the bell. If Elizabeth was working, she would slip the envelope through the brass slot in their door.

Instead, it was William who appeared around the corner and quickened his pace to greet her at the door.

"Delivery," she said, waving the envelope. "Not a last minute RSVP, I hope." She could tell from the envelope that this was not the case. Every invitation had been accounted for. The extras were sitting in a box in her office. One or two would be used as keepsakes—she planned to make a scrapbook for Elizabeth and include one—and the rest would sadly be recycled, not that there were many. Still, it was good to have a few on hand, just in case.

Kate had set aside one for her sister Charlotte. Why, she didn't know. Elizabeth and Charlotte had never been close, but the families were, and... Well, it was strange to think that Elizabeth was getting married and Charlotte wouldn't be in attendance. But it was also a reminder of what she had done and why she was absent.

"I was just about to head into town to meet my brother," William said, opening the door.

"I met him today," she said, carefully choosing her words. "You resemble him."

"Only in the physical sense," William chided, and Kate felt a twinge of disappointment. It was probably true, from what Elizabeth had said and from what she had seen. Alec was busy, and a little self-centered, while William was charming, hospitable... perfect. "I haven't seen him in a while. Hopefully we can catch up tonight if the party doesn't get too rowdy."

"My advice to you is no strippers, no gambling, and a full eight ounces of water before you go to bed," she said.

William gave her a rueful look, much like the expression she'd seen on his brother's face just a short while ago, she realized with a start. "Does any of that sound like something I'd want to do?"

Kate gave a small smile. "No."

When she'd first met William, he seemed like most of the other guys who floated through Misty Point in the summers. Attractive, boarding school educated, pursuing big jobs in Boston or New York. She'd thought he was just like Jake. The four of them went out a few times, usually at the pub on the pier. They seemed like the ideal set of couples back then.

But William was nothing like Jake. And for her best friend's sake, she was happy for that.

Later, William had admitted that he wasn't surprised to find out about Charlotte and Jake. Maybe he'd seen something that Kate hadn't. Or maybe he was just an excellent judge of character. He'd fallen in love with Elizabeth, after all.

"Trust me, all I want to do tonight is kick back with the guys, have a few beers, and probably drop into bed by eleven."

That sounded heavenly. "I'll promise to deliver Elizabeth by a reasonable hour then. Is she here?"

He pointed to the ceiling. "Upstairs getting ready. You want to go up?"

It was tempting, but not if she planned to change from her pencil skirt and work blouse. The Spanx were killing her, honestly, and she longed to roll them down and take a decent breath. She'd wear a sundress tonight. One with a forgiving cut and a flouncy skirt, even if she was starting to question whether she was getting a little too old for dresses like that. "Henry has a thing for dust ruffles," she explained, sparking a laugh from William. "I don't trust him not to lift his leg. I should be getting home soon anyway to get ready."

"See you tomorrow night then?" William asked.

Of course. Her parents were hosting the couple for a celebratory dinner. She'd managed to block that out. Everything had changed in the past year, and she had a sinking feeling that she wasn't living up to being the daughter she'd always been. She'd always been the straight-A student, the one to remember the Mother's Day cards, to always set the table (and clear it), and once she was an adult, to call every Sunday, even though she often saw one of them throughout the week.

But after last summer she'd become withdrawn. She'd gone from shopping for wedding gowns with her mother to avoiding her phone calls. And wrestling with guilt.

She gave Henry's leash a tug and decided to work out her anxiety instead of going straight home. She took their regular route, up over the hill where there was a slight view of the Misty Point Lighthouse, and then circling back down again, this time around a curved street that eventually led them back home.

She smiled to neighbors whose names Kate was starting to learn, and Henry happily chased a few bikes—a habit that Kate knew she would have to break soon, but bless him, he had *such* fun doing it!—and Kate was feeling nothing short of completely satisfied with her current circumstances when her blasted phone alarm had to go off, bringing her straight back to reality and everything that had brought her here.

Kate silenced the ringer with a frown and unlocked the back door. Henry wasted no time in scampering to his water bowl as soon as he was free from the leash, lapping eagerly as Kate dropped a few ice cubes into the bowl as a treat.

She set her phone down on the counter and contemplated it for a moment. She'd been feeling so much better lately, so much more at peace than she'd been in those first few horrible weeks and months after she'd been forced to call off her wedding, cancel the flowers and the venue, and go through the humiliating rounds of explaining to out-of-town guests why they needed to cancel their flight reservations, but there was no denying that memories still lingered, and going back to work, being reminded of weddings all the time was a trigger, as Wendy, her kind, white-haired therapist, liked to say.

As much as she liked Wendy, she also yearned for the day when she wouldn't feel the need to visit her anymore. But as her alarm was quick to point out, she wasn't there yet. And she had a scheduled appointment with Wendy in the morning, because Wendy was nice enough to offer Sunday morning hours to people like Kate, who couldn't break away from work, or who were in therapy partially because of their jobs.

The phone began to ring again, and Kate went to silence the alarm, only to see the familiar name appear on the screen instead. All at once, her throat closed up and her heart sped up and she felt like she had just run a mile, even though she was standing perfectly still.

At her feet, Henry squeaked his favorite turtle-shaped toy between his feet, signaling for her to play, and Kate gritted her teeth and turned off the phone, making the ringer, the name, and everything it symbolized disappear from this perfect little life she had built for herself.

She bent to gently tease the toy from Henry's mouth and then gave it a good hard toss through the doorway to the dining room, which still didn't have a table, where Henry bounded in delight. And then, before she forgot, she turned back on her phone and called Wendy's answering service to reschedule her appointment for tomorrow. It was last minute, and she might be charged, but right now the thought of sitting and rehashing the past was not what she wanted to do.

The call made, she picked up the plush turtle Henry had returned to her feet, happy to play, eager not to think about that missed call, or the others that had come before it.

Or the reason for why she couldn't bring herself to talk to her only sister.

★ ★ ★

Charlotte disconnected the call before the voice mail recording came on and reached for the candy bar she'd bought at the corner shop on her latest walk around the block, just ten minutes ago. The flowers were popping up, lining window boxes and gathering at tree bases, but it was hard to enjoy the sights when you were running on two hours of interrupted sleep, and each excursion into the outdoors only made returning to this small basement apartment all the more disheartening.

To think she'd imagined, when she'd first run off to Boston all those months ago, that she'd be living some glamorous life, high above the Common in a penthouse, taking leisurely strolls with her baby and boyfriend.

Only Jake had never been her boyfriend, had he? Nope. He'd been her sister's fiancé, and then he'd used her to end that. He made it clear when she announced her pregnancy that he wouldn't be sticking around for it. Or for her.

He'd gone back to Boston, and fool that she was, she'd followed him here. If she was close by, she figured they could talk, work things out. After all, there was a baby to think about. But the phone calls she made to him went unanswered, and the one time she'd shown up at his office had been too horrible to ever relive. And after that, she'd stopped. Stopped wishing. Stopped hoping. Started regretting. And started fearing.

And now, months later, and that lonely pregnancy behind

her, her baby was here. And she was still just as bad off as she'd been when she first left Misty Point.

She eyed her sleeping daughter as she peeled the paper back from the candy bar and sank her teeth into the sweet gooey filling, willing the baby not to feel her stare and wake up. Charlotte's feet hurt, and she didn't want to walk anymore, and besides, the sky was turning gray, and she'd detected a hint of moisture in the air on her last excursion. All she wanted to do was curl up on the couch and catch up on some much-needed sleep and block out all these stomach-churning thoughts that consumed her waking hours. So why was she calling her sister instead?

She must be delirious, she decided. This was what happened when you went for weeks with only a handful of hours of sleep here and there. You started calling people who didn't want to hear from you, in a misguided attempt to connect with another adult.

Or maybe, she thought as she miserably bit into the last of the candy bar and chewed, you started thinking of everything that had brought you to this point, and you dared to think you could somehow undo it, or make amends.

Not that she'd undo having her sweet baby girl, she thought, smiling fondly at the little bundle sleeping soundly. She was still buckled in the five-point harness of her carrier, snapped into one of those foldable strollers she'd found at a church yard sale two weeks before Audrey was born. She'd gotten chatty with the woman selling it, eager for any tips from someone who'd reared three rambunctious boys and still managed to look fresh-faced and content with her life, fighting the twinge of jealousy that her life hadn't taken such a traditional route, but was instead being taped and glued together piece by piece. The woman was all too happy to offer advice, and when she realized that Charlotte was on her own, the woman's eyes had gone all crinkly and she had all but given her the stroller for free, only accepting a few dollars at Charlotte's insistence. She'd thrown in the carrier for no extra charge. Apparently they wouldn't let you leave the hospital without one.

She closed her eyes. She'd taken her baby home in a cab. Just the two of them. And the whole ride she'd wondered what Jake was doing at that exact moment, and if he'd even listened to the voice mail she'd left him that day before informing him that he had a beautiful baby girl.

She'd given him chance after chance. She'd never shut that door.

But he'd shut it for her. That day in the office. Like she was going to take a paternity test? Who did he think she was?

But that wasn't the only reason she hadn't taken it. No, she wasn't that proud. Or stupid. No, the real reason was that she couldn't imagine it would make any difference in the end, unless she wanted to fork over a ton of cash for a team of lawyers. And where was she going to come up with that? Playing the lottery?

She'd considered it. Especially when the jackpot was especially big.

Charlotte swallowed the lump in her throat and turned away from the stroller, blinking at the empty wrapper in her hand. Some people were kind and good. But not Jake. And maybe, according to Kate, not even her.

She balled the wrapper into her fist, but she didn't dare cross the room to toss it in the bin. The floors creaked terribly, and Audrey's lashes fluttered at the slightest hint of noise.

Instead, she set the wrapper to the side, on the end table she'd salvaged from a neighbor who was moving, and flipped open her laptop to review her notes for Monday morning's interview. She hadn't yet figured out what she'd do with Audrey, and the numerous phone calls she'd left for her "ex" had gone unanswered and unreturned. She stared at the screen, waiting for her temper to subside. There was no use crying or getting upset; it didn't solve her current predicament, did it? She'd gotten herself into this situation fair and square, and this was why, all on her own, she would get herself on better ground.

She glanced over at her sleeping daughter. Make that get them both on better ground. Audrey deserved a wonderful life, and it was her responsibility to make that happen. Somehow . . .

Setting her laptop on the end table, she pulled herself up to a standing position and walked slowly across the room to the apartment's only closet, careful to avoid the creaky spots in the floorboards. She surveyed her options with a dispassionate sigh, and finally plucked a boring, plain black maternity dress from its hanger, *almost* glad for a reason not to have lost all that baby weight. She wiggled into it, alarmed and depressed that it fit just fine, instead of hanging like a sack like it probably should have by now, six weeks after Audrey's birth, and vowed to increase the speed on her daily walks and to stop eating pasta for dinner, even if noodles were one of the cheapest things she could buy and the money stretched for three meals.

She walked into the bathroom and stared at her reflection in the full-length mirror a former tenant had nailed to the back of the door. She smoothed her long auburn hair and then pulled it back in a low ponytail. She hadn't brought enough of her belongings with her to Boston—back in Misty Point, her parents' house was filled with shoes and clothes (not that she could fit into them these days) and all sorts of other things, like proper furniture, and . . . laughter.

Her eyes began to well up when she thought of everything she'd left behind. Everything she'd lost. She couldn't go back—not even for the clothes. When she'd left Misty Point, she'd left in defiance, and fear, and the horrible knowledge that she'd let down the two people she'd always tried to please the most: her parents.

She flicked off the light as the baby began to cry, no doubt hungry again, and blinked away the tears before they could fall.

She'd get back to Misty Point eventually. But she wouldn't go back until she'd cleaned up her life. And then she'd show all of them, especially Kate, that she had changed.

It was the only hope she had of them welcoming her back.

Chapter Five

⊗⊗⊗

Alec was still reeling over the conversation he'd had with his father that afternoon as he sat in the loud, noisy pub a few hours later. It was hard enough knowing how bad things were at the Montgomery Group without his father calling to remind him every few hours. With a heavy sigh, he adjusted himself on the hard wooden pub chair and looked over to William, laughing with some friends Alec had never met, without a care in the world. Somehow all the problems that they'd once shared had become Alec's burden alone. And unlike his brother, he wasn't in a position to just walk away, as much as he wanted to half the time.

Make that most of the time, he thought.

Lowering his eyes, Alec swirled the Scotch in his glass before downing the last sip, grimacing only slightly as the liquid burned its way down his throat. He raised a finger, signaling for a fresh round as another burst of raucous laughter emerged from the group.

In all his life, he had never seen his brother so happy. Clearly, life with Elizabeth here in this sleepy town was having a positive effect on him. The brother he knew back in Boston was focused and driven. The guy a few seats down from him was relaxed and carefree. For all William knew, Alec was doing just fine without him.

But he wasn't. For so many reasons.

Alec felt the familiar pulse of anxiety tense his muscles. The waitress handed him his drink and he took a sip, eager to set aside his worries for a night and enjoy an evening out. He'd been living in the office, often sleeping there, usually not seeing the light of day except through his corner windows when the sun climbed its way over the skyline. In theory, a week in Misty Point was the perfect opportunity to kick back, get a little beach time, maybe rent a boat for an afternoon.

He chuckled to himself. Like that would ever happen.

As the eldest of two boys, Alec had always borne the brunt of the pressure from their father. It was Alec who had been expected to step up and take over the family's financial planning firm. Alec who was supposed to preserve the legacy their father had built. And now it was Alec who was fighting to keep the sinking ship from going down.

Because that's what it was, really. Revenue had dropped by nearly fifty percent since last fall when William made his exit from the company, and though it had never been confirmed, he had his suspicions about where those clients had gone...And he knew damn well how important it was to get them back.

"When's Dad getting in to town?" William asked casually, raising his voice over the din of the pub. It was a dark room, with a nautical theme as Kate had pointed out, and Alec could see why his brother had chosen it. Located right on the shore with the water in close distance, it felt like a retreat from the hustle of city life back in Boston.

"Friday," Alec said. Probably without an hour to spare before the obligatory rehearsal dinner he was technically hosting. He wasn't surprised his father hadn't informed William of his itinerary—if it wasn't for Alec's continued involvement with the family's company, his father probably wouldn't have much to say to him, either. He'd never been the soft and feely type. They'd had their mother for that.

Alec rubbed at the back of his neck and took another sip of his drink. The evening wasn't going as planned. He had hoped for a chance to have a private conversation with William—something casual and nonthreatening about the state of the family business—but so far, it had been nothing but fun and games.

"I'm glad you could make it," William said, coming around to give Alec an affectionate slap on the back.

"Wouldn't miss it!" Alec replied, hoping his smile appeared as genuine as the one plastered on William's face. He took stock of his younger brother for a minute, allowing himself a proper look for the first time all evening, and felt a mild shock at what he saw. He'd only seen William once since he'd moved to Misty Point, and he had noticeably changed since his last trip to Boston. His hair was a little longer, his smile a little wider, and even the way he dressed was a little more casual.

Alec tried to dilute the bitter taste that was forming in his mouth with another swig from his glass. With each flash of William's grin and every echo of his boisterous laugh, the knot in Alec's gut tightened. He had half-hoped he would stride into town and see his brother nearly sick with nerves, just looking for an excuse to run back to his old life. But William seemed more confident than ever about his choices. And happier, too.

"Well," William continued, locking nearly identical dark brown eyes with his, "things seem pretty crazy at the office these days. I wasn't sure if you'd just be driving in and out on Saturday for the wedding."

Alec resisted the urge to tell him exactly how things were in the office. Now wasn't the time for it. "Even if I wanted to get a late start, that wedding planner you hired never would have allowed it."

William gave a knowing laugh. "Ah, Kate. So you've met?"

"Oh, we've met all right," Alec said. An image of the pretty brunette sprang to mind. She might be an irritant, but there was no denying her physical attributes. And maybe a little something else, too.

"What did you think?" William asked with a wink.

"Please." Alec shook his head studied the ice in his glass.

"What?" William chided, elbowing him in the ribs. "You can't deny it—she's a good-looking woman."

Alec swirled the drink in his hand, watching the caramel-colored liquid coat the ice. "I don't have time for women these days. Not on a serious level at least," he clarified.

"I used to say the same thing, and look at me now," William said.

It had only been a year since he'd met Elizabeth on a weekend sailing trip to Misty Point, returning to Boston with a goofy grin and a notable lapse in concentration that continued for the next six months until he'd surprised them all with his resignation. He was choosing the love of this woman over his own family. And he didn't even apologize for it.

Or consider the risks that went with it.

Alec met his brother's eyes and forced a slow breath before he spoke. "Yeah, well, you know I'm not looking to settle down."

William frowned. "Not every marriage ends like Mom and Dad's did."

Very few marriages ended like their parents' had. Most marriages ended in divorce, not... Alec drained his glass, lowering his eyes to the table. He didn't like to talk about his mother, and William didn't, either. She was a memory, and a private one, tucked away and treasured, and never shared.

"Are you just planning on staying married to the job forever?" William continued before Alec had a chance to dwell on his previous statement.

Alec flashed his brother a rueful grin. "Would that be so bad?" Now was the chance he had been waiting for. He pushed his glass away as he contemplated his wording. "We used to have a lot of fun back in the office, as I recall."

William tipped his head, smiling fondly at a distant memory. "Yeah," he admitted. "We did."

Alec studied his brother carefully, gauging his mood. "You ever think about coming back to the company?" He could only hope his tone sounded more casual than he felt. The noise from the pub helped disguise any hint of desperation that might have otherwise been heard.

William shifted his gaze to the table. "Oh, I don't know." He shrugged. "Sometimes, I guess."

Oh, really? Alec chose his next words carefully. "You know I'd love you back. What do you say? It could be like old times."

"Old times." William took a sip of his drink. "Thinking

about coming back and actually doing so are two very different things, Alec. I have a whole life here."

"But Boston is your home, William."

William shook his head. "No. No, it's not anymore."

Alec tried not to let his frustration show. "So you're saying this is your home now? That you plan to live in this little resort town permanently?"

Opening his eyes wide, William laughed softly. "Yes. That's exactly what I'm saying." Frowning, he held his brother's gaze as the room around them stilled. "Look, Alec, do you know what I did over the weekend? I went sailing with Elizabeth's dad. The weekend before, Elizabeth's brother helped us assemble a new porch swing. We do big Sunday dinners. Heck, we even go to Elizabeth's cousin's daughters' dance recitals. We have a yard and a garden, and we're planning to get a dog after the wedding."

"You could have a dog in Boston," Alec pointed out. *Not that he'd have time to give it the attention it deserved,* he thought.

Alec glanced at his brother, whose eyes seemed to hold the same sad understanding.

"Do you think I would have time to take care of a dog if I was still living that lifestyle? Much less a wife? Or...kids?"

"Kids?" Alec was grateful for the darkness of the room so his brother couldn't see the blood drain from his face. Clearing his throat, he said, "Okay, yes, you did work a lot of hours."

"Too many. It's no kind of life. That's why I worry about you."

"You know I love my job, William." And he did. Or, at least he used to. It was something he used to excel at—something that used to make his father proud. His father might not have given him much in life, but he had handed both sons that company. It was the one thing Alec had held on to—the one constant in his life that made him feel connected. But now... Alec sighed and ran a hand through his hair, pushing it back from his forehead.

His brother looked unconvinced. "Yes, but I'm just saying—there's a lot more to life than that job. Don't you want a family?"

The word tapped into his worst fear. "I thought I had a family." Now all he had was a father, who was more interested in spreadsheets than hearing about his day.

"You know what I mean."

"You mean a wife." Alec stared out the window onto the cobblestone street. It was late and a glow of gaslights illuminated the storefronts and bustling sidewalk restaurants. There was more going on in downtown Misty Point than he'd thought there would be. He tried to imagine William strolling hand in hand with a wife and a couple of kids, stopping at the ice cream parlor across the street, where families were gathered on benches. He shot a glance back at his brother. "You really think that Elizabeth's the one?"

William's eyes sparked. "Yes, or I wouldn't be marrying her. I thought by you coming here that you had finally accepted it."

Alec held up a hand. "Can you blame me for being shocked? You barely knew the girl, and it was our first time ever meeting her." He dragged out a sigh. "Look, I'm not here to cause trouble, William. I'm just looking out for you."

"I know," William replied, his tone a little more forgiving. "And so I hope you can understand that I know what I'm doing."

Alec leaned back in his chair, feeling depressed and nauseous all at once. Everything he wanted—everything he cared about—

was crashing down around him. He let his gaze drift lazily around the room before coming back to William. "You're really happy, aren't you?"

But he knew the answer; it was written all over his brother's face. His brother had found the one thing he had been missing all his life. By marrying Elizabeth, he wasn't just getting a bride; he was getting a built-in family—and the hope for one of his own in the future. When they were young, they used to kick the ball to each other in silence, observing all the other families at the park huddled around picnic tables or sharing a laugh. Even though Alec knew it was pointless, he had searched the stands at every one of his soccer games, hoping to see his father's face in the crowd. He could still feel the weight of that disappointment now at his age—nearly three decades later. It was the main reason why when William got around to playing sports, Alec made a point of showing up and cheering him on.

And look where it got him in the end. William had found a better replacement, and Alec was left behind.

All he had left now was the company, and God knew its days were numbered. He couldn't ask for his brother's help, as much as he wished he could. It was the reason why he hadn't picked up the phone and called him when this mess started six months ago. He knew William would help if he was directly asked, but Alec had pride, and he wanted William to come back because he wanted to, not because he felt compelled out of loyalty.

William had no idea the lurch he had left his family in. It was so easy for him to stand by Elizabeth and walk away from his own brother—had he really never paused to consider the ramifications of his actions? They'd lost two major clients in the past year: one to a high-profile divorce that broke up the asset pool and another to investment purchases against Alec's advice. Three other big clients had followed William in his departure—at the time, that hadn't seemed like a problem, but now it was. It was crucial to bring in new business, but they didn't have much time to hold on.

"You up for a round of golf this week?" he suggested. Misty Point no doubt had some excellent courses.

"How about Monday?"

Alec hesitated. Monday was his meeting with Mason Lambert. His entire reason for staying in Misty Point rather than leaving tomorrow. Well, that, and trying to convince William to rejoin the firm.

He opened his mouth, about to suggest they have drinks tomorrow night—just the two of them—when William cut in. "Hey, before I forget. Kate's parents are having us over for dinner tomorrow night. Why don't you join us?"

"Kate the wedding planner Kate?" Alec couldn't resist the twinge of interest that quickened his pulse, but it was soon replaced with that uneasy feeling that had settled in his gut since arriving in Misty Point. "That sounds like a family affair."

"And you're my family. Join us. They're nice. You'll like them. And it will give you and Elizabeth a chance to get to know each other better, too."

Alec didn't see how he could argue. He shook the ice around in his glass before taking another sip. Things were already off to a bad start. For some reason, a little part of Alec had hoped he could sweep into town and lure William away from Elizabeth and the life he had created with her. He had thought that blood was thicker than water, that William's bond to his own family could override any infatuation he might have for the woman he was so determined to marry. But William adored Elizabeth. He had asked her to marry him. William, the confirmed bachelor, was getting married to some pretty young woman from Misty Point, Rhode Island. A resort town with cobblestone streets and a downtown filled with ice cream shops.

If it wasn't so ludicrous, Alec would burst out laughing. But there was nothing funny about this at all. Not when everything Alec had worked so hard to build was crashing down around him. Not when the only person who could save him was the one person he couldn't ask for help.

* * *

Kate brought her thumbnail to her mouth and then, remembering her manicure, set her hand back firmly in her lap. She glanced at the screen on her phone, happy to see that the light was only blinking with a new email alert—and good news at that. The cut glassware Kate had special-ordered for the event was in transit, scheduled to arrive by Tuesday morning.

Kate breathed a little easier, but despite having another item to check off her list, she couldn't fight the frown that was pulling at her forehead.

Charlotte had called today. Again. Making that the fifth time in a month. And if recent history proved anything, this wouldn't be the last time. For whatever reason, her sister was determined to get in contact with her. As far as Kate was concerned, there was nothing left to say. What did you say to the woman who had slept with your fiancé and then run off to Boston with him, leaving you with shattered dreams and a broken heart? *Oh, so nice to hear your voice? Oh, that's ancient history; how are you?*

Yeah. She didn't think so.

As far as she was concerned, there was nothing to discuss.

So why did a part of her chest ache when she thought of that name lighting up her screen? When the sound of her sister's voice was so close, just a press of a button away?

It was nostalgia, she told herself firmly. For something they'd once shared. For a relationship she'd hoped to have with her only sibling and now never would. She'd imagined long chats about simple commonalities like recipes or movies or books, not men they'd both slept with.

But then, when had she ever been close to Charlotte, really? Their bedrooms growing up were side by side, but their worlds couldn't have been more far apart. Charlotte was headstrong, feisty, and openly selfish. A role that Kate now realized she'd probably contributed to, without even knowing it. Kate had been the responsible one. The good student. The neighborhood babysitter. The shy wallflower. And because of this, Charlotte could stand to be a little more reckless.

Yes, reckless. That's exactly what Charlotte was.

Kate forced a smile at Elizabeth and tried to focus on the present moment. Just because her dreams had been ripped from her didn't mean that her friend's wedding festivities should be any less magical.

She'd planned tonight's event according to Elizabeth's tastes, keeping in line with a color scheme of pink and going along with all her favorite foods. It was a small affair—just herself, the bride and the other two bridesmaids, Bree, and their good friend Colleen McKay. They had a prime table on the back half of the terrace at Grigio's, Misty Point's see-and-be-seen wine bar, and the restaurant had accommodated Kate's wishes for the pink rose centerpieces and votive candles. Strings of lights hung above and were wrapped around the potted trees that anchored the space. Quaint and intimate, it was just the kind of party Elizabeth wanted, no need for fanfare or limos or "wild nights" on the town, as Alec had joked.

"I wonder what the guys are up to tonight." She waggled her eyebrows at Elizabeth's eye roll, but soon the girls started throwing out suggestions, each more titillating than the next.

"Dancers?" Elizabeth repeated to Colleen, her jaw dropping. She gave a knowing shake of the head. "William's not into other women like that. I can trust him."

At this, her cheeks turned a bright shade of red and the table fell silent. Kate felt her own face begin to burn when she realized what was happening. Of course. They were tiptoeing around her feelings again, and as much as she loved them for it, sometimes, she wished they wouldn't.

"Well, I bet they get a poker game started before long," Kate said, breaking the ice. "If you need to spend the night with me, you're welcome to it, Elizabeth."

She hoped her friend didn't catch the inflection of hope in her tone. Spending time with Elizabeth had been the truest way for her to shut out the loss of her sister. And it had been nice to have someone to lean on for once. She always had to be the strong one in her family—the one who patiently filled the kettle for tea while Charlotte cried over the latest guy she'd been dating who had disappointed her. Kate never bothered to point out back then that at least Charlotte was asked on dates. And when Charlotte bustled down the stairs a week later, eyes as bright as her smile, asking Kate to zip up the back of her dress, Kate did so, knowing that in a week, when the excitement of this date wore off, they'd be back at the kitchen table again, Kate handing over the tissues, which Charlotte didn't even bother to throw away.

But with Elizabeth, the tables weren't so uneven. And when Kate had needed someone the most, it had been Elizabeth doling out the tissues.

Now it was Kate's turn to return the favor.

"Have you broken in your shoes yet?" Kate met Elizabeth's guilty smile across the table. "I don't need you sitting down halfway through the reception because your feet are throbbing."

"Don't worry," Elizabeth assured her. She tucked a strand of blond hair behind her ear and leaned back in her chair. "I'll wear them around the house tomorrow. I figure it can't be too bad of luck for the groom to see the bride's shoes before the wedding."

Kate wasn't a suspicious person by nature, but when it came to weddings, she wasn't taking any risks. "Just promise me he won't see the dress."

"Kate!" Elizabeth cried. "You can't honestly tell me you believe in all that superstition."

The conversation at the other end of the table stopped, and suddenly all eyes were on her.

Kate shrugged. "I just don't like taking any chances. Why tempt fate when enough can go wrong anyway?"

Across the table, Bree gave Kate a pitying smile, and all at once Kate was reminded of how she must look: not like the uptight wedding planner, but like the bride who never had a chance to walk down the aisle.

She reached for her Champagne and took a long sip, but her hands were shaking slightly, and the table had gone uncomfortably silent again. She wracked her brain for a casual way to break the ice, but this time, it was impossible. She was rattled, unsure of herself, dangerously close to that bad place she had only just escaped from.

Elizabeth tutted. "I promise he will not see the dress. Or the veil. And I will hide the shoes when he's around. Besides, with you as my wedding planner, what could go wrong?" She winked and reached for a slice of bread before hesitating and reaching for the veggies and hummus instead. "There will be plenty of time for carbs after the wedding," she sighed.

"Well, considering the last man who took me out to dinner was my brother, I don't mind if I do," Bree announced as she filled her plate.

"Hey, I'll gladly go out to dinner with your brother if you don't want him," Colleen joked, but Bree just shook her head firmly.

"The man is an eternal bachelor. If it weren't for our monthly dinners, he'd exist solely on microwaveable meals and takeout and boxed macaroni and cheese. You should see the way he hovers around the stove on holidays, hoping for a doggie bag of leftovers. I don't even think he combs his hair half the time."

Colleen settled back in her seat, looking completely unconvinced.

Kate and Elizabeth exchanged a secret smile across the table. Poor Colleen had pined over Bree's older brother, Matt, for years, always perking up when his name came up in conversation, even enrolling in a class at the local college that contained his name on the syllabus, only to drop out after the first lesson when she'd discovered he had a girlfriend at the time. Sure, Matt was handsome, but Bree was fair in her assessment, too, and from Kate's personal experience, a good man was hard enough to find even when he didn't come with a warning.

Colleen set down her glass. "What do you mean that the last man who took you out to dinner was your brother? Is everything okay with Simon?"

Bree stopped chewing for a moment. "Oh, everything with Simon is great. But you know..."

Kate's lips thinned. Yes, she did know. She knew an undeserving man when she saw one, although admittedly, more and more they all seemed undeserving. But Simon was a special case. How many nights did Bree sit beside him on the couch while he stared at the television screen, absorbed in a video game, of all things? Or perhaps worse—cartoons. How many times had he stood her up when she thought they were supposed to be meeting for brunch?

"I wonder if the guys are having fun tonight," Colleen mused.

"I can't imagine anyone having fun with Alec around," Elizabeth replied.

"Is he really that bad?" Bree asked as she refilled each of their four glasses with more pink Champagne.

"Maybe it will be better with him now that you and William are getting married," Colleen suggested.

Elizabeth shook her head. "I don't see him suddenly welcoming me with open arms. He didn't even congratulate me when we got engaged. He just sat there, practically scowling. He barely spoke for the entire meal. And he didn't even say goodbye or nice meeting you. Believe me, if it were up to him, William wouldn't be marrying me at all."

"He was probably just surprised," Bree argued. "Give him another chance."

Poor Bree, Kate thought. She really was too forgiving at times.

Still, when it came to Elizabeth's future brother-in-law, she had to agree with her cousin on this one. "He's here for the entire week. So maybe he's had a change of heart." But even as she spoke, she knew her words were unconvincing. He'd made it pretty clear to her that he was in town for business. Not that she'd be telling Elizabeth that.

She frowned as she picked up her glass. Business in Misty Point? She supposed it wasn't entirely impossible with the summer homes owned by neighboring Boston's elite.

"I met him today," Kate offered, and the surprise in Elizabeth's eyes made her wish she hadn't brought it up. Now they'd spend the rest of the evening talking about a man the bride couldn't stand, and this was supposed to be a happy night, one Kate had been looking forward to. A night without any men present, and the subject of men hopefully closed.

Elizabeth chewed on a carrot stick and eyed Kate carefully, gauging her reaction. "What did you guys talk about?"

Kate forced her expression to remain blank. She darted her eyes to the cheese plate to avoid Elizabeth's heated stare. "We went over the rehearsal dinner. He...had some great suggestions."

"And?" The word was spoken with so much intensity that Kate was forced to pull her attention back to Elizabeth's wide, unblinking eyes.

And...and he's totally gorgeous and reminds me entirely too much of Jake. Old Jake. The Jake I thought I was marrying, not the one who ran off with my sister.

She tried to properly consider the question, thinking back on her brief time with him. She pulled up an image of him, a tingle trickling its way down her spine at the memory of those penetrating dark eyes. "He looks a lot like William. I was surprised just how much. But you got the better brother," she added lamely, thinking of William's easygoing demeanor.

"You could say that," Elizabeth snorted. She tilted her head, not yet satisfied with the answer. "But what did he seem like to you? What was his mood like?"

"Busy," Kate said quickly, wondering why she was so compelled to protect this man. She should loathe him. She should find him detestable. And she did...sort of. "He seems distracted, I guess, and just really preoccupied with his career."

Elizabeth's lips thinned. "That's him, all right. All he cares about is that company. Making money. He doesn't care who he knocks down in his pursuit. When it comes to his work, he has no boundaries. William is so much happier running his own business."

"I know the type." The answer was bland, Kate knew, but it was safe. And true.

"Speaking of types," Colleen cut in, "I agreed to be set up on a date by my mother." She held up a hand and closed her eyes. "I know. I know. But she really sold him. Dark hair and tall and an attorney. We're having drinks tomorrow night."

"If it works out, you can bring him as a date to my wedding!" Elizabeth said happily, but Kate was quick to do the math, drawing up the seating arrangements she'd spent more than half a day planning. Colleen was a bridesmaid, along with Bree, but there were no extra seats at the singles table and the only open slot she had under the current setup was at the grandparents' table, and that wouldn't look right. She stifled a sigh, told herself to calm down, and decided to shelve this issue until tomorrow. She'd figure it out. She had to. It was Elizabeth's wedding, after all. And didn't one of them deserve a perfect day?

"Well, it's just drinks, and the referral does come from my mother, but... it seems promising." Colleen gave a shy smile, and Kate blinked, suddenly remembering how it felt to be filled with that kind of hope.

But then she remembered how relationships ended, and that was a sobering thought.

Still, with the possibility of Colleen bringing a date and Bree still clinging to Simon, that meant that Kate was the only one of their group going stag. To her best friend's wedding.

It wasn't lost on her that she would technically be paired with Alec all night.

All the more reason to hurry up and find a more practical date.

Chapter Six

B y nine the next morning, Kate had already clocked two hours at the office, half of which was spent working out the menu for a wedding next month, while the other half was devoted to redoing the seating arrangements for Elizabeth and William's reception, just in case Colleen's date went well.

She studied the guest list with a frown, noticing all the plus ones and the perfectly empty spot next to her own name. Really, she wasn't sure why she was so caught up in this. She'd gone to weddings alone before, back before she'd met Jake, and besides, she wasn't just the maid of honor at this weekend's event; she was also the wedding planner, meaning she didn't have time to attend to a date. It wouldn't be fair. She'd be too busy running around, making sure that the cake was angled just so for the camera, that the photographers were there to capture each tender moment, that the music was loud enough, and that the centerpieces were centered. She didn't have time for a twirl on the dance floor. She probably wouldn't even see most of the cocktail hour. She closed her laptop firmly. That settled it. She had a valid reason not to have a date.

And really, if she had a date, how could she keep an eye on the potentially troublesome best man? He was her focus this week. Other than the bride, of course.

Grabbing her bag and lightweight cardigan, she opted to walk the short distance from her office to the Beacon Inn to meet Alec for their ten o'clock appointment at the tuxedo shop. If she was sensible, she would put the sweater on and button it to the very top, just to be clear that she was running a professional errand only, but darn it if she didn't feel a little thrill as she walked down the street. It had been a long time since she'd been on her way to meet an attractive, single man...for any reason. It was probably the most exciting Sunday she'd had in...longer than she wanted to think about.

And that was all the more reason to keep her head on straight, she told herself firmly. All she needed was to remember the day her world had come crashing down, and all thoughts of romance scattered like sand on a sidewalk.

She was supposed to be going with Jake to the cake tasting; she'd been looking forward to it all week, imagining all the varieties they would try, how exciting it would be to settle on the perfect one. But they'd never made it to Colleen's Cakes. They'd never even made it outside. Ten minutes was all it had taken for their relationship to end—she remembered, because he was meeting her at eleven thirty, and when he walked out the door she remembered looking at the clock on the wall of her apartment. For weeks after, she couldn't stop thinking that it took months to build a relationship—and only a minute to destroy it.

She shook away the thoughts as she paused to stare at the

window display of the Book Stall, her favorite shop in town. There was no use going down this path. As difficult as it was, she had to listen to the wise words of advice that had felt a bit callous at first: everything happens for a reason.

Maybe it did. After all, if Jake hadn't cheated on her, she probably wouldn't have decided to get a dog to keep her company. The strange twist of fate that led Henry into her life wasn't lost on her. She grinned at the thought of him.

Who said you needed a man to be happy? Give a girl a dog, and she'd be loved for life.

Though it was still early, the streets of Misty Point were already filled with tourists ready to start their day. It was a warm morning, and sweet salty air filled her lungs, making it impossible not to smile a little as she walked past the shops on Harbor Street, despite the heaviness in her heart.

Kate hurried the rest of the way to the inn. The entrance from the street was long and winding, the green grass contrasting beautifully with the crisp white building and the bright blue sea behind it. It was Elizabeth's choice to have her reception here, and Kate couldn't have come up with a better choice for her best friend. A large tent would be set up on the lawn for the reception following the beach service, and, last she'd checked, the weather was still forecasted to be sunny all week.

Kate turned onto the brick-paved path that led to the streetside entrance of the hotel and shivered as she entered the lobby. She swept her eyes over the room as she wiggled into her cardigan, and seeing no sign of Alec, crossed to the front desk.

"Room 412," she said, recalling the room number Alec had given the bellhop yesterday. "I'm Kate Daniels. We have an appointment."

"Certainly." The woman behind the counter pressed the buttons and held the receiver to her ear. Kate watched with growing impatience as she waited for Alec to answer. The tux shop was technically open until five on Sundays, but when it came to wedding parties, they had a strict policy about prescheduled appointments. Finally, the woman said, "Mr. Montgomery? Kate Daniels is in the lobby for you." A pause. A long pause, Kate thought. And she wondered if she should be worried about that sudden pinch between the woman's brow. "Certainly, sir. I'll let her know."

The woman replaced the receiver without a sound and gave her a serene smile. "He'll be down shortly."

Shortly? Kate checked her watch and fought the urge to ask just how shortly, but instead admitted defeat and dropped into a nearby chair.

Fourteen minutes later, and nine minutes after Kate had started wrestling with whether or not to tap that elevator button and hunt him down herself, the doors of the elevator slid open and Alec appeared, looking considerably less polished than he had last time she'd seen him. His wavy brown hair was bedraggled, and there was a strip of toilet paper on his chin where he seemed to have cut himself shaving.

"How are you this morning?" she asked, standing to greet him.

"Oh . . . fine. Yourself?" He looked past her distractedly, giving her no chance to respond. "I need a coffee."

Not on her watch. "You can have coffee after the fitting."

"That's not until ten," he reminded her.

Kate held up her phone and pushed a button to light up the screen. "It's nine-forty."

"Where is this store? Another town?"

Admittedly, it was a ten-minute walk, but that wasn't the point. The point was that she was on a tight schedule, and as with yesterday, Alec didn't seem to want to take that into consideration. "Get a coffee, then. But make it a quick one."

His eyes seemed to glimmer. "Yes, ma'am."

He took off in the direction of the hotel café, his stride long and purposeful, and Kate struggled to keep up with him in her heels. "A table by the window, please. Or one outside, if there are any free," she heard him say.

"A table?" Oh no, no. This wouldn't do. She looked at him sternly. "We only have twenty minutes," she reminded him. "Ten, technically, if you factor in the walk."

He looked at her in amusement. "Did anyone ever tell you that you worry too much?"

She pinched her lips, hitched her handbag straps a little higher on her shoulder, and, noticing his chivalrous wave in the direction of the hostess, followed the woman to the table, wondering if Alec's eyes were on the back of her head or the back of her ass as they made their way onto the outside veranda.

Just in case, she stood a little straighter.

★ ★ ★

Alec watched as the waitress poured coffee into his mug, Kate's eyes blazing from under the shield of the stainless steel carafe.

He picked up the mug, trying his best to still the shaking of his hands, and drank back the full cup quickly, hoping it would dull the sharp pain that had been slicing through the space between his eyes since he'd woken to the call from the woman at the front desk just a mere twenty minutes ago.

Jesus, just how much had he had to drink last night? Too much, that was for sure. He wasn't used to it. A beer here and there, sure. A glass of Scotch on a particularly rough day, that was a given. But a night out at a bar? Those days had ended when William left town.

"So, tell me. How was the bachelor party last night?" Kate raised one eyebrow as her mouth curved into what might pass for a smile. He supposed it was the closest thing he'd get from her this morning.

"Not much to tell," Alec said, rubbing a hand over his forehead. A waiter passed him, carrying a tray of omelets, and Alec eyed them eagerly, wondering if he dared... and wondering what would happen if he didn't.

His stomach felt raw and scraped out and he was shaky and out of sorts. His hair was still wet, and Kate wouldn't stop staring at his chin.

"Do I have something on my face?" He laughed uneasily.

"You cut yourself shaving," she said, motioning to the spot where he'd nicked himself in his rush to get downstairs.

He rubbed his chin and frowned at the discovery. Jesus. He was more out of it than he thought. "If you'll excuse me for a minute, I'll go to the restroom and clean up." Pushing his chair back, he stood, feeling the blood rush to his head at once. He resisted the urge to grab the table for support, instead waiting for his vision to clear as he searched for the sign for the men's room.

Kate sighed as she reluctantly reached for the carafe and filled her mug. "Do you like your eggs scrambled or fried?"

He hesitated. "Excuse me?"

"Your eggs. I suppose it won't hurt if we're a few minutes late. And something tells me you'll feel a little better once you have something in your system to soak up the remains of last night's party." She slipped him a small smile and he grinned in return.

"Fried," he said.

Kate jutted her chin. "In the lobby, take a left at the elevators."

Alec smiled gratefully. "Thanks."

"Don't thank me. Can't have you sick all over the menswear," she remarked, but she was doing a damn poor job of hiding her smile.

When he returned, there was a pitcher of ice water and a plate of buttery toast on the table waiting for him.

"Your eggs will be up any minute," Kate told him. She clutched her mug in front of her with two hands, as if warming her fingers.

"Cold?" Alec asked as he eagerly bit into a square of toast.

Kate shrugged. "You get used to spending time in hotels in my profession. Besides, this beats the office."

"Cold air?"

"Cold boss." Kate grinned ruefully before hiding her smile behind the rim of her coffee cup, but the light in her eyes seemed to fade by the time she set the mug back down.

"Ah," Alec said a little begrudgingly. "I understand. People think working for a family business has its perks. But my father isn't an easy man to please."

He thought of the two missed calls from his father he'd already received today, the last one coming as he was scrambling to meet Kate. It wasn't like him to be unavailable, and his father didn't care that he was in Misty Point, partaking in William's wedding week plans. No doubt the man wanted some update on how things were going with drumming up new business or convincing his brother to come back to the firm, and as of right now, there was nothing to report on either front. But Alec would have to change that, and soon.

The waitress arrived and set a steaming plate in front of Alec, causing his stomach to churn. He pushed the plate away and Kate swiftly pushed it back.

"Eat it," she said with a hard look once the waitress had moved on to the next table. She reached for the pitcher of water and filled a glass to the rim. "Seriously," she said, softening her tone. "You'll feel better if you do. Trust me."

Alec lifted an unconvinced brow but reached for his fork. He folded the napkin into his lap and cut into his eggs. Watching her as he chewed, he remarked, "Has anyone ever told you that it's okay to smile once in a while?"

Kate bristled. "What's that supposed to mean?"

Alec shrugged, wondering why he was bothering to have this conversation with a woman he would probably never see again after this week. It was the remark she'd made about her boss, he realized. The twitchy look in her eyes she had every time she glanced at the clock. It was that five-pound binder full of plans for a party. A party that was supposed to be fun. "I'm just saying, you could lighten up a little bit. That's all."

"Lighten up? You don't even know me."

"Perhaps," he said, dousing his eggs with salt, "but I'm just going off what I see."

"And what do you see?"

Alec offered her a gentle smile. "Forget I said anything," he said.

"No. I want to know," she insisted, leaning over the table until he could see the flecks of green around her pupils.

Alec set down his fork with a heavy sigh. *Here it goes.*

"You had a steady boyfriend all through high school, went to the prom both years. Or maybe you didn't date at all. Too pretty and too standoffish. A tricky combo with adolescent boys. You come from a good family. Maybe you're an only child, but more likely the eldest. You were a good student, but you worked hard. You took your grades seriously, and you approach your career the same way. I'm guessing you ran for student council. You probably initiated bake sales for various fund-raisers, too. Your parents are probably still married, and I bet they still hold hands. So you believe in a fairy-tale ending and you expect one for yourself. That probably includes a big wedding, a European honeymoon, and a four-bedroom house in the suburbs with impeccably organized closets where you'll raise your two point five blond and blue-eyed kids with your equally preppy husband." He paused. "Am I right?"

She didn't blink. "What makes you think I believe in fairy-tale endings?"

Alec frowned. "You're a wedding planner. You mean to tell me you're not buying the dream you're selling?"

Her mouth curved into a slow, mysterious smile as she pulled back against the chair.

Alec took another bite of his eggs. Combined with the coffee and water, he was already feeling a little better. Not that he'd be repeating last night anytime soon. And not that he'd likely have opportunity or reason to again. None of his friends in the city were getting married anytime soon, either. And like him, they'd rather be able to get up early to hit the gym for a few hours before clocking a fifteen-hour workday.

Kate silently drank her coffee, saying nothing more about his opinion of her, and strangely offering none of her own about him.

"You'd better eat fast," she finally said. "That fitting is in less than ten minutes now."

"Tsk, tsk." Alec shook his head and glanced at her with mock disdain. "There you go again."

"Okay, you win," she said. "I am being a little...bossy—"

"A little?"

Kate grinned. "Okay a lot. I just...I want everything to be perfect. For your brother and Elizabeth."

"That makes two of us," he said through a tight smile.

★ ★ ★

Kate eyed Alec's plate, calculating that he had about six more bites to go. She signaled a passing waitress for the check. A few minutes late to the fitting was one thing. Half an hour late meant their appointment would be lost. And then...She sighed. Her week was jam-packed, as the week before a big wedding typically was.

"So how long have you known Elizabeth?" Alec asked as he slid the bill from Kate's side of the table to his own and picked up the pen.

"We've known each other since we were kids." Kate smiled fondly at the memories of those carefree days spent building sandcastles on the beach and collecting shells. The bike rides into town to get ice cream. "We lived next door to each other growing up. We live next door to each other again now," she added, and noticed that Alec's eyes widened at that tidbit. "I recently bought the house next to theirs."

Another slight narrowing of the eyes. No doubt he wasn't expecting that. He was probably circling the possibility of whether she was in fact attached and happily living with someone, or if she'd actually bit the bullet and purchased a home for herself. Admitted that she wasn't going to find a man anytime soon.

"I'm guessing you've probably heard some not so nice things said about me," Alec said ruefully.

"Oh, now, I wouldn't say that." She gave a watery smile and pushed the sugar bowl to the side, careful not to rattle the porcelain lid.

But Alec just chuckled softly. "Don't worry. I know my reputation."

She lifted her gaze to meet his sad smile, sensing he was waiting for her to say something. "And what would that be?"

"That I'm ruthless. Arrogant. Cold. You get the drift."

"Funny, I was thinking something along the lines of overly sure of himself, overly ambitious..." A few other choice adjectives that would be better kept to herself.

"Ah, so you've formed an opinion of me as well, then." He studied her, and Kate shrugged. "Go on."

Kate sighed. "We have an appointment."

"It can wait," he said, and something in his tone told her she had no choice but to oblige.

"Okay, you grew up in a wealthy family, didn't have to ask for anything, wanted for even less. You have good looks, and you rode them all the way through high school. You probably didn't even bother to ask most girls out, because they were busy asking you. And you liked it that way. You still date casually, but not seriously, and you don't really care how it plays out or who gets hurt. You're the same in business, which is your top priority. You like a fast-paced life with no strings attached. You think about kids, but not in the immediate future, but deep down you know you have neither the time nor interest for them, or a wife."

Jeez, where had that come from? *Jake*, she realized with a start.

A twinge of shame fell heavy, but only for a moment. Men like Alec and Jake weren't put in their place often enough. Maybe if they were, they'd be held accountable for their actions. Maybe if they were, she wouldn't be planning everyone else's weddings instead of her own.

★ ★ ★

Alec pushed his empty plate away and reached into his pocket for his wallet. The morning's fog had finally lifted and his mind was as clear as the sunny blue skies. He glanced at Kate as he slapped a fifty-dollar bill on the table.

"We should probably go," he said abruptly. He glanced down at his watch and frowned. "How long will this appointment take?"

"Depends on how cooperative you are," she said pertly.

Alec sighed and followed her through the door, plucking a peppermint candy from the dish on his way out. He popped it in his mouth as a warm, salty breeze hit his face, clearing his head almost to a state of normalcy. Now he remembered why he didn't go out much anymore. His life was his business, and he was jeopardizing the one thing that he revolved his existence around. It was a mistake he wouldn't be making again, at least not on this trip.

His phone vibrated in his pocket. Without a response to Kate's wide-eyed questioning gaze, he answered. He'd already ignored too many calls for one day.

He listened to his assistant's feedback and disconnected the call. "Change of plans," he said to Kate.

"Are you kidding me?" she asked, but her voice was flat with accusation.

Suddenly, his mind was racing with the implication of a meeting with Mason Lambert a day early—he'd been preparing for this meeting since he set it up three weeks ago, but he'd have to clean himself up, clear his head, and get into the right mindset.

"We're going to have to reschedule," he said distractedly, thinking of the notes he had upstairs in his room. He'd have to hurry to look over them. Mason Lambert was a sharp businessman. Any sign of weakness would be sniffed out immediately.

Kate's eyes were unnaturally wide as she stared at him. "What do you mean, we have to reschedule?"

"It's important," he said, raking a set of fingers through his hair.

"Your brother's wedding is important, Alec."

"I wouldn't be rescheduling if it wasn't important. It's my business. You have to understand."

"Business!"

He eyed her. Most of the time when women gave him that look it was because he was canceling plans a little more of the personal nature. "Kate, work with me here. I'm in town for a week. Tomorrow. I promise. Three o'clock work for you?"

She folded her arms across her chest, taking her time in giving him an answer. "I'll have to call and check, but let's plan on that. But I still don't see what could be more important than your brother's wedding," she was sure to add as she walked away.

Chapter Seven

Kate's feet were burning by the time she'd pounded her way back to Harbor Street, muttering under her breath as she wound her way to Colleen's Cakes, the bakery owned and operated by none other than her dear friend Colleen.

Thanks to Alec's cancellation, she was more than an hour early to check on the status of the wedding cake, but hopefully Colleen could squeeze her in. With any luck, she'd cross the cake off her list and return a few client calls before meeting Elizabeth for lunch.

She checked her texts to see if Elizabeth had replied to her suggestion that they meet a little earlier than planned. Excellent. She'd be heading out in fifteen minutes.

Kate took a calming breath before pushing open the door of the shop, but it was a pointless exercise. As soon as she entered the room, all the stress rolled from her shoulders and a smile teased her mouth as she breathed in the smells of vanilla and sugar.

The room was airy and light, with creamy white walls and

big windows. Kate made her way past the glass display case, admiring the birthday cakes and "everyday" cakes like coffee cake and death by chocolate cake and a colorful selection of cupcakes, and walked to the back of the room, where Colleen was hard at work piping pale green petals onto a buttercream frosted cake with a pastry bag.

"You're early," Colleen remarked. "Just give me a minute to finish these petals. It's for a fiftieth birthday dinner. You remember Mrs. Channing?"

Kate tried to connect the name. "Middle school art?"

Colleen grinned. "The very one. Hard to believe she's fifty, huh?"

Kate shook her head in wonder. Mrs. Channing was always so youthful and exotic, with her waist-length braid swinging against the back of her long, floral dresses. "Hard to believe we're thirty."

"Don't remind me." Colleen groaned. She rotated the cake and began swiftly adding the rest of the petals.

Kate watched the effortless movement, knowing just how difficult it was from her attempts at making fancier birthday cakes for friends and family over the years, and sighed. "Someday you promise to teach me how to do that?"

"It's not so tricky once you have the hang of it," Colleen said happily. She placed the piping down on a plastic sheet to set and wiped a loose strand of hair from her forehead with the back of her hand. "I wasn't expecting you until eleven thirty."

"I'm not catching you at a bad time, am I? I can come back." She could. And she would, if need be. But she'd learned the best way to stay on track was to batch her errands in one trip, and seeing as she didn't plan to leave the office tomorrow until the suit fitting...and there would be a fitting, if she had to kidnap the man and drag him there herself, so help her, there would.

"Actually, this is a perfect time. My morning customers just left, and I don't expect another wave until after lunch. And I could use a break before I finish this cake. I want to mull over the color scheme a bit before I add the gum paste flowers. Oh, listen to me! Thirty years old and I'm still eager to impress my art teacher." She waggled her eyebrows. "You want to see what I have so far for Elizabeth?"

Kate looked around at the empty tables and nodded eagerly. She trusted Colleen nearly as much as she trusted Elizabeth, and not just as a friend. She recommended Colleen to all her brides—the woman didn't just make the best cakes for miles around, but she was also organized and dependable, and she took pride in what she was making. Still...Kate was ultimately the fall guy if anything slipped through the cracks.

"Don't mind the mess," Colleen said gaily as Kate followed her through the stainless steel door into the kitchen. Cakes in various stages of completion lined the counters, some iced, some tiered, some sitting in their pans, waiting to go into the oven.

She pushed through one more set of doors, and Kate felt her tread slow. She'd been back here many times, but each time she felt the wave, the stir of nausea, the sense of dread, the slow, un-avoidable reminder that always made her heart hurt a little. Even now. Nearly a year after her wedding had been called off.

"You coming?" Colleen paused in the doorway and looked at her quizzically.

Kate smiled wider but her cheeks felt stiff. "Just caught up in all the cakes you have going on here."

She needed to get a grip. If she didn't, she'd have to find a new profession. And why should she let Jake rob that of her, too?

"If you think these are nice, then check these out. This is where the magic happens..." Colleen winked as she held open the door for Kate to pass, leaving no room for further hesitation.

Kate put one foot in front of the other and walked into the back room, where wedding cakes of all heights and shapes towered high around her, all belonging to someone, all waiting for their special day.

She walked over to a particularly beautiful five-tiered circular cake, covered in a creamy white fondant and lined with a lavender ribbon. "This is beautiful," she breathed, giving it a closer look. "That shade of purple is..."

"Perfect. I know. It reminds me of—" She stopped, her pale cheeks turning a shade of red that Kate knew had nothing to do with the heat of the ovens in the adjacent kitchen.

Kate turned away from the cake and the memories of her own wedding cake, or at least the design she and Colleen had come up with for it. Three round tiers, white fondant, lavender ribbon, and burst of flowers at the top to match the freesia she had in her bouquet. Make that *would* have had, she corrected herself.

"It's okay," she said, hating how familiar that sounded. How many times since she'd announced that the wedding had been called off had she been forced to smooth over awkward situations with those words? Somehow it was her job to eventually put on the bright smile and reassure everyone that it was fine; she wasn't bothered by the reminder of the love of her life cheating on her with her sister or the humiliation of calling off her wedding. She was fine; she was over it! No worries. No worries at all.

Only something told her no one was buying her brazen attitude. There was too much pity in everyone's eyes, and they twitched at the slightest potential reminder. Her parents tiptoed around her, eager to please, never mentioning their younger daughter in her presence, a look of desperation often taking over her mother's expression.

Everyone just wanted her to be happy. And everyone assumed she was not happy.

Would it take finding a new man to get them to all stop defining her by her past once and for all?

Unfortunately for her, the answer to that was probably yes. And more unfortunate was the fact that she had absolutely no interest in giving her heart away again.

"Well. Anyway." Colleen blinked quickly and gestured to her progress on Elizabeth's wedding cake, which, perhaps intentionally, looked nothing like Kate's.

Kate knew that at first Elizabeth had tried to tone down her excitement and even any discussion of her wedding around Kate, and eventually, as with everyone else, Kate had set a reassuring hand on her best friend's arm and said the same words she'd just given Colleen. "It's okay."

And this time, it would have to be. Her best friend was getting married. Two weddings wouldn't be ruined by Jake.

Elizabeth had chosen pink dahlias for her bouquet, and Colleen went with this inspiration for the cake, highlighting the white four-tiered creation with a cascade of perfectly piped petals. Kate looked at the drawing tacked to Colleen's corkboard and down at the sample layer she had created for approval.

"It's perfect," Kate announced, beaming in satisfaction. "And I don't need to taste it to know it tastes delicious, too."

"You want to try a sample of something? Lemon chiffon with strawberry and cream filling? I'm experimenting with new flavors." Colleen pointed to a particularly inviting slice of undecorated cake that was resting on the center island. "Go on. Otherwise, this sample just goes to waste."

Kate thought of the morning she'd had and the sad fact that she didn't exactly need to worry about looking svelte in that bridesmaid dress next weekend and shrugged. "Why not?"

"Oh, good. I was hoping you would say that. Now I don't need an excuse to have a slice myself." Colleen's dimples quirked as she reached for a knife and plated them each two generous servings before leading them back into the empty storefront.

Kate cut her fork through the layer of fondant and each of the three layers of cake. It barely even crumbled as she brought it to her lips. "Oh my," she said through a mouthful. She smiled as she swallowed and eagerly dipped her fork for another bite. "Who needs a man when there's cake?"

Colleen raised her arm. "Me! I need a man. Or, I'd like one, at least." She gave a sad sigh.

"Well, don't you have a date tonight?" Kate asked.

Colleen dragged her fork through the middle layer of frosting. "Oh, yes. I do. But...you know my mother. She tends to exaggerate a bit. Tall with dark hair could mean anything over her five-foot-two frame. And lawyer could mean something like...paralegal."

Kate laughed. It was true that Fiona McKay was slightly prone to dramatize, but she still wasn't prepared to let her friend off the hook so easily. "Does it matter if he is a foot shorter than expected and not quite as handsome? Sometimes spark is overrated." She raised a knowing eyebrow. "Jake kept my heart racing right up until the moment he disappeared without looking back."

"Yes, but some guys are good guys...even the handsome ones."

Kate bit her lip. She was getting cynical, and who was she to crush her friend's hope? The girl still believed in good guys and love and happy endings and all that other nonsense. Kate managed not to snort into her cake.

"Do you ever think about dating again?" Colleen asked. It was the first time her friend had dared to broach the subject, but she didn't look hesitant about bringing it up. This was a good sign, Kate knew rationally. It meant that maybe eventually everyone would stop dancing around her, nervous to accidentally offend.

"Nope." Kate swallowed another bite of cake, but it didn't go down as easily as the last one.

"But you're young and you have so much to offer. There are good guys out there."

"Really?" Kate looked up at her friend through hooded lashes. "Name one."

"William, for starters," Colleen suggested, and Kate shrugged. Maybe, she thought, and hopefully yes, but you could never be sure, could you? Still, if she were a betting woman, she would say that William was a keeper. She wouldn't be so happy for her best friend otherwise. "And your father. And my father. And Bree's brother has always been nice to me..."

Ah. Of course. "Matt is nice," she agreed. But she also agreed with Bree's assessment of her older brother. Her only male cousin was never with—or without—a girlfriend for long. A warning sign. A big one. "But be careful who you give your heart away to. Learn from me."

"I just hate what Jake did to you," Colleen said, growing angry. "Between you and me, I never liked the Lamberts. They think they own this town, even when they're glorified tourists. The turn their noses at hardworking people like me and my mother who are actually adding something to the community."

It was true. Jake's parents weren't the warmest bunch, and his father was hell-bent on him following in his footsteps, but Jake had been sweet... at the beginning.

"It wasn't just him," Kate said on a sigh. She and her friend exchanged a knowing glance. "Anyway, enough talk about that. I want to hear all about what you plan to wear on this date tonight, sparks or no sparks."

For the next ten minutes she listened to Colleen try to convince herself that maybe she could fall for the nice, safe, reliable guy even if they religiously split every bill to the penny like she'd done with the last guy she dated and even if they did discuss their dating woes to each other like only friends could the way she had with the guy before that, while Kate did her best to stop thinking about asking for a second slice of cake... and about all the reasons why Alec Montgomery was anything but a nice, safe, reliable guy.

★ ★ ★

Alec sat across from Mason Lambert among the bustling lunch crowd, trying as best he could to drown out the little voice in his head that kept reminding him how important it was for this meeting to go well. The patriarch of the Lambert family, Mason oversaw the Lambert family's entire real estate portfolio—which spanned coast to coast and included many of the most exclusive office and retail properties in the country. He was a tough man to crack, and rumor had it an even more difficult man to deal with, but getting him to agree to this meeting had been half the battle. Alec's assistant had been trying to arrange this meeting for weeks in light of his visit to town, and it wasn't an opportunity to be taken lightly.

"Isn't this fortunate timing?" Alec folded his hands on the table. "I happen to be in town this week for my brother's upcoming wedding. I'm glad we were able to set up this meeting."

"Thanks again for being so flexible with your timing. Business has suddenly called me out to Vegas for the majority of the week, and I'm catching the red-eye out of Boston tonight."

"Not a problem."

"I used to only spend my weekends here," Mason explained, "but my wife likes staying through the summers now that the kids are grown. She prefers the peace and quiet. My middle son also spends a fair bit of time in Misty Point, though he's been in the city most of the past year. It's a great little town."

It was. In fact, Alec couldn't find much to complain about. Other than the reason for his visit, of course. "Well, fortunately, our office is located in Boston, so should you decide to work with us, you'll have access to us around the clock."

"Planning on spending summers in Misty Point, too, then?" Mason replied.

"The occasional visit. My brother now lives here." But he wouldn't for long, if Alec had anything to do with it. Alec gave a polite smile and cleared his throat, waiting for the right moment to make his pitch. The last thing he needed was for the other man to see the desperation in his eyes. Garnering Mason Lambert's business was game-changing in itself, but when he came with the extension of five well-connected children...It was a game changer.

"I did my research, Mr. Montgomery, and I liked what I saw. I don't trust my money with just anyone."

Alec said nothing. His homework must only have been skin-deep. But then, the financial condition of the Montgomery Group was a well-guarded secret. Not even William knew how bad things were—yet. "Discretion is very important to us, Mr. Lambert. I can assure you that our client list is impressive, and privacy has never been an issue."

Mason looked at him thoughtfully. "Your brother is running a fine operation here in town. Small, but well respected just the same." He broke his stare to reach for the bread basket in the center of the table. He took his time in layering a roll with butter.

Alec took the bait. "William's a smart kid. Taught him everything I know."

Mason seemed to like this. "I'd like to sit down and have a proper meeting about this later in the week when I'm back in town. I'd like to bring one of my sons along as well. He oversees a large portion of my East Coast real estate holdings, and his involvement is therefore essential."

Alec loosened his tie, trying to drum up a memory of Kate's itinerary for the week. The only thing he could recall was the rehearsal dinner Friday night. Missing it would not go over well. "I'm available Friday morning if that suits you."

Mason's expression remained unchanged. "I'll be in touch. Dinner might be better."

"Unfortunately, I've committed to hosting a rehearsal dinner on Friday evening."

"And unfortunately, I need this matter wrapped up by the end of the week," Mason said. "We parted ways with our last advisor a few days ago, and I don't want to let this go for too long."

Alec frowned.

"If it's a problem, I understand," Mason said evenly. "I could just as easily take my business elsewhere."

Alec tried to gauge the man's knowledge and failed. If Mason had any idea how crippled the Montgomery Group had become since William's departure, he was doing a good job of hiding it.

His heart began to pound in his chest as he quietly regarded Mason across the table. He knew that he and Mason had a similar philosophy: business was business. It wasn't personal. And right now, he had the family's company to think about.

It was a hell of a lot more than he could say for his brother, he supposed.

"Friday won't be a problem," he said tightly.

"Good, so that settles it." Mason stood, signaling the end of the meeting.

Alec rose to his feet, his mind spinning with the possibilities of what he had just agreed to. He strolled down the steps of the marina restaurant, creating distance between himself and the agreement he had just made. Inside his pocket, his phone vibrated, no doubt his father calling to check in on the status of the meeting, but for once he ignored it, deciding business could wait. Victory was finally close, but it wasn't as sweet as he had thought it would be.

Chapter Eight

⌒⊶⊷⌒

Elizabeth was already waiting at Fiona's Tea Shop, the friends' favorite restaurant in all of Misty Point, even if Colleen did cringe at the less-than-subtle eye motions her mother made every time a man under the age of forty passed by the front window. Kate and Elizabeth had been coming here since they were first allowed to go into town on their own, pedaling their bicycles along the cobblestone paths and sailing through the doors in their finest sundresses and wedge sandals and frilly handbags, thinking they were the epitome of sophistication. Back then Colleen was still helping out her mother, but sometimes she joined them for a petit four or cucumber sandwich. That was when they still ordered the hot chocolate instead of the tea, but as they grew, so did their tastes, and the tea shop...well some things were meant to stay the same.

"Ah, Kate! So happy to see you, dear. I was just thinking of you yesterday." Fiona had an eager look to her eyes that made Kate a little uneasy. She drifted her gaze longingly to the table where Elizabeth sat, suppressing her laughter.

"Oh?" She managed a polite smile. Fiona prided herself on being a matchmaker of sorts, and she had no problem with approaching young men at grocery stores or the dry cleaners if she thought they might be a good match for her only daughter.

But with a date arranged for Colleen tonight, Fiona may have turned her attention to another target.

Please, no, Kate thought.

"Well, I was at my knitting club on Friday night, and dear Peggy Wright was telling me about this marvelous new dating site where you actually take a test, and like magic, they find someone who is one hundred percent compatible with you." Perhaps not getting the reaction she was hoping for, Fiona pressed, "It's guaranteed. Or your money back."

"I imagine they are reimbursing quite a number of people then," Kate said with a little smile.

Fiona pinched her lips. "An attitude like that doesn't suit a pretty girl like you."

No, it didn't. Fiona had a point there.

"Well, I took the liberty of writing down the information for you." Fiona walked around to the hostess stand and retrieved a slip of paper, which she pressed firmly into Kate's palm.

"Dating these days is so easy! If you're open to it." She winked.

"Well. Thank you," Kate managed.

"My pleasure!" Fiona cried. She watched carefully to see what Kate would do with the information in her hands. Because Kate didn't want to explain herself further, she decided to do nothing, but vowed to toss it as soon as she got home.

She wasn't looking for love. And she certainly didn't believe that a computer could find her perfect match from whatever guys happened to be registered with the system at any given moment.

No, real love, the love like her parents had, was special. And rare. And even then, when you thought someone really knew you and would stand by you, there was no guarantee.

And you certainly didn't get your money back for that.

Kate hurried to Elizabeth, whose cheeks were flushed from laughter. She was happy to see her friend had snagged their favorite table near the window. Fiona liked the space to be eclectic "but not quirky," and while some tables boasted iron chairs backed with colorful throw pillows or banquettes covered in plush velvet upholstery, Kate and Elizabeth had always gravitated toward the pair of high-backed sky-blue wing chairs nestled around a mahogany pedestal table and tucked right into the shop's bay window with a perfect people-watching vantage.

"I ordered the Earl Grey for us," Elizabeth said as Kate unfolded her napkin. She eyed Kate watchfully as Kate set the strainer on her mug and helped herself to the teapot. Fiona was a firm believer in the details, something Kate appreciated, especially when that included sugar cubes and a miniature set of tongs. When she had finished preparing her first cup of tea—two lumps of sugar and a splash of cream—Elizabeth said, "So . . . aren't you going to tell me?"

Kate gave her a rueful smile, knowing exactly what her friend was asking and wondering how on earth she had managed to wait so long to inquire. She would have been bursting to know how the cake checkup went, and she knew that Elizabeth was, too, even if she was restraining herself from the emotions that were no doubt charging through her. "I thought you found it bad luck to see your cake in any form before Saturday."

"Oh, maybe I'm being silly, but I want my wedding day to feel, well, special. It just wouldn't be as magical if I saw the bouquet and the cake beforehand, would it?"

Kate couldn't agree more. Picking everything out and seeing it all were two very different experiences. A wedding day was meant to be a day of firsts—and onlys. Her happiest brides were the ones who had allowed for a touch of surprise on their big day. "It was perfect. Colleen is putting extra effort into this one. I can tell."

"Don't tell me any more!" Elizabeth said quickly, but she looked pleased as punch as she added a dollop of clotted cream to her scone. "I can't wait to see the flowers."

"I'll be checking on everything beforehand, so you can trust me, everything will be exactly as you envisioned. There won't be a wilted petal in the bunch, you have my word." She swallowed back the thought that there was only so much that was in her control. Flowers, cake, the music swelling at the exact moment the bride started her march down the aisle—this was all her responsibility. But everyone playing their part...There was only so much in her power. As Alec had so perfectly demonstrated this morning.

She eyed the three-tiered serving tray and finally selected a salmon and cream cheese sandwich on a thin rye bread, crusts carefully removed. Cake followed by high tea. Why not? It wasn't like anyone would be paying particularly close attention as she walked down the aisle or anything. And she had her Spanx...

Elizabeth set down her knife. "Is everything okay? You're frowning. You're worrying me!" She gave a nervous laugh, but Kate saw the fear in her eyes.

She was being unprofessional, letting her guard down because she had a personal relationship with the bride. Elizabeth may be her best friend, but she was also her client, and she deserved the best service Kate could offer.

Thinking fast, she said, "Oh, no. I was just thinking about something Colleen said earlier. She's going on that date tonight, but I have a feeling her eyes are only for one man."

"Matt." Elizabeth raised a knowing eyebrow. There was no denying the fact that Matt was attractive—if Kate could really think of her cousin that way. Captain of the lacrosse team and straight-A student to boot, what wasn't to like? Smelly socks all over his bedroom floor, Bree was quick to point out back then with a wrinkle of her nose. And there had been the time he'd pulled the ladder from their tree house, leaving Kate, Charlotte, Bree, and Elizabeth stranded with no food or toilet until her mother had come back from her shift at the library, proclaiming she would never give the responsibility of babysitting over to the giggling Matt again.

Whenever they told that story, Colleen got a wistful look on her face, as if she wished more than anything that she too had been the victim of one of Matt's childish pranks.

"Well, I'm happy she's giving it a try. And who knows, she may end up liking him more than she thought." Elizabeth took a sip of her tea. "In fact, you could learn something from her."

"Me?" Kate studied the serving tray and selected another finger sandwich from the bottom tray, opting, per tradition, to save the sweeter varieties for the end of the tea.

"We don't talk about this often, but well... I think you should force yourself to get out there a bit more. It's time, Kate."

Twice in one day, Kate mused. This wedding was sparking something. Or perhaps stirring something up.

"I have no interest in dating," Kate said, but there was reluctance in her voice that she knew her best friend could sense. "Why put myself through that again?" The ups and downs, the excitement, the nerves, and then the comfort. Yep, that was when things fell apart. When you got comfortable.

"Because you might find yourself blissfully happy, that's why." Elizabeth beamed a smile only a person madly in love could pull off. A part of Kate wanted to shake her head and think, *You wait and see,* but the other part of her dared to believe that her friend was right... that someday she, too, could be as happy as Elizabeth was.

"And if I don't?" There was always that risk. And now she knew just how badly it could hurt.

Elizabeth sighed. "Then you tried. But if you don't... You're thirty."

Kate cringed. "Exactly."

"I meant that you have a lot of years ahead of you. Do you really want to be alone forever?"

"Of course not," Kate said automatically. She hadn't thought of forever. *Forever* was a big word, a word she used too much in her profession.

"Then why not dip your toe in the dating pool, see what fish are in there? You may be pleasantly surprised." Elizabeth picked up her scone, giving her a knowing look before she took a bite from it.

"And I might end up right back where I am."

"Or you may end up realizing that not every guy is as bad as Jake."

"I don't know who I'm angrier at some days. Jake. Or..." She couldn't even say her name.

"Charlotte was always a flirt," Elizabeth said. Unlike the members of her family, Elizabeth didn't refrain from her honest opinions about Charlotte. "Remember that time back in high school when I had a pool party and Charlotte showed up in a string bikini? She was fourteen but more sophisticated than the two of us combined."

"She always did like nice clothes," Kate murmured. She remembered that day. Kate had worn a modest one-piece, with shorts on top. But then, Charlotte had always been far more interested in her nails, hair, clothes, and fashion magazines than things like studying or preparing for a test. From the age of twelve, when she first discovered her love of boys in a precocious and alarming way, she devoted her spare time to her appearance.

Kate, on the other hand, had been a fan of clear lip gloss and functional ponytails. And books.

"The guy I liked couldn't take his eyes off her. And of course she fed right into it, giggling and setting her hands on his arms. Arching her back. She knew I liked him. She didn't care. And he was seventeen. That didn't matter, either."

No, of course it hadn't. Charlotte enjoyed being the center of attention. Enjoyed winning affection. And Kate had indulged that for far too long.

"You deserve a guy who only has eyes for you. He's out there. You just have to be willing to find him."

Kate sighed. Technically she knew that few guys could top Jake's indiscretions. And she didn't have any other sisters they could sleep with, either. But the thought of giving her heart away only to have it trampled on... "I'll think about it," she said, hoping that would be enough to end the discussion.

But Elizabeth didn't seem finished yet. Her eyes sparked as she sat a little straighter. "Why not ask that photographer...Phillip, was that his name? Why not ask him to the wedding this weekend? He's cute."

"He is. And he's also a professional contact," Kate reminded her. She was on thin ice as it was with Meredith, no need to jeopardize things further by the possibility of a romance gone wrong. "Besides, I'll be busy working this weekend. I may be your maid of honor, but I'm still the wedding planner."

"Just keep an open mind," Elizabeth urged.

"I'll try," Kate said, even though she felt just as closed off now as she had before they started this conversation.

Elizabeth's expression tightened as she refilled her teacup. "There is one thing I should mention. You know your parents' dinner tonight?"

"Yes?" The Daniels and Jones families had been friends for so long that her parents were nearly as excited about this weekend's wedding as they had been for hers. Kate couldn't help but feel a little bit of hurt over it, even though she knew their hearts were in the right place. Elizabeth was like another daughter to her mother; she'd seen her grow up, been there every step of the way, even through the dramatic teenage years. But she knew her mother probably wished it was her turn to see her daughter happy.

I am happy, she wanted to tell her mom, and she did, many times. *Happy on my own.*

Elizabeth sighed heavily. "William invited Alec."

"He did?" Kate realized she had cried that out a little too

loudly, if the pinched-lip look of disdain the older women at the next table shot her was any indication. "I mean, of course he did. Why shouldn't he?"

She hadn't considered the possibility that Alec would be there tonight. She immediately wondered what she should wear, and then just as swiftly gave herself a silent lecture. Who cared what she wore?

"I suppose it's only right, but I'd be lying if I said I wasn't dreading it a bit. William claims his brother will like me just fine once he gets to know me. Says we got off on the wrong foot. He claims it was his fault for introducing me to his family the same night he announced he was moving away and leaving the firm."

Kate tipped her head thoughtfully. "Well, that could cause for a teensy bit of bad blood." She laughed. "Still, I understand your apprehension. When it comes to the groom's family, it's imperative that they make you feel welcome."

Which was something the Lamberts had never done, she thought.

★ ★ ★

Charlotte pushed the stroller into the park and sat down on the nearest bench. Honestly, one would think with all this walking that she'd be back to herself again. She frowned down at her stomach and then lifted her hand to her hair, which hadn't been washed in more days than she could remember.

She'd have to remedy that. Tonight. She'd planned to use Audrey's afternoon nap to do things like shave her legs—but that would probably take an hour, she thought, chuckling.

Still, her laughter stopped as her heart grew heavy again. She was a pretty girl. She knew it. Men knew it. And she knew they knew it. It was how she ended up in the position she was in, she supposed. A single mother. With a forest growing under her armpits.

She laughed again, and then, realizing she was laughing to herself, quickly stopped.

She gazed down into the stroller and touched her hand to Audrey's forehead—gentle, and oh so careful not to wake her—hoping that she hadn't over- or underdressed her. She didn't have air-conditioning in her apartment, or money for a window unit, but the baby was so tiny, and it didn't seem right not to cover her up, snuggle her in a blanket, but at the same time . . .

She had a sudden longing to call her mother. She would know what to do. But she couldn't call her mother—not to tell her she had a baby. If she did, she'd be in the car before Charlotte had even had a chance to explain. And she wasn't ready for that, yet. Because she had to explain. And first . . . First, she had to turn her life around.

She glanced back at the stroller again. If she didn't know better, she'd think Audrey was smiling a little in her sleep. She knew from all the books she'd borrowed from the library that babies this young technically couldn't smile, but she didn't care to believe that just yet.

Coming along the path were two other women pushing strollers. From the legging capris to the tight tank tops and running shoes, it was clear they were power walking, not aimlessly strolling the sidewalks on end hoping their babies would settle down like Charlotte did most days. She watched them impassively as their ponytails bounced on their shoulders. They were talking animatedly, engrossed in a story that one was clearly caught up on, something about what one of their husbands had done.

"He put him to bed in his clothes," the blond one was saying. "My only night out in two years and he puts him to bed in his clothes."

The brunette shook her head knowingly. "What did he have to say about it?"

"He said he thought they were his pajamas. But he was wearing them all day, I said!" The blonde was pushing a double stroller. A toddler was snuggled next to a baby a few months older than Audrey. Catching Charlotte's eye, she gave a tight smile and continued her story, her voice fading as they walked over the hill and disappeared behind the branches of a willow tree.

Charlotte wistfully watched them go. No doubt they would finish their lap and go home to their husbands, who put their children to bed in clothes instead of pajamas, and all would be forgiven. They'd make dinner: chicken nuggets for the boy, homemade veggie purée for the baby, who would spill it all over the floor, and pasta for the adults. There would be bath time and story time and then maybe a glass of wine for Mom, and then they'd fall asleep in their comfortable bed with their crisp white cotton sheets, and their baby would probably sleep through the night. They'd awake to the sun, not the sound of crying, and then it would be breakfast time and work time and all the busy little things that added up to a day.

While Charlotte . . . She pressed a hand to her cheek, realizing that she was crying. Horrified, she grabbed a corner of Audrey's flannel blanket and dabbed her face, for once grateful she'd given up on mascara.

She could still have that life. Not with Jake. Not with any man, maybe. But she and Audrey, they were a family. And with any luck, she'd soon be reunited with the rest of her family, too.

It all started with that interview.

Right. First thing. The legs. Then the hair. And what had she ever been thinking, giving up mascara?

Chapter Nine

━━∞∞∞━━

At six o'clock that night, Alec rolled to a stop outside a brick Colonial house a few miles inland from town and double-checked the address William had texted him earlier. There were only two other cars in the driveway, no sign of his brother's vehicle, and Alec wrestled with whether he should sit and wait for William to arrive or kill the ignition and face the wrath of Kate on his own.

Never one to dance around tough subjects, he turned the key, grabbed the bottle of red wine he'd picked up at store in town, and closed the car door. The path to the black front door was lined with rosebushes, and something told him that Kate was going to be just as prickly tonight as one of the thorns.

Every choice came with a consequence, he told himself as he reached out to touch the doorbell. And if a chance to turn his family business around meant a little attitude from the uptight wedding planner, so be it. It sure as hell beat the alternative.

From behind the closed doors, he heard the muffled sounds of footsteps and the turning of the locks. He grazed his back teeth together into a bracing smile, waiting for the narrowed eye and pinched lips, but he was startled to see a pleasant-looking woman of medium height and stature smiling back at him. Her blue eyes crinkled at the corners, and she wiped her hands on her apron before extending a hand.

"You must be William's brother! My, I'd notice the resemblance anywhere." The woman smiled. "I'm Maura Daniels."

Kate's mother. "Then this is for you," he said, dropping her hand to extend the bottle of wine that promised to have a smooth finish with hints of chocolate and a blackberry undertone. "I can see the resemblance with you and your daughter, as well."

Maura patted her shoulder-length hair and gave a pleased, girlish laugh. "We're all out back. Come on in."

Alec followed her through the hallway, passing a living room and dining room on each side of the curved staircase, and photos of young girls at various ages that lined the wall, satisfied to notice that his hunch was right. She was the eldest. And no doubt a bossy older sister to boot.

Maura led him into a sunny kitchen, where a large oval table was covered in desserts and the island space was a mess of cutting boards and trays, and casserole dishes ready to go into the oven. Alec shifted uneasily on his feet as Maura open a set of French doors that led onto the wooden deck where people were already gathered. This was a quintessential family home. A little cluttered. A little busy. Lived in. Loved.

He didn't belong here.

Happy to be outside again, he scanned the deck for his brother and, seeing no sign of him yet, accepted the beer Maura was offering him from a cooler.

"I need to check on the rice!" she said in a voice that explained this was somehow urgent, and then disappeared back into the house, leaving him alone with the beer and the heated stare of Kate from across the deck.

He gave a sheepish smile, and not seeing much of a choice, put one foot in front of the other and made his way over to her.

"Thank you for having me," he said, determined to keep things pleasant.

"I'm surprised you found the time to be here," Kate replied. She looked out over the yard, where Alec spotted a tree house wedged between the branches of a large maple tree. "And to clarify, this is my parents' house, not mine."

It was clear that Kate hadn't forgiven him for rescheduling the fitting. Jesus. Clearly this appointment was more important to her than he could have imagined. Not that he had been in a position to cancel or attempt to reschedule with Mason Lambert.

He took a sip of his beer, trying not to think about the next meeting. A meeting that could move the company back on steady ground. But a meeting that could cost him his relationship with his brother.

"Did you play in that thing growing up?" Alec gestured to the tree house, happy for a reason to change the subject.

Kate blinked, disarmed by the question, and then followed his gesture to the makeshift ladder leading up to the largest branch of the old tree. For a moment, her expression softened, but her eyes went flat when she looked back at him, and then down at the drink in her hands. "I haven't played in that thing for years. I'm probably a bit too big for it now."

"And here I thought it might be a nice place to hide." Alec grinned, but she didn't match the effort.

She tipped her head, looking at him thoughtfully. "You're not much of a party person, are you?"

Alec sipped his drink. "Not really."

"Huh."

"Not what you were expecting?"

"Just surprised is all," Kate said.

Alec leaned back against the deck rail, giving her a knowing smile. "I see. Doesn't fit in with your big opinion of me, does it?" He took another sip of his drink, finding that, like earlier this morning, he was starting to enjoy himself.

"I didn't say that," she said hotly.

"No, but you thought it. Tell me, why is it that you don't like me? You're friends with my brother. Are we really all that different?"

At this, she gave him her full attention. "I think you are. And for Elizabeth's sake, I hope you are. With your track record, you won't even make it to the wedding!"

She was sharper than he'd given her credit for. "I apologize again about today. If it could have been avoided, I would have rescheduled. I promise I will be at your service tomorrow at noon."

"Three," she corrected.

"Three." He took a long pull on his beer before flashing her a grin.

Kate bristled. "I should go help my mom in the kitchen. William and Elizabeth should be here any minute," she added, before brushing past him.

★ ★ ★

Alec wasn't sure who was less pleased by the table arrangements in the Daniels dining room: Kate or her best friend, Elizabeth. As soon as he slid into the chair next to Kate's, she had awkwardly inched hers away by gripping the seat and jostling a bit. And Elizabeth, well, her attention was nearly solely on William, who was jovial and loud and disturbingly right at home in this cozy little house.

Alec cracked his lobster, listening to a lively debate about a renovation of the Misty Point Lighthouse, surprised that his brother had such opinions on the matter. He'd naïvely assumed that William was only in Misty Point because of Elizabeth, possibly even missing the pace of Boston, but it seemed more and more obvious that William liked the town here, and worse, he was becoming a part of it.

He eyed his brother thoughtfully across the table as he chewed, noticing the color in his cheeks, the bronze hue of his arms, the golden highlights in his hair. And he realized that the person he was looking at didn't fit in well in Boston.

Well, time to change that.

"That lighthouse has been standing since the nineteenth century," Jeff Jones was saying. "It's a town mascot. A symbol of our longevity."

"Exactly, meaning there's two hundred years of rot and rust to clean up. What's wrong with sprucing the thing up a bit?" demanded Kate's father, Frank, growing red in the face. It was clear that this was a subject of much debate, and perhaps not just at the table.

"I like the way it looks," William volunteered. "Whenever I think of Misty Point, I think of that lighthouse. It would be a shame if it changed. After all, that's where I proposed." He leaned in to plant a kiss on Elizabeth's check. The table all but cooed, and Alec could only stare in wonder.

"And what do you think, Alec?" Frank said as the table fell silent. All eyes were on him, waiting for an answer. Jesus, this was worse than the boardroom, Alec thought, wishing he had a tie to loosen.

"Oh, I couldn't say. I'm not familiar with the area. I don't think I have much right to an opinion on the matter."

"Nonsense!" Jeff cried out. "Your brother is marrying my only daughter. That makes you family now."

Alec skirted his gaze to Elizabeth, who looked down at her plate, leaning a little closer to William, and back at her father, who was grinning happily. He chewed the lobster in his mouth, finding it had gone rubbery and cold, even though it was cooked perfectly.

Family. Was he part of this family, technically speaking? This strange group who talked over one another and went back for years? William was. He fit in right at home. He was one of them now.

And damn it if Alec didn't envy him for it.

But Alec, he didn't fit in well. Didn't know how to ease into this laid-back, cozy lifestyle the way William could. He felt stiff and awkward and out of place. It wasn't how they'd grown up. It wasn't what they knew. But it was William's world now. And it could be his, too. If he accepted it.

"I say renovate," he said, reaching for his wineglass. "The only way for progress is to move forward, not stay rooted in the past."

He started at his own words as he set his wineglass back on the table. Where the hell had that come from? He was glued to the past, after all, wasn't he? Still living in Boston. Still manning the family company. Still haunted by the memory of his mother. He lived the life he knew. He didn't take risks. And he certainly did make changes. But William did. Big ones.

It was clearly the answer Kate's father wanted to hear, from the pleased look on his face. Kate, too, he noticed, seemed to slant him a look of approval from the corner of her eye. A wink, he couldn't help notice, was passed from mother to daughter.

"Aw, now, I'll give you a pass on this one, but next go around, you stick with us," Jeff joked, and Alec felt his gut stir uneasily. There it was, a suggestion that he was part of this now. Even by extension.

"We're sorry your father couldn't join us tonight," Sally Jones said. "But then, Elizabeth tells us he's a busy man."

"Too busy," William cut in. All the ease in his face had been replaced with tense lines. His jaw was tight as he reached for his wine, giving Alec a long look.

"He'll be arriving on Friday," Alec said. "For the rehearsal dinner." He stopped chewing, thinking of his last conversation with Mason.

"Then we'll all be together," Elizabeth's mother said, but her smile slipped as a strange silence filled the room.

Alec looked at William, who was focused on cutting his lobster, and then to Kate, who sat with her hands in her lap, her jaw clenched in what seemed like anger.

Confused, he looked over at her parents, who also stared at their plates, her father in overt discomfort if the pull at his collar indicated anything, and her mother with so much sadness that he suddenly realized that he was missing something.

Elizabeth's mother was blinking her eyes in overt desperation.

Her mouth was working out something, but no words came out.

Alec said, "I was hoping for sushi for the rehearsal dinner, but Kate had the sense to talk me into something a little more . . . elegant."

From this he elicited a grateful smile from Kate. "Yes, well, we compromised. I think everyone will be pleased," she said, giving Elizabeth a meaningful stare.

The gesture wasn't unnoticed by Alec. Even though he'd tried to make more of an effort with the bride before dinner started, she'd been pulled away, and it was clear she was wary around him. He knew he could easily make up for their last and only meeting by apologizing, or showing her how enthusiastic he was that she was marrying William. But he couldn't exactly do that, either, could he? Not honestly, at least. He couldn't say he was sorry for getting the shock of his life that night in Boston all those months ago when William sprung not one but two inter-connected bombshells on him. And he couldn't exactly pretend he was excited for this wedding, when because of it, William was here, in Misty Point.

"Well, if everyone's had enough, I'll bring out the dessert. Homemade blueberry pie and ice cream," Maura said, standing to collect their plates. Kate stood to help her, giving Alec a quick view of the curve of her hips as she walked around the table gathering dishes. He stood to help, but Maura set a heavy hand on his shoulder, pushing him back down.

"You're our guest. Sit. But you can help next time." She grinned, and Alec relaxed into his chair, feeling strangely at home and strangely nostalgic all at once.

All his life he'd dreamed of a family meal like this. But it was his brother who was lucky enough to find it.

★ ★ ★

Kate knew it was silly to feel uncomfortable in your own childhood home, but she couldn't help it, she did. Her conversations with her parents were stilted and surface level, and they certainly never spoke of Charlotte. She rarely came back here since her sister had left, but she'd made an exception tonight for Elizabeth's sake. And then things had to get awkward . . .

She sighed as she started another pot of coffee for the guests who lingered on the deck, chatting away while fireflies blinked in the darkness. Every time she thought she was over it, something had to set her back. And tonight, she couldn't stop thinking, just as she'd done at Christmastime when there was no way she could not spend the day with her parents, that someone was missing from the group.

And from the look in her mother's eyes, she had felt the exact same way.

Unscrewing the top from the bottle of cream, she emptied some into a ceramic pourer her mother had had for as long as Kate could remember. She was just about to set everything up on the tray when she saw Alec coming in through the sliding glass doors.

Damn it. She skirted her eyes, trying to look busy, but there was almost nothing left to do. She wondered if it was too late to pour the cream out and start over, just so she could focus on something other than that handsome face or that broad smile that made her heart flutter way more than it should.

Maybe he was just coming in to use the restroom, she thought, only half hoping this was the case.

But no, instead, he walked over to the island, leaned against it, and said, "Need any help?"

Kate blinked quickly. "No. But thanks. I think I have it."

She eyed the coffee machine, whose drip suddenly felt painfully slow, and all but willed it to hurry the heck up. But as the saying went, a watched pot...

"I can carry the tray for you," he offered.

My, wasn't he eager to be of assistance tonight? No doubt feeling a bit guilty over canceling the suit fitting, perhaps? A pleased smile formed on her lips at the thought of it.

She started to protest, but then decided against it. Doing so would only drag out an argument she really couldn't afford to have. No, the best thing for her—professionally speaking—was to be on good terms with the best man. Professionally speaking only, she reminded herself.

"Thanks," she said. "It's almost done." She shot a warning glance at the coffee machine.

The kitchen felt silent and still and the muffled sound of laughter through the windows only underscored the feeling that she was alone in the house with Alec. She tried to think of something to say, something that wasn't solely about the wedding, or something she needed him to do for it, but found she was suddenly overwhelmed, and if she dared to admit it, a little nervous, too.

He was a sort of nice guy, she was beginning to realize. Annoying. Impossible. But still...kind of nice.

"You never mentioned a sister," Alec said mildly.

Kate stiffened and reached for the coffeepot before it had finished brewing. Despite the automatic stopper, a few drops drizzled onto the hot plate and sizzled. "It never came up." She felt her hands shake as she transferred the coffee to a carafe.

She hated that her parents still kept the photos up in the hall. At first she had found it insensitive, but then she figured it would be a bigger statement and reminder to take everything down. But now, now she wondered if it was a source of denial. Or hope. That their family could someday be what it once was.

That didn't seem possible.

"Why isn't she with us tonight?" Alec asked.

She couldn't make her hands stop shaking, and she was starting to worry she might spill the hot liquid all over her fingers. She set the coffeepot back on the burner, where it continued to brew.

"She's in Boston, actually. She, um, lives there now." *With my ex-fiancé.* She could just imagine them dining in the best restaurants, crawling into bed together at night, walking through the Common.

"Boston?" Alec raised an eyebrow. "Interesting."

"It's not far. A lot of people from Boston have summer homes in Misty Point."

"That they do," Alec said. "Who knows, might end up with one myself someday."

This was surprising. "Really?"

"With my work schedule?" He laughed, but there was a sadness in his eyes she'd noticed earlier, at the dinner table, where he'd been surprisingly subdued.

He lifted the heavy tray effortlessly and jutted his chin to the door. "Mind grabbing that for me?"

Kate slid it open and let him pass, thinking that for someone who came from a world so different from this, he seemed almost at home here.

Not that she was going to get used to having him as a regular fixture or anything.

★ ★ ★

"Alec seemed like a nice young man." Maura slanted a suggestive glance at Kate as she sank her hands into the soapy dishwater.

"Mom..." But Kate couldn't help but smile. A little. Alec had been the perfect gentleman all through dinner, even if he did seem a little out of his element.

"Is he bringing a date to the wedding?" Maura tried again, and this time, Kate had to burst out laughing, giving her credit where it was due. "What?" her mother asked, feigning innocence. "I'm just making conversation."

"No, you're just fishing," Kate scolded. She sighed as her mother passed her a stainless steel pot to dry. She'd take the nagging over a conversation about Charlotte any day. Even though her mother never broached the topic, she was still uneasy, waiting for the day when a piece of information she didn't want to hear slipped out.

She ran the towel over the steel pot. Maybe that was why Charlotte was calling so much. Maybe she and Jake were getting married. Maybe her mother knew. Maybe she told Charlotte to reach out to her first. Maybe she was about to drop the bomb.

Or maybe Kate was being paranoid.

She felt shaky as she continued to dry the pot. For all she knew her sister was calling to get back her favorite red pumps. Shoes mattered to her. More than sisterhood.

"He is coming to the wedding alone," she said, forcing herself to stay focused on the conversation. *Just like me.* "But don't go getting any ideas. I've had to deal with him these past few days, and he's been nothing but grief."

Well, not entirely.

"How so?"

"He canceled today's fitting at the last minute. Claimed a last-minute meeting came up."

"Well, he is giving up a whole week of work," Maura pointed out as she turned on the taps.

"True." Kate begrudgingly watched as her mother rinsed a pan. "But it was last minute, days before the wedding, and you know how important it is to stick to a strict schedule."

"I know how important it is to you that this wedding go off without a hitch." Maura gave her a gentle smile. "Relax, honey. And try to enjoy it. This is your dearest friend's wedding."

Kate gave a small smile. Guilty as charged.

"So, other than reschedule a suit fitting, what is it that this man has done to so greatly annoy you?"

"He's not nice to Elizabeth, Mom. He doesn't approve of William marrying her. He doesn't think she's good enough." She and her mother exchanged knowing glances. "Doesn't that sound a little familiar?"

It was a sore subject that Jake's parents had never warmed to Kate, clearly frowning on her middle-class townie status. She had tried to overlook it, told herself that it didn't matter, that what mattered was Jake and his loyalty to her. But in the end, she didn't even have that.

"He seemed nice enough to her tonight," her mother pressed. "And he was a very polite guest."

Kate couldn't argue with that. "But you saw how stiff and almost uncomfortable he was. No doubt our house is not what he is used to."

"Oh, I have no doubt at all about that," Maura said. "But just because he was out of place doesn't mean he was looking down on us. Look at William. He's different than..." She stopped short of saying the name they were both thinking. "He grew up with a silver spoon, and he fits in right at home here."

"True," Kate agreed. "He moved here permanently, after all. And he opened his own business. I think he made a choice to have a different life than the one he grew up with."

"But not his brother?"

Kate shook her head. "He's all business. He clearly really likes his life in Boston, and everything that comes with it."

"That's too bad," Maura said, looking genuinely disappointed.

"Too bad for him," Kate said, "but it has nothing to do with me. In case you were wondering, he was never going to be an eligible suitor. He's too... handsome."

Her mother laughed. "How can anyone be too handsome?"

But Kate knew. She'd learned from experience. "He's rich, good-looking, and successful. Some women might think that's three things he has going for him, but I know better. That kind of combination... That's nothing but trouble."

Her mother stopped washing the dishes and looked at her sadly. "Oh, honey. Someday the right man is going to come along and make you believe in love again."

Kate pinched her lips. She wanted nothing more than to correct her, to say that no, no, he wouldn't... almost as much as she wanted to believe that what her mother was saying was true.

"And when that happens..." Maura hesitated. "Well, maybe you and Charlotte can—"

She shot her mother a look of warning. Her heart was hammering in her chest. "Mom—"

"I know, I know. It's just... What can I say? I want my girls to get along."

"Too late," Kate said in a clipped tone. Her cheeks were hot as she turned to open a cabinet door and add a plate to the stack. She wanted to run, grab her keys, and sprint out the front door.

But she was curious. And it could be months before her mother dared to mention Charlotte again.

"Do you ever speak to her?" Kate dared to ask. As soon as she said it, she wished she hadn't. She didn't want to know. Not really. But at the same time, she didn't want to wonder anymore. And she certainly didn't want to answer one of those calls to find out firsthand what was up.

No, if there was news, it would be better to hear it now. From her mother. Her mother who loved her and wanted the best for her.

"No. Once or twice," her mother admitted. "But the calls were brief. She didn't have much to say."

Kate didn't know whether to feel betrayed that her mother and Charlotte had spoken or grateful that there wasn't any more news that could hurt her. She wondered if she should tell her mother about the calls from Charlotte, but then she would be forced to explain that she had deliberately chosen not to answer or return any of them. And then her mother might worry more.

Because of course her mother worried about Charlotte. They all had. Charlotte was flighty and silly and funny. But Charlotte was also very irresponsible.

And that had finally all caught up with her, hadn't it? Except Kate had never expected that she would be caught up in it.

Chapter Ten

It was raining the next morning, despite the forecast, and Alec fought off the disappointment that his golf plans with William would have to be delayed, or canceled. He looked out the window of the desk near the window where he'd been working since five that morning, watching the waves crash against the rocks that hugged the shoreline.

Back when they were kids, they'd spend some summer weekends at their house on the Cape, but after their mother had died, those weekends ended. The house was boarded up and eventually sold. Their father claimed he was too busy to get out of the city, but Alec was old enough to know better. The house, and everything in it, reminded him too much of their mother. And despite what he said, and despite how he acted, he'd never forgiven himself for what happened to her. And why should he?

It was easier to forget, he supposed. He'd tried to do that himself eventually. And it was easier when that house and all the memories they'd shared in it were gone. The Boston brownstone had been their home, yes, but the Cape was where they'd laughed, and played, and behaved like a real family ... at least for a little while.

God, he hadn't thought of that place in years. Now he couldn't stop.

Alec looked away from the window, swallowing back the ache in his chest. It was Monday, and even though he was now staying through the week, from a glance at Kate's tightly packed schedule he could see that the chances of getting time alone with his brother seemed less likely than he'd hoped. With the golf outing he had never officially agreed to now off the table, he made a snap decision and texted his brother, seeing if he was free for lunch instead.

An hour later, he was pulling up to an unassuming brick building at the edge of Misty Point's main stretch; the only thing differentiating it from the dentist next door was the plaque on the wall: WILLIAM MONTGOMERY, FINANCIAL SERVICES.

Alec shook his head. If his father could see this ...

Only he wouldn't see it. And if all went as planned, soon this plaque would be replaced with something else. Something more fitting. An orthodontist's office, perhaps.

The door was unlocked, and he pushed through it into a small, windowless lobby. The receptionist desk was unassuming—and empty. A single frosted glass door was ajar, until William appeared in the frame.

"You're here!"

That he was. In a hundred years, Alec never could have imagined he'd be visiting his brother's offices anywhere other than the third door on the right, corner view, facing northeast, opposite end of the hall from his own. Instead, he was standing in this tight space, feeling large and out of place, just like he had last night in Kate's parents' house, while his brother, like last night, seemed right at home and perfectly at ease.

"I gave my assistant the week off," he said, explaining the empty desk. "I'd hoped to do the same, but... Well, you know how it is."

Did he? The office culture he knew was tense and heated, with closed-door meetings and analysts running numbers. While this... this was quiet and unassuming and as peaceful as a therapist's office.

He thrust his hands into his pockets and followed William into his office, which boasted the same subdued atmosphere as the lobby in a much larger space. A meeting table occupied one end, while two comfortable visitor chairs faced a large wood desk. William had hung seascapes on the warm gray walls, and, more humbly, his Harvard and Princeton diplomas hung in a corner, partially obscured by a plant.

"It's not much, but it's prime real estate, right in the center of everything. And check out this view." William turned to face the wide windows, where sailboats drifted by, so close Alec felt he could reach out and touch them, divided only by a stretch of grass and some jagged rocks.

"Impressive," he said, and it was. Understated but traditionally furnished, it was a peaceful place to be. A confident place. More inviting than the class-A office they occupied in the city. Or, rather—he corrected himself—he occupied.

After William had left, he still found himself looking up from his computer screen at eight at night, his stomach grumbling, his eyes strained, and pushing back his chair to go find his brother. It was usually halfway down the hall that he stopped himself. Saw the dark room. Remembered it was empty. That his options were going back to work or grabbing a quick burger at the mediocre steak house on the ground floor of their building. But it didn't taste the same without William sitting beside him at the bar, sipping a beer, putting perspective on the day and setting all the craziness aside.

Those nights had meant a lot. Maybe more than William could ever know.

"I'd be lying if I said it was the same without you," Alec said, hating the truth in his words.

"Ah, come on, you were always happier there than I was. You like the fast-paced pressure. You thrive in it."

It was true that Alec loved the rush that followed landing a new client, but that feeling was quickly replaced with something else once the work that came with it set in. Pressure. Stress. Unhappiness, he realized.

"So you like running your own practice?"

"I love it. It's steady, but it's more satisfying, too. I make my own hours. I choose who I want to go after. It's the same job, but in many ways, it doesn't feel that way at all." William hesitated for a minute. "Wouldn't mind having my brother around, though."

Alec looked at him sharply. Was he referring to the Boston office or this place? He considered the possibility that William was feeling him out, suggesting he come work here, and for a moment he felt a twinge of excitement, until he realized that was an impossible scenario.

The Montgomery Group was a family business, left to Alec— and once William—once their father retired. If he walked away now, what would become of the company? William was settled, happy; his life was full of other things. But his father . . . the business was all he had. And as much as Alec hated to admit it, it was all he had, too.

He'd sunk too much into it to walk away now.

"Well," William said, shoving his hands into his pockets. "Hungry?"

"I'm starving," he said, following his brother back out into the reception area and through the front door.

It was still raining, and he didn't have an umbrella, but he didn't care that he was getting a little wet. Alec was just happy to be out of that office. Away from the temptations it held.

★ ★ ★

It was raining. But that was not the problem, not really. No, the real problem was that the forecast had not called for rain today. Just like it was not calling for it Saturday. Or Friday. Or Thursday, the night of the lawn party. All outdoor events.

Kate sat at her desk and chewed on her nail, forgetting about her week-old manicure until she saw the damage she had done.

Always a fan of lists, Kate's therapist had suggested she use this habit to her advantage, claiming that it broke down her worries and fears and made everything feel a bit more manageable. Remembering this tip, Kate opened a fresh document in her word processor and began typing. Problem one: It might rain on the wedding. Solution: There are tents. Problem two: There could be a hurricane...

She stopped typing and set her head in her hands. There were so many things that could go wrong that there was no sense wasting her time typing them. And all it would take was just one for Meredith to find a reason to give her the boot.

She'd successfully dodged her boss all morning and, after checking Meredith's calendar, was happy to see she would be gone for vendor meetings for most of the day.

A break from the office before her next appointment might do her some good. With that in mind, she made a quick call, grabbed her favorite umbrella, and ten minutes later was sliding into a seat across from Bree at Harbor Street Café for a late lunch.

"I'm really happy you called," Bree admitted as she bit into her stacked veggie sandwich. "I've been so busy filling orders, I haven't allowed myself a lunch break in a week. Is it just me, or does it feel like everyone is getting married?"

Kate raised an eyebrow. "You're asking me that?"

Bree laughed. "Sorry. I know I have no room for complaint when you're surrounded by it every day, but you know what I mean."

"Well, it is June," Kate pointed out. "But I do know what you mean. It's hard not to feel left out sometimes." She sighed, hating that little twinge of loneliness she felt every so often.

"Well, at least you were engaged," Bree grumbled, and Kate was almost happy for her friend's lack of discretion. Bree could be blunt, but it was a relief from the usual tiptoeing that people seemed to do around her.

"To a cheating ass," she pointed out, and the girls shared a laugh. "Still, I don't know what's worse. Having that wedding day within reach or feeling like you might never have one."

"Exactly," Bree said. She looked up Kate, her expression turning a little nervous. "I have something to ask you."

Kate stopped pushing the lettuce around her plate and gave

her cousin a hard stare. "Oh no. You haven't gone back to the house to shut the windows yet."

Bree laughed. "I asked my brother to do it on his way to the college this morning."

Then what could it be? Something with Simon? She doubted very much that the man had pulled his eyes from the TV long enough yesterday to get down on one knee. No, this wasn't about her wedding planning services. Meaning, it was personal. "This sounds ominous."

"Only if you want it to be," Bree replied. She pursed her lips together, taking a big breath. "I want to set you up."

"Oh, no." Kate was shaking her head so hard, her hair was swooshing at her shoulders. "No, I told you, I'm fine on my own for now."

"But don't you want a date for the wedding this Saturday?"

"I don't have time for a date," she said. "I'm working the event, too, remember?" Besides, there was no room in the seating chart.

Bree gave Kate a scolding look. "Technically I'm working the event, too. And Simon will be there."

Ah, yes. Simon. Simon with his glasses and lanky physique and long stride. He was sort of adorable and harmless-seeming. At first. Still, Kate understood why Bree had fallen so hard for him. It's just that she wished she could find someone better.

"It's just, he's really handsome, three years older than you, and I think you two would really hit it off."

Despite herself, Kate asked, "And how did you meet him and why have I never heard of him before?"

"Well, I met him when I was making a delivery."

"Someone sent him flowers?" Kate stared at her cousin, incredulous.

"No." Bree dragged out the word, rolling her eyes. "They were for his mother. He's staying with her for a bit. She's not well, you see. And since he's not from around here—"

"He doesn't even live in Misty Point?" Kate poked at her salad.

"Seattle." Catching Kate's widened eyes, Bree hurried to say, "But he's so nice. And he could probably use a friend."

"I appreciate you thinking of me, but no." Kate sighed at the mere thought of this less-than-ideal arrangement. "The man lives across the country. I don't need any complications right now. What I need is a strong, sensitive man who is deeply loyal and devoted and happy just to sit by my side." She chewed on a carrot stick. "Come to think of it, I've just described Henry. So there you have it. I already have the only man I need."

"A dog is not a man." Bree pursed her lips in disapproval. "Changing topics, how was the dinner last night?"

Kate wondered if she should mention that Charlotte's name had finally been broached and then decided she was having far too nice of a time to upset herself two days in a row. Lunch with her cousin was always a nice time, even when Bree was trying to set her up on a date with a man who would soon be returning to Seattle.

"It was a nice time," Kate admitted, realizing that it was. Though he had been quiet through the dinner, Alec was a perfect guest, something that should probably make her relax a little about how the rest of the week would carry out. "I think it was the first step in helping Alec and Elizabeth have a fresh start."

"Oh, I don't know about that happening between now and

Saturday," Bree said. "Last time I talked to her, she was still quite upset by the reaction they gave when the engagement was announced. She's sure they don't think she's good enough to marry into their family."

"I hate to think that was the reason for their reaction," Kate said sadly, but she knew from experience that it was all too possible. She frowned a little, thinking of how Alec had broken the ice when that awkward silence had filled the dining room.

"Speaking of last night, do you know how Colleen's date went?"

Bree's mouth twitched. "He was tall and dark all right. And nineteen years old."

Kate gave a whoop of delight. "Nineteen? I thought he was a lawyer."

"An *aspiring* lawyer. You know, when he grows up someday? Colleen said he picked her up in his mother's car. And he had a bouquet of flowers for her. From the grocery store." Bree tsked.

"That's sweet." Kate pressed a hand to her heart, but she was laughing.

"It's statutory!" Bree exclaimed. She shook her head. "Colleen seemed pretty upset when I saw her this morning on my way into work. I think she was looking pretty forward to this date. Now the focus is back on my brother, of course."

Kate tried to imagine the fight that had broken out between Colleen and Fiona over this setup. She made a mental note to stay away from the tea shop for a while.

"Well, I guess I don't need to worry about the change to the seating charts, then."

"Not unless you heed your ever-so-wise cousin's advice and try out this guy I highly recommend." When she caught Kate's expression, her own softened. "I just want what's best for you. That's what family is all about."

Was it? Once Kate might have thought so.

She checked her watch. The afternoon was getting away from her. "I have a meeting with the best man himself today. I should call to let him know I'm on my way." Kate pulled her phone from her pocket and scanned through her contact list for the Beacon Inn. Glancing across the table at Bree, she said, "Now don't go getting excited. This is just a fitting. I'm not looking for anything." Or anyone.

But if she were...

Nope. Alec was all wrong. Cute. Rich. Married to his job. And as if that wasn't enough, he lived in Boston. And she hated Boston now.

She asked to be connected to his room and waited, setting her fork on the side of her plate and taking one last sip of her iced tea. She checked her watch. She'd have to leave right from the café if she wanted to get there in time.

"Ms. Daniels?"

Kate frowned as a man who was certainly not Alec came on the line. "Yes?"

"Mr. Montgomery has asked not to be disturbed."

She felt her jaw slack. "Yes, but we have an appointment."

"I understand that, miss, but there is nothing we can do. Perhaps you can try back again later."

Oh, she would do just that. She turned off the phone and checked her watch again as a crash of lightning lit the sky, making her jump. So much for the rain. A storm had rolled into town the day the best man had set foot in Misty Point.

* * *

Charlotte nervously tapped her foot on the carpeted floor, resisting the urge to check her watch. Audrey would be getting hungry soon, and she hadn't planned for this interview to go on for so long. She'd only given her upstairs neighbor, a lonely widow with three cats named Mrs. Jansen, two bottles, which she'd thought would be more than enough, considering Audrey slept so much. Honestly, who knew that newborns could sleep so much! Of course, Audrey mostly slept during the day, and usually only on walks, but she could sleep for hours if you pushed her around the park. Charlotte had practically memorized every tree and flower and bench plate.

"You don't have much work experience." The man interviewing her—God help her she'd never exactly caught his name—frowned at the paper she'd printed out in the library yesterday afternoon on one of her walks. "And I see a recent gap here. Tell me, what have you been doing since you worked at...Lighthouse Beach, is it?"

Oh, just following my sister's fiancé to Boston on the off chance he'd want to claim his child, Bob.

Bob! Yes, that was his name. Charlotte smiled in relief.

"I recently moved here from Rhode Island," Charlotte explained. Her stint as a parking guard at the beach in Misty Point was short-lived and not exactly relevant, but it was something, and she needed to give this everything she had. She paused to clear her throat as she thought fast. "I've been getting set up in the city, and finalizing some, uh, personal situations."

"And how do you like Boston?" Bob asked, reaching for his coffee mug.

"I love it," Charlotte fibbed. She'd always dreamed of getting out of Misty Point, reveling in the energy of the city on their annual weekend getaways to New York and Boston when she was growing up. She'd happily followed Jake to Boston, eager to start a bustling, busy life, excited to give her unborn child the glamorous experiences she so longed for herself.

But after ten months in that dark and depressing garden apartment that smelled a little too much like the Thai place next door, she longed for the feeling of lush, cool green grass between her toes, the salty air in her face, and the wind off the sea in her hair. She imagined Audrey at various stages of girlhood splashing in the water, clutching a plastic shovel with her chubby little hand, or running back to her with a pail full of shells. That was the childhood she wanted to give her daughter. Only now...How could she?

"Do you get out much?" Bob was now asking.

"Oh." Charlotte jutted her lip, again wise enough to answer correctly. "Enough. I'm a bit of a homebody, though." These days...

"Well, check out Little Italy if you haven't already. I'm partial to a good pasta dish myself."

Charlotte narrowed her eyes marginally.

"Well," Bob continued, sliding her resume to the side of his desk. "Would you be able to start tomorrow?"

Charlotte suppressed the gurgle of glee that threatened to pop right past her lips, and instead swallowed hard, managing a very professional, "That shouldn't be a problem. Thank you. Thank you for this opportunity." *And this paycheck!* she thought giddily.

Her mind began to spin with possibilities. She'd buy Audrey

that sweet little pink sundress she'd seen in a shop window on one of their walks. She hadn't dared to walk in to the boutique, given the state of her credit card balance. But now . . . Now she'd give her daughter something pretty, not just something practical. And who knew, she might be starting off as an insurance assistant, but before long, she might be an insurance agent herself.

Sure, it wasn't exactly the glamorous type of position she'd always dreamed of, but she wasn't dumb enough to think that dreams came true anymore.

But some did, she thought, thinking of that sweet baby waiting for her at home.

Charlotte stood, forgetting momentarily that she was wearing a maternity dress and that she had so carefully disguised her stubborn stomach bulge by carrying her handbag in front of her into the office.

Bob eyed her abdomen. Charlotte didn't move. She knew what he was thinking. Probably wondering if she was pregnant, and how far along. Legally, he couldn't ask; she knew that much. She licked her lips to cover her smile when she thought of how shocked he'd be to hear the real truth. That she was actually quite thin, or at least she used to be, and that no one ever told you that your tummy didn't just instantly deflate back to normal as soon as the baby was born.

But then, there were a lot of things they didn't tell you.

Deciding to end the mystery and save further speculation, she grinned and said, "I'll have to treat myself to some Champagne tonight to celebrate!"

Bob frowned a little and then, seemingly relieved, grinned at her. "Your boyfriend will have to take you somewhere special."

"Oh. No." Charlotte shook her head, but there was a traitorous twist to her heart. "I'm on my own..."

Was it just her or did his smile almost turn into a leer? She laughed uneasily, feeling her back teeth graze as she began to edge toward the door.

So it wasn't ideal. It was a job. And right now, she didn't have much of a choice.

Chapter Eleven

⊶∞∞⊷

Clutching the receiver in her hand, Kate closed her eyes as the phone rang a second time down the line. *Please don't be—*

"The Beacon Inn, this is Raymond."

Raymond, she finished her thought with a close of her eyes. She had now spoken with Raymond four times in forty minutes, and the last two times she had detected a telltale hint of amusement in his tone. She contemplated quickly hanging up and then decided against it. Who cared if she looked like a stalker? Saturday was quickly approaching, and it was her responsibility to make sure everything fell into place. If the best man didn't want to cooperate, then it was her job to hunt him down and make him.

"Alec Montgomery's suite, please," she said briskly, wincing with the vain hope that the hotel worker didn't recognize her voice.

"Mr. Montgomery has asked not to be disturbed, Ms. Daniels," Raymond said flatly.

Kate willed herself not to say something she would live to

regret or might prompt Raymond to officially file a restraining order. The menswear shop had been generous enough to offer her another time slot for the fitting, but they had been clear that anything past five o'clock would make it impossible for them to promise the suit would be ready in time. Alec had to be present for that appointment, but how could she guarantee anything when he was making it impossible for her to even contact him? Of all the things to go wrong, this one was too ridiculous to have even predicted.

"Would you like to leave a message?" Raymond continued.

She had already left two. A third wouldn't make a difference, and she had the sinking sensation she was becoming the brunt of some joke behind the front desk of the hotel. A place where she was known, and a place she would be frequenting again soon.

Very soon, she thought, narrowing her eyes.

"No, thank you," she said, placing the phone back on its cradle. She leaned back in her chair and focused on the beautiful arrangement of white hydrangeas in the ivory vase on her desk. She considered calling Elizabeth, or William, to ask for Alec's cell phone number, but it would only cause them alarm.

No, she would have to figure this one out on her own, and if Alec was determined to isolate himself in that hotel suite, then he would be sorely surprised to discover he was about to have company. He may think he was in Misty Point for business, but he had some unfinished business with her, too, and blocking her calls would only buy him so much time.

And your time is up, Kate thought, standing to gather her files. Without further contemplation, she plucked her tote off the hook behind her door and darted out into the summer afternoon. A cool breeze was blowing in off the ocean, and she shrugged into her cotton cardigan before heading to her car. It was showing signs of being a beautiful night...surely this meant the evening couldn't end in complete disaster.

"Where are you going?"

Kate whirled to see Meredith pulling herself up to full height at the corner of the street; her signature extra-large cappuccino was clutched in her hand with a grip resembling a bird's claw.

"I have an appointment with a vendor for the Jones-Montgomery wedding." She could feel her heart pounding within her chest. Even when she wasn't doing anything wrong, Meredith had an amazing way of making her feel like she was hiding something.

"Which vendor?"

"The menswear shop. I want to be sure all the groomsmen are accounted for." And the best man.

"What time is your appointment?" Meredith asked pertly.

Kate struggled to come up with a response. Three o'clock had come and gone and it was now coming up on four. "I planned to stop by before they closed for the day."

"Hmm, well, they're open until five, so come back inside for a minute. I have something I need you to do for me first."

Kate glanced at her watch and back to Meredith, who stood impassively on the sidewalk, her stone-cold eyes blazing, her lips thinned with disapproval. She wasn't being left with a choice.

Planting a smile on her face, she followed Meredith back into the cool, pristine offices of Bride by Design. She lifted her chin as Meredith led them past the curious receptionist and down the hall to her magnificent office. The other assistants and planners seemed to stop typing so they could watch out of the corners of their eyes, pretending not to stare. Was it just her or had the corridors fallen silent? They were all thinking this might be it: the day she got the axe.

Tonight she would add forty bucks to that Future jar. She might not even bother with a two-week notice when the day finally came. And she'd solicit all of her clients' friends to her new start-up. Discreetly, of course.

She smiled at the image of Bride by Design all boarded up.

Maybe she'd take over the lease!

Meredith's assistant gave her an especially pitying smile, no doubt mistaking Kate's smile over her fantasy for a friendly grin.

Of course, this kind of look was nothing new. She'd seen the change in the way everyone treated her since she'd come back. The pitying glances, the hushed voices, the way they all tiptoed around her in the kitchen while they made their coffee, speaking to her as if she were a child, in upbeat, chipper tones, as if encouraging her to live through the day. It was humiliating, and a sad reminder of what had brought it about. She'd been jilted. A word that was feared at Bride by Design.

Kate beamed back at the assistant, showing that she didn't have a care in the world. Just following her boss into her office for an impromptu meeting. Yep, nothing amiss. Nothing to be worried about. Nothing at all.

Except that she was suddenly worried. Meredith wasn't one for cozy chats or office gossip. When she called you into her office, it was because there was a problem.

And her Future jar certainly wasn't full enough just yet.

She hovered in Meredith's doorway, watching as the woman took brisk strides to her oversized desk and pulled open a drawer. "One of my brides just came to me with the most beautiful square of lace," she said, holding out a small handkerchief for Kate to see. Kate nodded her recognition and reluctantly ventured farther into the room, happy when Meredith didn't ask her to close it. The carpet felt too plush under her feet, the floor-to-ceiling French doors flanked by dove-gray velvet drapes let in a blaring light that made her feel exposed, and the glint in Meredith's eyes made her stomach tighten.

"It's lovely," she managed, reaching out to finger the lace.

"We'll need three yards of it," Meredith said flatly. She uncurled her fingers from the cloth and tucked her ivory satin skirt under her as she took her seat.

Kate remained standing, scrutinizing the lace with narrowed concentration. "It looks antique," she observed.

Meredith shuffled some papers on her desk, saying distractedly, "I'm sure it is."

Kate blinked at the fabric as she considered Meredith's request. "How do we know that amount of yardage is even available?"

Meredith's smile was cool as she looked up at Kate. "We don't."

Now she understood. It was a setup. An impossible task. And one with consequences, no doubt. Kate stared at Meredith, remembering the time that she had fallen off the top of the pyramid during the homecoming game and only laughed good-naturedly. When had Meredith gone from a good-time party girl to an uptight bitch?

It was on the tip of her tongue to ask. And she might. Someday. When she gave her notice.

"I'll do my best," she said, knowing better than to make a promise she might not be able to keep.

Meredith's laugh was thin. "Do better than that. And don't

bother coming in tomorrow unless you've found it. Three full yards."

So here it was. It wasn't all in her head at all. Meredith wanted her out. And this was her final test. "Tomorrow?" Something like this could take days, if not weeks, and she still had a dozen things to do for Elizabeth's wedding—including a very inconvenient trip to get the best man fitted for his suit.

"Yes, tomorrow." Meredith patted her tight chignon before lowering her eyes to the stack of mail on her desk. After a long pause, she lazily dragged her eyes back to Kate, feigning surprise at seeing her there. "Still here? You should really run along before the men's shop closes, Kate. I wouldn't want Saturday's best man missing a suit, after all."

Turning before she showed any emotion, Kate walked out of the office, past all the ogling assistants, whom she was sure to say hello to through a gritted smile, and out onto the cobblestone street. Sensing their stares through the window, she contemplated popping into the coffee shop across the corner for a latte to underscore just how breezy she felt but instead plucked her sunglasses from her tote and pretend-dialed Elizabeth. She was laughing gaily into the dead phone as she slid into the driver's seat, but by the time she'd started the ignition and rolled to a stop at the corner, out of sight and safely away from the office, she was struggling to hold back tears.

This was it. She was sure of it. Meredith was determined to punish her, and she'd finally found a way. There was no way that Kate could find that lace and focus on this Saturday's wedding and all its festivities, much less the other clients she was busy with at various stages of their wedding planning.

She'd just have to accept the fact that this was the end of the road. She'd still follow through with overseeing Elizabeth's wedding, even if she was unemployed before the big day. She might not see the big check she'd worked hard for, as that technically went to the company, but Elizabeth would want her to finish the job as much as Kate would want to see it through.

And unlike her other clients, a true friend wouldn't care about her fallout with Bride by Design or question her capabilities.

With a heavy heart, she parked the car at the Beacon Inn and followed the path to the front porch, no longer so consumed with getting this suit fitted. It would get done, and then what? She could go back to the office and work for the rest of the night, or she could accept the inevitable.

Bypassing the front desk, where a man with dark hair was tapping at a computer, his brass name pin obviously displaying RAYMOND, even from a slight distance, Kate walked straight to the elevator bank and pressed the button for Alec's floor.

Ignoring the DO NOT DISTURB sign, Kate knocked firmly on the door three times and held her breath. From far into the room she heard a curse, followed by a shuffling of papers.

She waited. No response. Hesitating to wonder if he was staring at her through the peephole, she bit her lip and tapped again. Three sharp raps. She had come this far.

The locks turned so fast that she wasn't prepared for the sight of him—tall, a little weary looking, and not entirely pleased to see her. She had the distinct awareness of her stomach starting to flutter. *Oh, stop that!*

"Well, isn't this a surprise," he remarked, his mouth lifting a bit at the corners.

Kate narrowed her gaze, searching for a hint of sarcasm or disdain, and came up blank. Could he genuinely be so at ease with her showing up like this?

"I'm sorry to show up unannounced." She fought to keep her eyes from lingering on his square jaw, on his deep, warm eyes, and the T-shirt that hugged his chest. "I tried calling, but they wouldn't put me through."

"Oh. Sorry about that," Alec said, opening the door wider. Kate raked her eyes over his strong, muscled frame as he padded barefoot into the suite. She assumed this was an invitation to follow and closed the door behind her. "I had them do that in case my father tried to call."

He bent over the coffee table and gathered the papers that were strewn over the polished surface. Stuffing them into a large file folder, he straightened to face her, scratching absentmindedly at his taut stomach, where her eyes were now determined to linger. "We have an appointment today, don't we? What time is it now?"

"It's after four," she said.

He blinked and shot her a look of guilt that made it impossible to stay mad at him for long. "Damn. I lost track of time."

She should be annoyed. She should be furious, really. But maybe it was the knowledge that she was losing her job, or maybe it was the way he looked in those jeans and T-shirt, but she realized she'd lost the will to fight.

"It's open until five if we hurry," she said hopefully. "Any later and they can't promise they'll have it ready in time for the wedding."

"So you're leaving me no other option, then?" Alec raised an eyebrow.

"Not really, no," she admitted, holding her breath and saying a silent prayer that he wouldn't put up another fight. Without that suit... Oh, she couldn't even think about it. "I wouldn't be here if it wasn't this important." Instead she'd be home, enjoying a pint of mint chocolate chip ice cream with extra chocolate chips while watching one of those house-flipping shows that so easily passed the time, with sweet little Henry at her side.

"In that case, let's hurry," Alec said, and Kate let out a sigh of relief. "But I have one condition," he added, his deep brown eyes turning dark with mystery.

Kate bit back a sigh. She should have known he wouldn't make it so easy. That he would find a way to keep things on his terms. "What's that?"

"Have me back before six. I have work to do."

Kate let out a pent-up breath. For one fleeting, exhilarating second she had thought the request was going to be a little more... personal.

She should have known a man like Alec had a one-track mind.

Chapter Twelve

It was a routine part of Kate's job to oversee dress alterations or veil fittings, and there was that time she had to convince a most bewildered groom that he really didn't want to go with the kilt, especially since he wasn't even of Scottish heritage. But overseeing the best man's fitting? This was a first.

"Still questioning my decision to go with seersucker?" she asked, standing to give him the once-over in the most professional capacity possible, even though her gaze kept pulling to the waist of his pants and back to the gleam in that deep-set gaze. And she didn't know which was worse to look at, really.

When the salesman had first pulled out the blue pinstripe seersucker suits that Elizabeth and Kate had decided on for the groomsmen, Alec had visibly scoffed. When the accompanying pink tie was revealed, his groan had been heard throughout the store.

"I've learned that everything around here is a little more casual than I'm used to." He turned obligingly as the tailor pinned the shoulders of the suit jacket.

"And that's precisely why you should roll with it. If William wanted a big, posh, evening wedding, he would have gotten married in the city." Which was precisely what Jake had wanted. Or his parents did, at least.

She silently chastised herself. That should have been her first warning. You can't change a person. You had to just accept them for who they are. Or in the case of her ex-fiancé, *see* them for who they are.

"Turn around and let me have a look at it," she said once the tailor had finished pinning the pants. Standing behind him, Kate eyed the span of his shoulders.

She pulled on the hems of the sleeve, her thumb inadvertently grazing his wrist. She snatched her hand back so quickly that he turned around to give her a puzzled look.

So he was well built. So were mannequins.

She pressed her lips together, deciding not to even bother looking at the pants properly—they'd do, they would just have to—and said quickly, "Turn around."

"Yes, ma'am."

She tried to ignore the twinkle in his eye. "The bow tie's all crooked," she said.

"I'm more of a square knot type of guy," Alec said.

"Bow ties are underrated." Too often her grooms didn't even want to wear them.

"Ah, so you're into nerdy, professor types then?" He cocked an eyebrow, his eyes deep and dark and a little too intense for her comfort.

She locked on to his gaze, willing herself to stay strong even though that broad grin made her knees go a little weak. "I don't have a type."

"Ah, but I think you do," he challenged. "Go on. Tell me your type."

You, she thought to herself. *Someone like you.* And that was exactly why she needed to keep a cool head.

She shrugged, taking a step back to survey his reflection in the mirror. "I guess you could say I'd be drawn to someone with traditional values. If I had a type."

"So someone who wants to get married, then?"

More like someone who means it when they say they do, she thought.

"You're all done," she said, backing away.

"If you'd told me that getting frisked would be part of the experience, I wouldn't have canceled our appointment yesterday." He winked and, before Kate could recover from her shock, disappeared back into the dressing room.

Catching her reflection in the mirror, she realized her mouth was slightly open. She closed it firmly, rolling her eyes at what a boyish flirt he could be and reminded herself not to be pulled into it. Men like that got through life on their money and charm, and she would serve herself greatly to remember that.

Kate plucked her red pen from her handbag and scratched the fitting off her eleven-page list, but her heart felt heavy again as she quickly ran her eyes down the sheet, leafing through the stapled papers to calculate what else needed to be accomplished before the end of the day. This time tomorrow, none of it would matter, technically speaking, not if she didn't find that lace.

Except it would matter to Elizabeth. And it still mattered to her.

"We should probably get going," she said when Alec emerged

from the dressing room. "You said you needed to be back to the hotel by six, and Henry will be waiting for me."

Alec's brow momentarily furrowed. "Henry." He seemed to mull the word.

Kate tipped her head toward the door. "Ready?"

She fumbled to find her keys in the bottom of her handbag. She kept her eyes lowered in her search, but all the same she sensed his gaze on her. The man made her nervous.

Keys in hand, she walked briskly to the car.

She watched as he crossed around to the passenger side, noting the contours of his broad back and biceps. The way his dark hair glinted in the sun. She knew Henry would be eagerly waiting for her to get home—it was almost dinnertime after all—but she had irrational longing to prolong the afternoon. Perhaps take the long way back into town. Perhaps manage a flat tire . . .

And that would only end in disaster. She wasn't about to start losing her head all over something as superficial as physical attraction.

That was all it was, after all.

"Big plans tonight, then?"

Kate's heart sank when she thought of how she would be spending her night, searching for a piece of material that probably didn't even exist. Or she could just not bother. She could instead put on her pajamas, maybe even slather on a face mask, and watch a marathon of *Frasier* in bed. Jake had never been a fan of televisions in the bedroom. That had been the first treat she'd bought for herself in her new home.

Her home. How would she manage a mortgage payment if she didn't have a job? She chewed on her lip as she watched the road, Meredith's words as loud as if she were in the car with her. Had she really meant it when she said not to bother coming back tomorrow without three yards of that ridiculous, extinct lace? Maybe she should call her bluff, take Henry for a nice long walk along the shore tomorrow instead, and then stop for a lobster roll at that new food truck near the pier.

Would Meredith call, once the brides started emailing and the vendors started leaving messages, begging her to come back? Or could Meredith handle everything without her?

Her lips curved into a smile as she considered this approach.

"What's so funny?" Alec asked.

Kate slid him a look. "Ever think about getting revenge on someone and how you'd like to go about doing it?"

Alec gave a surprised laugh. "Who's the guy?"

"Actually, it's a woman. My boss."

"Ah, the mean lady."

"She's hardly even a lady. We went to school together, but we didn't hang out in the same circles." And they still didn't.

"What kind of revenge do you have in mind?"

"I do a fair bit of fantasizing about my resignation speech," Kate said. "Mostly in the shower every morning."

Her cheeks flamed. Why'd she have to go into detail?

"You think you ever will?"

"One of these days I just might," Kate said, but deep down she knew that wasn't true. Charlotte—Charlotte would quit. Charlotte wouldn't take Meredith's crap, either. But Kate had always been the rule monger, the one who went along with the flow, careful not to disrupt the peace, head down, working hard.

For a moment she wished she could be more like her sister.

And not just because Charlotte had Jake.

Charlotte also had chutzpah.

But she was also selfish, Kate thought, narrowing her eyes to the road. She didn't think things through. Didn't think ahead. If she had, would she have slept with Jake?

Guess Kate would never know. Who needed to know?

They fell into silence as she merged onto the road leading back to the inn. Beside her, Alec fiddled with the radio, shifting uncomfortably in his seat. He seemed agitated and restless. Something was bothering him. Kate glanced at the clock. Sure enough—she had less than five minutes to spare to get him back to the hotel.

"So, big plans tonight?" Alec asked again.

"Oh." Kate contemplated the question and how best to answer it. She decided there was no reason to lie and say she had a date or some exciting social event in town. Lying would indicate that she was trying to impress the man. And why on earth would she want to do that? "I'll probably just get some work done."

"But won't... *Henry* be waiting for you?"

At his name Kate smiled. No matter how bad the day went, he always managed to brighten her mood. "Yeah, but he'll be fine. He likes to keep me company while I work."

"Hmph."

Kate slipped her eyes to the right, startled by Alec's reaction. She watched him carefully as they sat at a red light and he stared silently out the window.

"So what do you and Henry usually do for fun around here?" Alec finally asked, his tone weary but vaguely curious.

It was an odd question, but Kate humored him. Heck, it was better than driving the rest of the way to the hotel in silence. And it sure as hell beat fretting over that damn lace. She chewed her lip, considering the origin. Was it Irish? Belgian? Maybe she could track down an antiques dealer...Or maybe she wouldn't bother at all. Maybe she'd drop it off tomorrow with her resignation letter.

And then what? That's where the fantasy ended.

Charlotte would never ask herself, *Then what?* Charlotte lived in the moment.

She shook her sister from her thoughts. There was no use comparing the two of them. They were very different people. She would never be like Charlotte. And Charlotte would never be like her.

She wouldn't want to be like her, Kate mused. To Charlotte, Kate was no fun.

Maybe Jake had felt the same...

"Oh, we like to go for walks," she said, thinking of her cute little dog and feeling better at once. "Sometimes we go to the beach." Not often enough, though. Once this wedding was over, she was taking a much-needed weekend off. That was, if she wasn't unemployed before then.

After a heavy pause, Alec said, "How long have you two been together?"

Kate frowned in confusion and after a split second she burst out laughing, laughing like she hadn't laughed in weeks, if not longer. Laughing until her ribs ached and her eyes teared. She darted her gaze to Alec, whose mouth had thinned in bewilderment. "You thought...you thought Henry was my boyfriend? Henry is my *dog*."

Alec's eyes widened ever so slightly and then his face spread into a smile. "Oh. I guess that explains why he wasn't at dinner last night."

Kate was still laughing as she pulled to a stop at the intersection. "Thank you for that. I needed a good laugh."

"How about a drink then? I've had a day."

Kate's heart skipped a beat. A drink? With Alec Montgomery? Technically there was no harm in it, she supposed.

Sensing her hesitation, Alec pressed, "If you need to go home and walk Henry, that's fine. I like dogs."

"Oh...I don't know..." She trailed off, unable to find an appropriate excuse. Her eyes searched the oncoming traffic for an answer.

"Hey," Alec bantered. "I came to the suit fitting, and I didn't even bat an eyelash at that pink bow tie—well, maybe just one," he said, catching her eye. "I at least deserve a reward for that."

Kate fought off a smile and failed. Pulling up to the stop sign, she knew she had a decision to make. To the left was home. To the right was the center of town.

She thought of the lace tucked into the side pocket of her handbag. She thought of her mortgage and her bills and Meredith's smug smile.

And she thought of Charlotte. Even though she didn't want to.

Screw it. The lace could wait. For today, she was living in the moment. And she might just have a little fun doing it.

★ ★ ★

Kate lived in a small Cape Cod–style house on a quiet, tree-lined street. Recalling that she had mentioned William and Elizabeth lived next door, Alec couldn't resist skimming his eyes over the hedge of pink rosebushes to the slightly larger white house on a green stretch of lawn. He tried as best he could to imagine William living there and failed, despite his brother's transformation. Only a few short months ago, William was living in a sleek loft condo with sweeping views of the Boston skyline, and now he was expected to believe that William lived here? The house had window boxes, for Pete's sake. Did his brother cut his own grass?

Alec frowned and followed Kate along the path to the front door of her house. An immediate yapping was heard the moment she slid her key into the slot and the door opened upon the smallest ball of ivory fur Alec had ever seen.

"Hi, Henry!" Kate cooed, dropping her handbag to the floor and kneeling to greet the little dog, who was spastically licking and jumping at her as quickly as his little body would permit. Kate laughed and closed her eyes as the small animal burrowed his way into her neck and licked eagerly at her face.

"Hey, little guy," Alec said, reaching down to give him a pat.

Henry darted across the room, his eyes dancing with excitement as he grabbed one toy after another in his frenzy. When nothing was good enough, he rolled onto his back on the rug and frantically waved his front paws in the air until Kate silently obliged and rubbed his stomach.

"He's a little hyper, but he's still just a puppy," she explained.

Alec's gaze shifted from the grinning dog to the curve of Kate's thighs, long and smooth and toned. He looked away.

He was only in town for a week. And he wasn't in town for that.

He glanced around the room. Cozy and eclectic furniture in shades of whites and blues gave it an airy, beachy feel. A pile of magazines was stacked in a basket, and there were several framed photos on a bookshelf in the corner. All of Henry, he noted, with a twinge of satisfaction. "How long have you had him?" Alec asked, coming around to sit on the edge of the white-slip-covered sofa.

"Oh...about seven months or so..." A strange expression shadowed Kate's face, but she quickly replaced the faraway look with a proud grin as Henry bolted up and ran to his overfilled toy bin once more. Sniffing around a bit, he selected a small yellow fleece duck and carried it back to Kate with a wiggling bottom, his tail happily slapping the floor.

Kate pulled the toy from his mouth and tossed it across the room, and he sprinted at full speed to retrieve it, squeaking it several times before proudly carrying it back to Kate and placing it at her feet.

"Did you teach him that?" Alec asked, genuinely curious.

"Yeah," Kate admitted with a smile. "Henry and I are pretty good pals," she said, stating the obvious.

"I can see that." Alec watched the way the puppy stopped what he was doing, anticipating Kate's next move with intense expectation as she edged to the other side of the room.

"Did you ever have a dog?"

Alec shook his head, his voice low with regret. "No. But we had a summer house on the Cape when we were young, and the neighbors had a golden retriever. My brother and I loved that dog. We were always sneaking treats from the kitchen for him, tossing him sticks...My mom always said it was the perfect dog. Playful and sweet. But he went home at the end of the day." He gave a sad smile. He hadn't thought of that dog in years. Or those long, lazy summer days.

It was this house, he realized. And this town. And that dinner last night.

"William never mentioned you had a house on the Cape," Kate said with interest.

"Oh, well, he's younger than me, and we didn't have it for long. My dad sold it years ago..." Alec swallowed hard, wishing he had never brought it up. Now it was there, the image he'd tried to banish. The one that William had found a way to re-create.

"That's too bad." She paused and then gestured toward the back of the house. "How about that drink? Lemonade? Beer?"

"I'll take a beer," he said, standing to follow her into the small, bright room. He leaned against the doorjamb as she busied herself with the glasses and beverages: a glass of white wine for herself, a beer for him.

"I should just take Henry out back quickly. It's fenced in, but I like to keep an eye on him." The little dog was now dancing at her feet.

Alec watched them out the window above the sink for a moment, finding it a bit overprotective that she was walking a dog in the backyard, on a leash, not that he'd be saying anything to that effect. Kate was uptight. But she wasn't unlikeable.

Not unlikeable at all, he thought.

He slid his eyes to his brother's house, noticing the large, shiny grill on the back deck. It was becoming increasingly easy to picture William there, flipping burgers and throwing summer barbecues with a grin on his face. If he closed his eyes tight enough, he could almost imagine himself doing the same.

Chapter Thirteen

⸺⸺⸺

Alec had settled himself on Kate's small flagstone patio when she came around the side of the house a few minutes later after a brief walk, Henry eagerly tugging the leash as he ran ahead of her. He didn't know much about dogs, but from what he could tell, this one wasn't exactly well trained. Not that he'd be telling Kate as much.

"Did it look like my brother was home?" Alec asked mildly as Kate locked the gate before setting Henry free. He could have explored the entire yard, but he chose instead to stay close at Kate's feet. Alec smiled. So maybe that was why she went out into the backyard with him. Maybe he would have huddled near the screen door otherwise.

Kate pulled out the chair beside him and craned her neck over the hedge that separated the two yards. "I don't think so. It's a busy week for them. I hope they went out to dinner for themselves before the festivities pick up. It helps to break away from the excitement sometimes and focus on each other. It's easy to lose sight of the point of the wedding with all the activity and hype."

"I take it you speak from experience?"

Kate flushed a little. "Not personally. But I've been in this business long enough to see my share of bridezillas, if that's what you're asking." She laughed. "Weddings can strangely bring out the worst in people." Her eyes darkened for a moment.

"What made you decide to become a wedding planner?"

Kate gave a small smile. "Oh . . . it's sort of a silly story."

He arched a brow. "Well, now you have to tell me. Or I'll be up all night wondering."

Kate sighed. "I was like most little girls, I suppose, always playing house with my dolls, or acting out my wedding day with dandelion bouquets and my mother's old lingerie." They both laughed. "Elizabeth and I would rope her poor brother into playing the groom and my sister—" She stopped for a minute. "She would be our flower girl."

"That sounds sweet," he said, trying to recall similar type of imaginary play as a kid. He came up blank. When it came to free time, he and William seemed to float along a little restlessly. There were organized sports and trips to museums, but the only time they really got to run around and be kids was when they were on the Cape, building sandcastles and forts and splashing in the water.

"I built up weddings to be quite magical," Kate said, rolling her eyes, even though the smile never left her mouth. "And then one day I asked my parents if I could see their wedding album, and my mom told me she didn't have one. She and my dad had eloped, I guess. It made me sad. The first thing I did when I was old enough was convince my parents to redo their vows. They protested at first, but I could tell my mom secretly wanted to do it. She let me plan all of it with her, the flowers and cake, and we held it right in our backyard, under a tent. I'll never forget that look on her face that night. It was like she was falling in love all over again. She felt special. And she deserved to feel special. And she deserved to have that feeling captured and shared." Kate reached for her wineglass and took a long sip. "Anyway, that's why I decided to join Bride for Design. I probably won't be there much longer, though."

"Ah, so you're planning on putting your shower fantasies to the test?" He stopped. "That didn't come out right."

Kate's cheeks were as pink as the flowers growing in the pot behind her.

She sputtered on her drink. "It's just a pipe dream. I'm hardly in a position to leave."

"Why not go out on your own?" Alec asked. After all, people did it. Look at William. But then not everyone could, he thought, thinking of himself. "You clearly know what you're doing."

"I just bought this house. It wouldn't be...responsible."

"Not a risk taker, then." He could say the same.

"No. I...never was." Kate shrugged. "Now more than ever, I just like to know what I'm getting into."

So they shared something else then. The dread of uncertainty. And there was plenty of it recently.

"Still, I could always see if a hotel is looking for an event planner or something..." She trailed off, looking out across the yard, suddenly leaning forward in panic. "Wait. Where did Henry go?"

"Shouldn't have taken him off that leash," Alec said. The yard was fenced in. Why not let the poor dog roam free?

She craned her neck to peek into the kitchen, where the

screen door was ajar. "He usually doesn't like to let me out of his sight."

"He's probably under one of the bushes," Alec said mildly, but Kate's eyes were darting.

"He's used to my undivided attention," Kate said.

Alec hesitated before asking, "So it's always just the two of you, then?"

Kate looked back at him. "Just the two of us."

Alec watched her carefully, wondering what a woman like Kate was doing without a line of eager men standing at her door, waiting for their turn. Unless the door wasn't open.

"Ever think about letting someone new in?" Alec didn't know why he had asked that question. But he was curious.

"Not lately," she said firmly, and hurried along the grass. "Henry! Henry!"

There was panic in her voice now, and Alec stood, stepping across the lawn to stand next to her. He swept the yard; the fence seemed secure, the wood panels tight with little space underneath. "I doubt he—"

"Oh, there he is," Kate said breathlessly. Her could hear the smile in her voice as she turned to the half-open kitchen door, where little Henry was staring back at them, something purple in his mouth. "What do you have, little guy? Come here and let me see."

The dog slowly came out onto the patio, and only when Kate's sharp gasp cut through the faint sound of crickets that were starting to chirp did he resume his earlier energy and take off across the yard, carrying a pair of lace underwear in his mouth as he shot past them.

Kate's face was almost as bright as her lingerie, but Alec could only laugh. He laughed until his ribs ached as Kate chased the tiny white ball of fur around the yard, barely missing each time until Henry finally decided he'd had enough fun and dropped the garment from his mouth before darting back into the house, where he could be heard happily lapping water from his dish.

"You asked if I ever considered adding another member to this household?" Kate raised an eyebrow. "Well, I think Henry has answered your question very concisely. He clearly considers himself the man of this house."

Alec glanced down at Henry as he came back outside to see what all the noise was about and bent down to scoop him up. The little thing couldn't have weighed more than seven or eight pounds, and he immediately curled into a little ball, nuzzling his face into the depths of his own fur. Alec patted him tenderly, wishing all at once that he could have had a dog like this. He'd always wanted one, but there was never time, was there? A dog required care and effort and love. Someone to be there at the end of the day. Much like a wife. Much like anything worth having.

Just as William had said.

Alec let his eyes roam over Kate's face. He wanted to kiss her right then, or hold her hand. Or sit here all night long and then come back again tomorrow.

But that wasn't his life, was it? That was just the life he wished he had. The life he never knew he wanted. Until now.

★ ★ ★

Kate set her wineglass on the patio table and looked out onto the yard, where fireflies were just beginning to flicker. She supposed she should get up, fetch some matches for the citronella candles or offer up something to eat. Or she could go inside and start searching for that elusive lace.

She glanced at Alec. Maybe it was because she didn't want to face reality, or maybe it was because she was having a surprisingly nice time, or maybe it was because she had never had a man over to her new home and wasn't sure when she would again, but she wasn't quite ready for him to leave just yet.

She licked her lips, pulling in a breath for courage. "Are you hungry? I could order a pizza."

Alec glanced down at his watch, his eyes widening. "It's late. I didn't mean to keep you so long."

Kate shrugged away her disappointment. "It's okay."

"Really? Don't you have more work to do tonight?"

Kate drew a long sigh. "Yes. No. Well, too much in fact. My boss needs me to do the impossible. Track down three yards of some antique lace. I don't even know the name of the pattern. All I have to go off is some handkerchief."

"A handkerchief?" Alec looked as puzzled as Kate felt, and something in his expression made her feel less alone. It *was* a crazy request.

"Yep. Here." She stood and walked through the screen door to the kitchen, where her handbag was still on the counter. She reached inside and plucked the square of material from the bottom, feeling her heart sink as she studied the lace. It looked positively ancient.

Alec had followed her inside and now stood before her, frowning down at her hand. He reached out a finger, gently stroking the edge of the material as he studied it, and in doing so, caressed the palm of her hand.

Stiffening, Kate tossed the lace on the counter, barely missing the sink. Lucky for that—Meredith had an eagle eye, and the slightest stain would undermine any success with fulfilling her request.

"She wants three yards of this," Kate explained, feeling her frustration mount as she picked up the precious hankie again. She didn't want to spend her night like this, in a vain attempt to locate the impossible. It was a setup, a game, no doubt. Something Meredith had cooked up to be sure she finally had a reason to fire her.

When she glanced up, Alec was watching her. Kate shifted uneasily on her bare feet, just waiting for him to say something about how silly or ridiculous this was. That it was only lace. That it was just for a party. That she was just some silly party planner.

"Then we'd better get to work," he said instead.

"We?" she said shyly, tipping her head. She couldn't fight the grin that played at her lips.

Handing her the handkerchief, Alec nudged his head toward the living room doorway. "You get your laptop; I'll get the rest of that wine. And I'll order that pizza while I'm at it. Something tells me this might take a while."

Unable to contain her smile, Kate walked into the living room and nestled down onto the floor with her laptop on the coffee table and Henry at her side, listening as Alec placed the order for their dinner.

He settled across the coffee table from her when he ended the call.

"Thanks for helping me," she said quietly with a smile that she hoped expressed the genuine gratitude she felt.

"Your boss seems like a real pill," Alec mused.

Kate grinned as she waited for her computer to boot up. "She is."

Alec handed her a glass of cold white wine and raised his glass to hers. "To a fresh start then?"

Kate wasn't sure if he was toasting her pipe dream of ever leaving or being on better terms with her boss of if he was alluding to something that seemed to be brewing between them.

Whatever the intention, she liked it. A fresh start. Wasn't that all she had been searching for all these months?

Kate clinked her glass with his and took a long, slow sip, eyeing him over the rim of her glass.

This was what life was all about, wasn't it? Starting over. Moving forward. Fresh starts. But as alluring as the idea of it sounded, a greater part of her was terrified. She'd taken great care in locking her heart up and protecting it from the harshness of the world.

But Alec was slowly bringing her walls down, whether she liked it or not.

Chapter Fourteen

⸺⣿⣿⣿⣿⣿⣿⸺

The next morning, Kate strode briskly through the office and straight to Meredith's office. It had been a long, almost sleepless night—it was past one in the morning when she and Alec had finally tracked down the elusive antique lace—but strangely, she didn't feel tired, only invigorated.

Her confidence had dwindled over the past few months, and not just thanks to Jake. Her professional belief had slipped, too, but piece by piece, she was getting it back, becoming more like her post-jilted self with each day.

And a little part of it was thanks to Alec.

Still, the thought of stepping into her boss's pristine office always made her stomach ache a little. Pulling in one last breath for courage, Kate straightened her spine and tapped twice on Meredith's half-open door before poking her head around the edge of it.

Her boss glanced up. "Well, this is a surprise," she said with an icy laugh. She patted her tight chignon and leaned back against her chair, her gaze steady.

Kate just smiled as she walked over to Meredith's desk and held out the handkerchief. Her boss's eyebrow arched in question. "It's Alençon lace. French. From the turn of the twentieth century."

Meredith's face pinched as she snatched up the material. "I could have told you that."

"I know you had asked for three yards of it, but unfortunately I wasn't able to track down a piece of that exact pattern in that exact size."

Meredith smirked. Of course.

"I found four yards," Kate took great pleasure in stating. "It was being used as a tablecloth. Pristine condition. I went ahead and paid for overnight shipping, so it will be here tomorrow. I also found a tailor who can cut it down to size without disrupting the pattern. Unless four yards would be better?" It took everything in her to maintain a neutral expression.

Meredith's eyes flashed, but she said nothing. Instead, she turned back to her computer screen: a signal that this conversation—and perhaps the possibility of Kate being fired—was closed for the day.

"Don't let your focus stray from the true task at hand. You should be concentrating on the Jones-Montgomery wedding first and foremost."

"Of course." Kate nodded.

"And how's that going?" Meredith suddenly asked, swiveling in her chair.

She should have known it wouldn't be this easy. Maybe Alec was right. Maybe she should just quit.

But to work as an event planner in a hotel...It wasn't the kind of personal experience she valued. She loved taking two people through the entire journey, spending months with them along the way, not just making sure everything came together on the big day. "Everything is on schedule," she said tightly.

Meredith looked unconvinced. "What about the musicians? They know the time to arrive for setup?"

Kate resisted an eye roll. The wedding was now four days away. No wedding planner would allow such an oversight at this stage. Swallowing a sarcastic remark, Kate nodded and Meredith scribbled a note to herself. "What time are they setting up the tent?"

"Ten o'clock."

Meredith tipped her head. Her forehead crinkled. "Why so early?"

Kate stifled a sigh and said, "I wanted to be sure to have enough time to oversee it, since I have to help Elizabeth get ready in the afternoon."

Meredith lips drew into a thin line but she said nothing. She had already vocalized to Kate that she felt her maid of honor status was a conflict of interest, and one that forced her to participate in the wedding rather than solely oversee it. As if she wasn't under enough scrutiny as it was, now Meredith had an extra reason for thinking that something was bound to go wrong. Kate knew that Elizabeth would forgive her, but Meredith would not. Big names were coming into town for this wedding—the groom was a well-known man, and many influential guests had summer homes in Misty Point, as Meredith kept reminding her. As if Kate didn't already know...

"Run me through the schedule leading up to the ceremony." Meredith stared at her patiently.

So much for the conversation being over, Kate thought

grimly. She swallowed the bitter taste in her mouth. Pride didn't go down easily.

"After hair and makeup, the bride and female half of the wedding party will gather at Elizabeth's parents' home at three. The cars will arrive at four thirty to bring us to the beach for the ceremony."

"And where are the dresses now?"

"They're at the shop. I'll be picking them up and personally delivering them Friday before the rehearsal."

Before Meredith could continue with her interrogation, Kate volunteered, "The groomsmen will gather at William and Elizabeth's house at three thirty and be transported via limousine to the beach, scheduled to arrive fifteen minutes ahead of the bride's car."

"What's the situation with the best man?"

Kate's pulse quickened at the mention of Alec. The image of his easy grin and warm brown eyes hadn't faded since he'd called a cab and bid goodbye last night, much as she wished it would.

"What about him?" she asked, her tone sounding intentionally vague. She cleared her throat, wondering if she looked as guilty as she felt.

"He's up to speed with the process? Where to stand? Speech? You know how some of them can be..." Meredith gave her a pointed look, and Kate almost slipped into a smile, forgetting for a moment that they weren't on the same team here, not really, and inside stories and conspiratorial grins had no place in this office.

Alec's questions haunted her, drawing up all the things she asked herself every day. Could she really continue like this, and for how long? She loved wedding planning, but was it worth this cost?

She couldn't think about this now, not when her best friend's wedding was days away.

"Kate? It's imperative that the best man cooperate. We don't need another Ross Davidson on our hands."

A prickle of panic made Kate stand a little straighter. No one at Bride by Design could ever forget Ross Davidson, the red-haired troublemaker from the Keough wedding last summer. Thanks to one too many drinks before the ceremony had even started, he had cat-called when the bride and groom had their first kiss, and then tripped the maid of honor on the way down the aisle. No attempts at sobering him up before the reception had been successful, and he was determined to give a speech he hadn't prepared in advance, sprinkled with less-than-flattering comments about the bride's weight and tasteless sexual innuendos about their forthcoming honeymoon.

Kate shuddered. "I can assure you that Alec Montgomery doesn't have a drinking problem," she said with confidence. If the bachelor party proved anything, it was that Alec was not the partying sort.

She smiled softly. He was sort of a homebody, in a way. Surprisingly.

"And his speech is acceptable? You've seen it?"

She blinked at her boss, wondering how she should answer this one. She had been so concerned with getting his suit fitted and making sure he was satisfied with the rehearsal dinner that she had overlooked this rather important detail. Normally a wedding planner wouldn't have to think about something as personal as this, but given Elizabeth's concerns, she had reason to make sure everything would be fine.

She chewed her lip as she considered the status of this elusive detail. Would Alec have taken it upon himself to write something up? She highly doubted it, based on what she'd seen of him this week. If there was a general trend throughout this process, it was that Alec was very passive when it came to his best man responsibilities.

She said the only thing she could. "It's all under control."

Meredith accepted the answer with a quick nod of her head. "Good. Now how did the call with the caterers go last night?"

Kate stared blankly at her boss for only the briefest of seconds before her blood stilled.

Oh my God, the caterers. She had made a mental note yesterday to call the caterers last night, and she had forgotten. Between the suit fitting and that damn lace, she had once again failed to fulfill one of the most basic tasks on her list.

She couldn't lie her way out of this one—Meredith would be sure to know, if she didn't already. Kate eyed her boss warily, gauging if this was a trick question, and decided to answer as honestly as she could. "I wasn't able to connect with them last night. I'll call them now."

Meredith gazed at her icily. "You do that."

Kate inhaled sharply and exited Meredith's office on shaky knees. She would call the caterers. Of course she would. But first, she would call the best man.

★ ★ ★

Alec finished looking through the notes he had gathered from his meeting Sunday and settled back into the stiff armchair, glancing around his hotel suite. The day had been less productive than he had hoped, and the looming deadline of his next sit-down with Mason Lambert was weighing heavily.

It wasn't like him to not be able to focus. From a young age, he'd used it to push through life. When his mother had died, he'd focused on his grades, something she'd taken seriously and the one thing that felt as if it was within his control. He made a goal to never get anything lower than a ninety percent that year, not even in art, or science, which he'd always struggled with, and with that goal in mind, he'd become fixated, distracted. When the emotions started creeping in, he thought of that report card and what he wanted it to say, and all at once the image in his mind was replaced with something attainable. Later, in business, he could sit in his office, hell, even sleep there, without thinking of the outside world, without wondering what events he was missing or what parties he could go to, what women he could be dating. It was a skill, he thought. But it was also, perhaps, a curse.

He wished it could be different—that he could be more like William, calm and casual—but he couldn't. Alec worked hard to be sitting at the top of the Montgomery Group. Too hard sometimes. Especially now, when it didn't seem to be paying off.

He rubbed a hand over his jaw, realizing he'd forgotten to shave today. He'd been too busy working, and not only because so much was on the line. Something had shifted in him last night at Kate's house. And the night before at her parents' home. Something he needed to shut out.

And so he'd spent the day focused on the meeting with Mason. It beat worrying about the state of his family's company or wondering if William would ever rejoin him. And it beat thinking about Kate, and her little dog, and how much happier he'd been in her living room than he'd ever been in that over-air-conditioned corner office.

But now his concentration had expired. Admitting defeat, he closed his laptop and walked across the room, wishing he could be doing something else right now. Something involving sitting in Kate's kitchen with a nice cold drink and funny little Henry on his lap. He stared out the window to the vast stretch of ocean. The tide was rolling in, and large waves broke against the rocky shoreline, creating a bubbling white foam in their wake.

His chest tightened when he thought of the way Kate had looked when she'd waved him off last night, standing in the glow of the porch light, Henry tucked happily in her arms, his tail wagging with contentment. The way she'd smiled and wiggled her long, feminine fingers in a wave. The way he had fought with everything in him not to lean over and kiss her but instead jammed his hands into his pockets and hurried across the stone path, wishing he could stay.

But he hadn't. Instead he had come upstairs to this room, and he had barely been able to think about anything else since.

His phone rang and he crossed the room to answer it, hoping it was Kate.

"Hi..." It was Kate. And the way his spirits rose at the sound of her voice confirmed the obvious. He liked her. And he really shouldn't be spending this week thinking about a girl from Misty Point when all hell was breaking loose back in Boston. "How are you? I hope the hotel remains comfortable?"

Alec frowned at her formality. He'd thought their evening had been enough to undo any damage Elizabeth's disparaging opinion may have caused, but maybe he had misread things.

He sat back on the bed and put his feet up, hoping to get to the bottom of this once and for all. "And to what do I owe the honor of this call?"

Kate seemed to hesitate. "I hate to bring it up, but I'm sitting here going through the wedding checklist and I was wondering if you had your speech written?"

"The speech." Alec couldn't fight the disappointment in his chest. So this was the reason for her call. Business. For once he was on the other side of it.

"The best man speech," Kate said, and Alec could just picture her chewing on her bottom lip as she waited for his response.

Alec glanced over at his papers on the coffee table. Among the shuffle of business papers was a draft of the speech he'd planned to give at the wedding. *It couldn't be less heartfelt,* he thought grimly.

He sighed as he shifted his eyes away from the handwritten notes. He wished things could have been different—that the speech he gave could actually mean something. But he didn't believe in marriage. Hell, he didn't even believe in love. And he certainly didn't believe that William and Elizabeth would stand the test of time. No one could, and the odds were already stacked against those two. They came from two different worlds, and as much as William might like the laid-back beach life for now, there was a part of him that would always need something more.

Alec closed his eyes. He couldn't think about this anymore.

"How about dinner tonight?" he said. "I could really use your help on this speech, actually."

Wasn't a lie, per se. His speech was forced at best, and who better to help rewrite it than the woman who knew his own brother better than he did these days? A woman whose days revolved around William and Elizabeth's happy union?

"I have a meeting with the caterers tonight," Kate said, but Alec wasn't about to let that excuse stop him.

"Tomorrow, then."

Silence stretched down the phone line. "What did you have in mind?" Kate finally said.

He hadn't thought that far ahead, but he wasn't about to let this opportunity slip away. "There's a bistro just down the street from the hotel that has some sidewalk tables."

"I know the one," Kate said, and though she still hadn't agreed, Alec took it as an answer.

"Tomorrow then. Seven o'clock." He quickly ended the call before she could protest.

Chapter Fifteen

Charlotte sat at the metal desk in the front of the small, street-level office that housed Bob's insurance business. She had hoped there would be a steady flow of traffic throughout the day, or at least a few clients stopping by for a meeting.

Since she first arrived at nine o'clock, after bidding goodbye to Audrey and Mrs. Novak, who was kind enough to accept a delayed payment once Charlotte received her first paycheck, it had been just her and Bob. Alone. In a very small office. For the second day in a row.

Charlotte studied the computer screen, cringing as she heard Bob end his phone call, hoping he wouldn't open his office door and start getting chatty again. She'd politely listened to him beat his chest about his golf and skiing abilities yesterday afternoon, and of course, there were the endless strategic questions about her personal life, which she'd craftily dodged every time.

Aside from teaching her how to use the not-so-complicated phone system, there was the internal database he'd vaguely run through with her this morning. Now, as Charlotte clicked around and never ended up on the page she was supposed to be, she started wishing she'd asked a few more questions.

Still, that would have required more time alone with the man, and she didn't need that.

What she needed was a paycheck, though. *Eye on the prize, Charlotte.*

The door to Bob's office opened with a creak, and Charlotte muffled a groan, her eyelids fluttering in annoyance. He lingered in the doorframe, either checking up on her work or looking for attention. Swallowing a sigh, she pivoted her chair. It was the latter.

Bob, it seemed, was in need of female companionship. He was single—he'd been sure to mention that yesterday morning, about thirty-four minutes into her first day, when he'd suggested they close for a bit and stroll down the street for a coffee. It had seemed so innocent at first, even when he'd insisted on paying, but then there'd been the suggestion of lunch. She'd been smart enough to pack something perishable—a polite excuse that had made poor Bob's shoulders slump. She'd stolen the few minutes he'd gone to lunch today to call to check on Audrey, smiling when she heard her soft cry in the background, and she'd scooted off to the bathroom when she saw him strolling down the sidewalk, a crumpled takeout bag in his hands, his suit looking rumpled.

Bob was not an alpha male. Or very smooth with the ladies. Bob, she was starting to realize, was a bit of a sleaze.

"Just adding these contacts to your database," she said pleasantly, keeping her eyes fixed on the screen.

"Oh, you're on the wrong screen," Bob commented, coming

to stand beside her chair. Charlotte swiveled it when his leg brushed her thigh. "Here, let me show you."

Before she could react, he moved his hand onto the mouse, his fingers skimming hers before she could snatch them away. Gritting her teeth, she folded her hands in her lap and focused on breathing through her mouth as she watched him expertly maneuver the database. He'd really overdone it with the cologne today. And she'd thought nothing could top yesterday...

"I think I understand now," she said first chance she could, eager to get some space.

"I'll wait while you add this contact to make you sure it's clear."

Oh, please don't, she thought.

Technically, this was a reasonable thing for him to say. Charlotte knew this, objectively. But she also knew that something didn't feel right. For example, did he really need to stand that close?

A little unnerved, she added the next contact on her list. Some poor sod who would be cold-called tomorrow during the dinner hour, no doubt. She grinned when a little alert popped up on the center of her screen letting her know she'd succeeded.

She glanced up at Bob, seeing this as his cue to move, but he wasn't looking at the screen. No, Bob's eyes were too busy ogling the mildest hint of cleavage he could make out through the scoop-neck blouse she wore.

Charlotte felt her cheeks heat with fire, and she abruptly pushed her chair back and stood, waving her mug with enthusiasm. "Coffee break," she said, forcing a stony grin. She brushed past Bob and waited until she could hear him settling into his office chair and picking up the phone to make more cold calls before tucking into the bathroom.

Don't quit. You can't quit. She told herself this over and over. She *would* quit. Once she found something else. Something better. But now ... She was out of options.

Fighting back tears, she tried to imagine coming in here again tomorrow, and the day after, and the day after. And she tried to imagine going back to that dark apartment, and not being able to buy Audrey that sweet little dress after all.

And she thought of her bedroom back in Misty Point. And the wind in her hair and the sand in her toes.

She pulled her phone from her pocket. She could call her parents. She hadn't told them about Audrey yet. Hell, they'd never even known she was pregnant. At first she was too ashamed, and then too nervous that she would make things worse, and then ... Well, too much time had passed.

She'd tell them. She would. But there was someone who deserved to know the truth first.

She scrolled through her list of contacts, finding Kate's name. She could call her. She might actually answer this time. And then what?

What would she say? *I'm sorry?* How lame was that? Maybe something like *How's this for irony?* No, too flippant. Or how about *Well, misery loves company.* No, too callous.

She chewed on her fingernail, sighing deeply. She couldn't hide in here forever; Bob would no doubt start wondering ... or knocking. She wouldn't put it past him.

She pressed the button before she lost her nerve and with a shaking hand brought the device to her ear. Kate just needed to hear her out. She needed to know the truth.

★ ★ ★

Kate stared at her phone and with a pinch of her lips, silenced the ringer.

She finished typing her email to a potential client, made sure to include links to her portfolio, and sent it off. She scratched the item off her list and stared at the next item on her agenda, but her mind didn't absorb any of the words.

Charlotte wasn't going to stop. She was going to keep calling, and keep trying, and...

Kate couldn't deal with this right now. Not when she had a wedding in a matter of days, a job on the line, and a date with a guy who was all wrong for her in an hour.

She shook her head clear. It wasn't a date. No, it was a meeting. A meeting, she told herself firmly.

She stared at the phone, waiting for a beep that would signal a voice mail, holding her breath until enough time had passed and she was certain that there wouldn't be one.

Small favors, she thought. It was hard enough to see her sister's name keep popping up on the screen. Knowing that there was a message, with her sister's voice, trapped in this device?

She pushed back her chair and smoothed her skirt. She walked to the kitchen, got a glass of water even though she wasn't thirsty, and came back and emptied it onto her desk plant.

She wouldn't think about Charlotte right now. Or why she was calling.

She would stay busy. Return a few more emails, clear her desk, and get ready for her dinner *meeting*.

She worked for half an hour more and, once she was sure that Meredith had left for the day, slipped into the bathroom. From her bag, she pulled out a brush, deciding just a touch-up would do. But her heart was starting to beat a little faster when she realized she would have to leave soon, and when she found herself reaching for the blush, she stopped herself.

What was she doing? Primping for this guy? She hadn't even really agreed to this dinner, had she? No, she hadn't. She had technically inquired about his suggestion, and he had taken that as a yes.

She muttered under her breath. Yep, arrogant. Used to getting his way.

Still, it would be rude to cancel, and she did need to discuss that best man speech, just in case, and really, he had helped her out the other night. She sighed. Truth be told she enjoyed his company. There. She'd said it.

In her head. No way would she ever be making those thoughts known. To Alec. Or anyone.

Kate looked down at her cell phone, curiosity over her sister's call piquing her interest for only a second, before she tossed it into her handbag and then reached for her lipstick. She swiped it over her lips quickly, telling herself it was only because she was going out in public and not because of her dinner date. Make that dinner *companion*.

Checking her reflection in the small mirror one more time, she reached behind her head and plucked at her hair clip, allowing her hair to fall freely around her shoulders.

She smiled, noticing the way her eyes were alive and dancing. She hadn't seen that look on her own face in a long time, and the shock of it made her worry a little. She was getting carried away. Excited. And she couldn't take another fall right now.

Kate watched as her smile faded and she quickly slammed the

compact shut as she caught a glance of her frown. She had struggled too hard for too long to just end up hurt again.

Before she could talk herself completely out of the night, Kate grabbed her handbag and hurried out of her office. She still had a job to do, and that included making sure the best man gave an appropriate speech. Given the strained relationship between Alec and the bride, Kate could only assume that Alec needed all the help he could get.

"Kate!"

At the sound of her name, she stopped walking and glanced across the street, where Elizabeth was standing at a crosswalk, waving to grab her attention. Kate's stomach knotted.

"Hey!" She managed a watery smile and held up her hand, waiting as Elizabeth jogged across the street in a pale pink cotton shift dress, looking every bit the radiant bride-to-be that she was.

"I knew that was you!" Elizabeth gushed, and gave her a peck on the cheek. Pulling back, she skimmed her eyes over Kate and exclaimed, "You look all dolled up!"

Dolled up? So much for not trying to make an impression. Kate looked down at her A-line work skirt and sleeveless top. She had the sudden urge to wipe off her lipstick with the back of her hand.

"Hot date or something tonight?" Elizabeth winked.

Kate's cheeks burned with guilt and she struggled to find an explanation that her best friend wouldn't see through. "Ha-ha," she said lamely, but Elizabeth wasn't buying it.

Elizabeth's eyes turned sharp. "Oh my God. You *do* have a date! I *knew* our little talk over tea sunk in. So go on," she urged. "Tell me more. I need details, and lots of them."

Kate lowered her gaze to the cement below her strappy sandaled feet (she should have stayed in her work pumps; then she might have dodged this awkward moment!), knowing that this time, she would have to come clean. She couldn't hide from Elizabeth forever, and she didn't want to, either. It didn't feel good. Besides, Kate was Elizabeth's wedding planner and Alec was the best man. It made sense that she would have to meet up with him.

Even to her own ears, the excuse sounded weak. Very, very weak.

"It's nothing," she stammered. "A business meeting. No biggie." *No biggie?* Yep. Couldn't lie to her best friend.

"But you're all gussied up! You have on fresh lipstick. And your hair..."

Kate's hand reflexively darted to her head. "What's wrong with my hair?"

Elizabeth's lips curved into a satisfied grin. "I knew it!" she squealed. "You wouldn't care what your hair looked like if you weren't going somewhere special. Now dish. Who is he? Anyone I know?"

Oh, he's someone you know all right. Kate took a measured breath and locked Elizabeth's curious gaze with her own, gauging her friend's reaction. "It's Alec," she finally admitted.

The smile immediately fell from her friend's face. "Alec?"

So much for admitting her muddled thoughts that had no business being there in the first place. Kate thought fast. "It's his best man speech. I wanted to meet with him to look it over, just to be sure it's okay. You know how guys are." She rolled her eyes to drive home the point.

Elizabeth stared at her pensively before her shoulders shrank with obvious relief. "I was a little worried about what he would get up and say on Saturday. Thanks for looking out for me and William."

Kate laughed nervously, feeling sick with herself. "Of course." She swallowed hard before saying, "You know I would do anything for you, Elizabeth."

"I know." Elizabeth nodded. "Heck, you're spending your evening with Alec Montgomery of all people, for my sake. If this isn't the sign of a true friend, I don't know what is."

Kate gritted her teeth into a smile. "I should probably get going," she said, motioning to the WALK sign.

"Well, don't let him get to you," Elizabeth said as Kate began to edge away. "He has a way of getting under people's skin."

"I won't," Kate replied. But the problem was that he had already gotten under her skin. Just not in the way Elizabeth could have ever expected.

★ ★ ★

Alec was leaning against a light pole when Kate approached. He was dressed in khaki shorts and a crisp white T-shirt that accentuated every ripple in his chest, and Kate's resolve since her conversation with Elizabeth had already weakened. Considerably.

It had just been too long since she'd touched a man, that was all. It was a natural reaction that surely anyone would have to someone of the opposite sex after all this time. Especially one who looked like Alec.

"Hey!" He flashed her a big grin as she closed the distance between them.

She brightened at the sight of his friendly smile, wishing the response wasn't so automatic. "Hey."

Alec gestured to the door of Bistro Rouge. "It's full, but the wait should only be a few minutes."

"I don't mind," Kate said, glancing at the customers who had filled the stretch of sidewalk tables that were tucked behind tall planters overflowing with colorful blooms. It was a romantic restaurant, one of the best in Misty Point, but she knew better than to assume this was why Alec had chosen it. He was visiting town, it was close to his hotel, and from an outsider's point of view it probably just looked like a decent place to eat. Besides, he was probably used to picking the finest options. It was surely nothing more than that.

And she shouldn't wish it to be.

Just thinking of how betrayed her friend would feel to know that Kate was siding with the enemy was enough to make her come up with an excuse and leave. Going through with this dinner at this cozy little spot would make her the worst kind of friend there was. She knew too many people like this already, and she didn't want to follow in their example.

She stole a glance at him, taking in the strong width of his back as he casually studied the menu outside the restaurant, his hands thrust in his pockets, his hair wavy and dark and just begging for her to tangle her fingers through... *Stop it!*

She opened her mouth, knowing she had to say something, but not knowing quite what, when she saw him. *Jake.* He was coming around the corner, laughing that laugh, smiling that smile, without a care in the world. He was rounding the bend, coming in her direction. She watched in frozen horror, not knowing whether to hide or run. Her mind ran wild with every worst-case scenario. Was he coming to the restaurant? Would he speak to her? What would she say?

What was he even doing here? He was supposed to be gone, long gone.

And then she remembered. The phone calls. Charlotte. Panicking, she darted her gaze, searching for her sister, not knowing what she would say if she saw her. There were many things she could say. None of them positive, of course. But silence . . . silence had been the best option. Until now.

"Alec." Her voice locked in her throat, coming out strained and forced.

He turned to face her, his eyes growing wide at the sight of her. "Are you okay?"

"I need you to do me a favor," she whispered urgently. Her heart was pounding as her eyes zipped from Alec to Jake and back again.

He hadn't noticed her. Not yet. But he would. And soon.

Alec rolled his eyes in a joking way. "Do the best man duties ever end? What do you need me to do now? Arrange flowers? Frost the cake? Oh . . . I know. Kiss the bride?"

"No. Kiss me." She blinked, shocked by her own words. It was rash, impulsive, and completely desperate. She was probably sending him all the wrong messages. But she didn't even care.

For once, she wasn't thinking about the ripple effect of her actions. Or what she would say in five minutes. All she could think about was the here and now. And that if she didn't have time to run and hide from the people who had publicly humiliated her, the most she could do was prove to Jake—and Charlotte—that she was over it. That they hadn't hurt her. That she was just fine.

Alec's smile vanished from his face, replaced with a look of surprise. "What?"

"Kiss me," she repeated breathlessly, her mind racing. She hadn't even contemplated the possibility that he might turn her down, laugh in her face, storm off. It would make it all worse—seal her humiliation. "I need you to kiss me. Right now."

Alec's expression was frozen and for a moment Kate was struck with the horrifying thought that he would drag this out, or turn it into a joke. She didn't have time for that. But then his brows lifted and his lips curled into a devilish grin. "If you insist," he murmured, reaching down to scoop his arms around her waist in one smooth effort.

His kiss was anything but shy as he pressed his lips to hers, pulling her so close to his chest she could feel the heat of his body through his shirt.

Her knees went a little weak as she let herself go, and for a moment she wasn't even thinking of Jake or Charlotte at all. She wasn't thinking of the hurt, the pain, or what would happen next, when they broke apart. She wasn't thinking of anything.

Abruptly, she stepped back. A flicker of what she recognized as desire passed through Alec's eyes and she inhaled deeply, forgetting that they were in a public space, smack in the center of Harbor Street, that people were watching, and that the person she had wanted to witness this could be standing right beside her by now. All she knew was this moment: the heat of Alec's skin still close to her, the way his cotton T-shirt felt under her fingers, the way the shape of his body felt under her palms. The way his strong hand still rested on the curve of her hip. The way she wanted it to graze lower...

She turned and scanned the sidewalk, looking for any sign of the ghost that had caused her such a fright.

"I'm sorry, Alec, I have to go."

She'd been reckless. Careless. This wasn't her. This was something Charlotte would do.

Charlotte. The calls. She was back. In town.

She hadn't realized fully until this moment just how much she truly didn't want to talk to her.

Alec lifted his grip on her arm, halting her in her tracks, his voice husky and rushed as he said, "Is everything okay? Kate? Have I done something?"

"I have to go," she said, not bearing to look at him as she turned and fled, down a side street, her eyes wide and watchful, searching for any sign of her sister.

She needed to get home. She needed to be away from here, from the people and the possibilities of running into Jake. Of seeing him and his smiling, smirking face. She needed to get away from the lure of Alec's voice, calling after her, his tone filled with so much worry and confusion that she wasn't sure she could keep going.

Or if she even should.

Chapter Sixteen

A_{ny} doubt that Meredith was trying to drive Kate out of Bride by Design was reaffirmed the next morning when she asked Kate to cover a meeting she had at a potential wedding location for a new client.

"Bluestone Manor?" Kate couldn't believe she'd heard that right.

"Is there a problem?" Meredith asked calmly.

Damn straight there was a problem. Bluestone Manor was a two-hundred-year-old mansion set at the top of the breakers, with a breathtaking view of the sea. It was also the place Kate was supposed to be married. And the place she hadn't been to again since she'd had to cancel the reservation, getting back only a fraction of the deposit her parents had so generously given for the wedding.

Kate shifted uneasily on her feet, suddenly aware that she hadn't answered the question yet and that her boss was staring at her with a look of naked impatience.

"No problem at all," Kate said tightly.

"I would have gone myself, but I have a conflict with Sally Schofield," Meredith clarified, making it clear that even though Kate might be filling in for this venue viewing, she was not taking over the account.

Still, Kate thought, she couldn't afford to mess this up, and that was exactly what she would do if she let her emotions get the better of her.

She left the office quickly with the signature soft pink folder Meredith handed her for Bride by Design's newest clients. A year had passed since she'd been to Bluestone Manor, but the drive up the winding, tree-lined path to the edge of Misty Point felt familiar, bringing her back to a time and a place she'd tried so hard to forget. To feelings of hope and excitement and possibility. Had she known the last time she'd visited for her menu tasting that it would be her last, that the salmon they'd selected would never be eaten by their guests, that she would never have her picture taken with Jake against that stone wall in the rose garden or under the weeping willow at the far edge of the grounds?

Of course she hadn't. She'd been too caught up in the excitement, the beauty. The details. She'd stopped listening to the little voice in her head that told her Jake might not be the one. That something didn't feel quite right.

The road was nearing the peak of the cliffs, and Kate steeled herself as the large stone mansion came into view. She pulled the car to a stop, allowing herself one long look from a distance, one last chance to accept what had come of those dreams, before she shook the cobwebs clear and drove over the gravel path to the discreet parking lot, tucked out of view from the mansion by a dense boxwood hedge.

Her legs felt unsteady under her as she made her way across the path to the front door and into the expansive lobby, set up like an old English library, with warm wood tones and soft lighting and fresh cut flowers overflowing from crystal vases.

The couple was waiting at the base of the curved staircase, whispering to each other in excited tones as she approached. "Eve and Christopher?" she asked, just to be sure. "Congratulations on your engagement," she said, shaking their hands. "I'm Kate Daniels, a planner at Bride by Design."

Eve, a pretty brunette with big green eyes, nodded. "Meredith mentioned you would be meeting us. She said you were quite the expert on this place."

Oh, did she? So this was payback for doing her job and finding the lace, it would seem.

"I am quite familiar with Bluestone Manor," she agreed. And just for Meredith's comment, she was going to give them a tour to top all others.

With that mission in mind, she led through the many rooms of the house, describing the history of the home as they walked, and stopping to point out the little details that she'd always thought would have made her own wedding day so special.

"There's an option to have the reception in the main ballroom or here," she said, leading them into the dome-ceilinged conservatory at the back of the house.

She didn't need to look at them to sense their excitement, but even so, she couldn't seem to steal her eyes away. The groom was a little out of place, as most of them were, taking the bride's lead, standing just a bit behind. But it was her face he was looking at more than the surroundings, as if her wish—her happiness—was what mattered the most.

Kate felt a tightening in her throat, and she cleared it. Awkwardly. "If you'll excuse me, I'll let you have a look-see, and then I'll be back to get your thoughts."

She hurried down the hall toward the bathroom. She knew her way, of course. Her cheeks were flushed when she caught her reflection in the large mirror above the marble sinks. Her eyes were wet.

This was a test. The worst one yet. And she was going to pass it.

She took a few long breaths, forcing herself to imagine how much worse it would have been to end up married to a philandering cad, not just merely engaged to one. It was definitely better to focus on that than, say, the cherub-cheeked children they might have had, running along the sand... And really, Jake might not have even wanted children. Every time she mentioned things like that, his brow would knit and he'd grow strangely quiet.

Yep. A red flag. A big one.

Better off without him.

Before she slid back into that bad place again, she pulled open the bathroom door and walked slowly back to the conservatory. She hovered in the doorway as the couple walked around the room hand in hand, admiring the lead-paned windows and gilded sconces. A year later, the room was even more beautiful than she'd remembered, not that she tried to think of it much. The glass-enclosed space lent panoramic views of the rose garden to the stretch of vibrant green grass leading to the cliff, and the bright blue sea beyond. A grand piano was tucked in the corner. To its side was where the band would play, and over near the row of mirrors on the sole windowless wall in the room was where the head table would be positioned. She'd imagined sitting at the center, looking out onto her guests and the beautiful view beyond.

Nope. Not going to go there. It wouldn't do her any good now, and today she had something to prove. Not to Meredith. Or Jake. Or Charlotte. But to herself.

It was time to get over the pain of her past once and for all. And what better way than to face the ghosts right here, where they haunted her the most?

By the time she'd led the couple through the rose garden and watched them walk off to their car, looking back a few times to take in the building, she felt completely sure that not only would they choose Bluestone Manor for their wedding location, but also that Meredith would find nothing to complain about.

But somehow, that wasn't enough anymore. Instead of fantasizing about walking back into the office to see Meredith pleased with her work, or perhaps even miffed by it, all Kate could think about was how much better it would feel to march in with her resignation letter.

"Kate?" a voice called out as Kate began walking back into the lobby to retrieve the manor's updated brochure to bring back to the office.

She turned, smiling weakly when she saw Gretchen Trager coming toward her. She'd been hoping to dodge her old contact at the manor, but it would seem that luck was not on her side these past twenty-four hours. The universe was determined to throw her old life back in her face. And she had no choice but to confront it.

Kate gave Gretchen a hug hello and pulled back, about to ask how business was going when she saw the head tilt. Of course.

A year may have passed, but despite everything that happened between their last meeting and today, one thing was still on Gretchen's mind.

"How are you?" she asked, squinting with obvious compassion.

"I'm great. How are you?" Kate managed to smile a little wider, eager to proceed with normal, present-day conversation, and not go back to that dark time in her life.

But Gretchen wasn't buying it. She paused, her eyes roaming Kate's face as her neck crooked a little lower. "I've thought about you," Gretchen continued, and Kate gritted her teeth into an even wider smile. She had an urge to make up an excuse (Off to see a fake boyfriend, perhaps? One by the name of...Henry?), say goodbye, and turn to go. But despite her delivery, Gretchen was being kind, and Kate couldn't overlook that.

"It's been a busy year, but not as busy as this summer will be. But then, I don't need to tell you that." She gave a lame laugh, hoping to draw on the camaraderie those in the business had for spring and summer seasons, when, at least in Misty Point, most people chose to get married.

"So you're keeping busy then. Good. Good." Gretchen was nodding, her gaze still one of far too much sympathy.

"Busy, busy," Kate said, feeling her pulse quicken. The grandfather clock was beginning to chime, just like it had the first time she'd come here with Jake, hoping to convince him that this was the perfect venue for their wedding—far better than that sterile and stuffy hotel his parents preferred. He'd agreed just as the clock began its first bell and kissed her right there in the lobby. Now, hearing those bells, she was right back there for a moment. Full of hope and anticipation and joy. So much joy.

"I should actually run," she said, waving the brochure awkwardly for no reason other than her head was spinning and she wasn't sure what to do with her hands. Suddenly the lobby felt stiflingly hot, old and musty. She needed to get outside, breathe in the sweet, salty air, and be alone. Away from the head tilts and the soft voices and the squinted eyes and the subtle head shakes. "Wedding season beckons."

For some, she thought, blinking quickly.

"Of course, of course. I'm relieved to see how well you're holding up," Gretchen said, reaching out to give her hand a squeeze.

The hand squeeze. Yep, it was officially time to leave.

The clock continued to chime as she marched through the front door, the bells fading into soft, sorrowful reminders as she made her way to the car and drove away, and she kept driving, without any route in mind, until Bluestone Manor and all the wonder it had once held was far behind her.

* * *

Charlotte sat on a park bench eating her lunch of salt and vinegar chips and a cheese sandwich. A year ago she wouldn't have been caught dead eating like this, but back then she was still young and carefree and, well, boy crazy.

Still, this paunch wasn't going to disappear on its own. She'd have to start eating better. It would be part of her new life plan. Once she had her life figured out, that was.

Suddenly the door she'd trained her eye on opened. Her

heart skipping a beat, Charlotte sat a little straighter and quickly brushed the crumbs from her lap. She held her breath, waiting for her moment, as a man she did not know casually pushed through onto the sidewalk and hailed a passing cab.

Charlotte slumped back on the bench, miserably bringing the sandwich to her mouth. She didn't know why she was so disappointed. After all, was she really looking all that forward to seeing Jake the Snake after all this time?

That was an affirmative no. Sure, she'd loved him once. Or thought so. Now...she wasn't sure. How could she love a man who would take advantage of her like that? He had used both Kate and then her, and he had no interest in that precious little girl he had never even met. In a perfect world, she wouldn't need his help, or anyone else's for that matter, but it wasn't a perfect world, and she'd learned that lesson the hard way.

Ten thousand dollars. That's what he had given her that day she'd shown up at his office. Not ten thousand dollars to help his baby. Not ten thousand dollars to take responsibility or offer help. No, Jake had given her ten thousand dollars to go away and never bother him again.

And because she was alone, and pregnant, and broke, and because he looked so angry with her, questioning if the baby was even his and making it so clear that he wanted no part of any of this and wouldn't come around and change his mind, she took it.

And now...all these months later, it was nearly gone.

She checked her watch. Forty-five minutes until she was due back in the insurance office. Forty-five minutes to turn her life around and demand justice once and for all.

As she waited, she fed some birds the crusts of her bread, one eye locked on that shiny brass door, knowing he would appear at any moment. And when he did, she'd go up to him, ignore the surprise in his eye, and tell him not to worry, she wasn't here for him; no, she was here for Audrey, their daughter, and for the child support he owed her.

She swallowed hard, shifting on the hard park bench that was making her back hurt where they'd stuck that awful epidural needle in her back. It had made so much sense this morning on the bus ride into work. The thought of going back there was so terrible and her future had felt that dim that she finally realized she had no other choice.

She'd avoided Jake all these months. Let her pride stand in the way of her well-being. But it wouldn't stand in the way of her daughter's well-being.

She blinked, realizing what she was saying. She glanced over at the door again. She could wait all day, or she could cross the street and ask the receptionist to buzz his office, maybe threaten a little scene if he didn't comply—that man had always cared far too much about his image, God knew.

Or she could stand up and leave. She could swallow her pride the way she should have, the way she wanted to, the way she'd been trying to do. Neither Jake nor Kate had taken any of her calls in months, but this wasn't the park bench she should be sitting on. No, the real person she needed to confront was her sister.

Jake might cough up more money, so she could keep living in that awful apartment, scrambling for work, still wondering how to make things right. But Kate...Kate could offer her a family again. The family she wanted to give her child.

Kate wasn't going to answer her phone calls. That much was

certain. So that left her no other choice. She'd have to face her head-on.

Charlotte stood up and tossed her half-eaten bag of chips in the trash. She was never one to dillydally once she'd set her mind to something. And one thing was now decided.

It was time to go home.

Chapter Seventeen

⸺⧟⸺

Elizabeth was already soaking her feet in bubbling, rose-scented water when Kate pushed through the door of the salon fifteen minutes later than their designated meeting time.

"Sorry, sorry," she said a little breathlessly as she eagerly shed her shoes and hung her handbag on the coat hook. It wasn't like her to be tardy for anything, but if the past year had taught her anything, it was that she was human. And she'd just needed a few minutes to collect herself before she proceeded with her day. And that had meant going home and taking Henry for a walk, with an extra lap around the park.

"No problem. I'm just sitting here, luxuriating." Elizabeth smiled and closed her eyes. "No one tells you that one of the perks of getting married is being able to pamper yourself for days beforehand. This is the most relaxed I've felt in weeks."

"And it will probably be the most relaxed you'll be until Sunday morning," Kate said, knowing from professional experience only just how anxious her brides became as the ceremony grew closer. That was when the phone calls usually poured in. Everything was second-guessed—the dress, the venue, the flowers. Sometimes the groom. More than once an inebriated bride had called Kate on the eve of her wedding, saying she had spent the last forty minutes Facebook-stalking her ex and wondering why she ever ended it...But then, the next morning, all was right again. Smiles returned. Dreams came true. Everything proceeded as planned.

It was only in the rarest of cases that cold feet led to a cancelation.

In Misty Point, there had only been one reported case, actually. And she'd had a front-row seat.

Kate sank into the reclining chair beside Elizabeth. Even though all the women in the bridal party were having their hair, makeup, and nails done the morning of the wedding, it had been Kate's suggestion weeks ago that she and Elizabeth steal a little time for themselves in preparation for the lawn party tonight and the rehearsal dinner tomorrow.

For the wedding, the girls would all be wearing pale pink polish, and Elizabeth was going with the same, but for the next two days, Kate had a sudden urge to break with tradition. She selected a pretty lavender color for her toes and a paler version of the shade for her fingers.

"Thought I'd go a little wild." She winked at Elizabeth as she dipped her feet into the tub, sighing as the hot water eased her muscles.

"I needed this," she admitted. She made a mental note to treat herself a little more often. It was something her therapist had suggested, back when she'd first gone to see her, when she'd finally admitted to herself that she wasn't holding herself together as much as she wanted. "Do something nice for yourself at least once a day," Wendy had encouraged. And at first she had. But once she was back at work, it was too difficult to find the time, and eventually the habit faded away.

"Bad day?"

"Meredith sent me to Bluestone Manor." Kate met her friend's knowing eyes.

"That bitch," Elizabeth said, sparking a laugh from Kate. "Do you want to talk about it?"

"Yes. No." She didn't know, really. "It was strange," she said. "Being there. It stirred things up."

"Of course. These types of things aren't easy to get over."

Kate nodded. Elizabeth was so understanding. Others were impatient, eager to just see her happy and settled. But what no one seemed to understand was that it wasn't just about Jake. Or finding a replacement.

It was about Charlotte.

"I saw Jake last night," she blurted, even though she hadn't been sure she would mention it.

Elizabeth's eyes popped. "He's back in town?"

"It appears so." Kate shook her head. "I guess it was bound to happen. It's summer after all. You know how much time he spends here in the summer." It was where they'd met, after all. The summer was full of memories of sitting on his boat, watching him at the helm, the wind in her hair, a glass of wine in her hand, and not a care in the world weighing on her shoulders. Eating lobster rolls on the beach, her toes in the sand, Jake laughing at something she'd said. His skin tanned, his eyes so green.

Well. No use harping on that. She wiggled her toes in the warm water, fixating on the rose petals.

"Did he say anything to you?"

Kate shook her head. "I don't even know if he saw me."

"Was he . . . alone?" Elizabeth's eyes were wide.

"When I saw him, yes." Kate shifted slightly in her seat so she could give her friend her full attention. "Tell me the truth. Is my sister back in town?"

"God, I hope not!" Elizabeth said, then clamped a hand to her mouth. "I'm sorry. She's your sister. It's just, well, you know I haven't forgiven her."

"And neither have I," Kate said, relaxing back into her chair. She leaned her head back and closed her eyes. Tried to shut out the world for just one moment. It was no use.

"But if she is town, you're bound to run into her."

Kate's stomach turned a little queasy. "I know."

They fell silent for a moment. The only sound that could be heard was the flicking of Elizabeth's magazine, which seemed to grow angrier with each turn of the page.

"You know, what I find the most unforgiveable is that she never even tried to talk to you about it. She never even tried to make it right. She just let Jake end things and then off they both went to Boston a few weeks later!"

Kate gave her a rueful look. "Well. What was she supposed to say?"

"True." Elizabeth huffed out a breath and closed the magazine. Clearly even celebrity gossip couldn't distract them right now. "I have to say that even though Charlotte was always a little wild, this was pushing it, even for her. Her own sister!"

Her own sister, Kate thought bitterly.

"Well," Elizabeth said. "Maybe they've broken up. If you only saw Jake, he could be in town alone." She gave a smile of encouragement, but oddly, the thought didn't please Kate.

Where was Charlotte, and why was she calling? She could find out today, maybe even right now, if she'd call back.

Yeah. No thanks.

"Was this right after I left you?" Elizabeth asked after a long pause.

Kate winced as the woman doing her nails brought a pumice stone to the bottom of her foot. She's always been too ticklish, and now the woman frowned in disapproval as Kate curled her toes. She laughed, grateful for the diversion. "I'm sorry," she said, "it's just..."

Elizabeth rolled her eyes. "She's too ticklish," she told the woman, who only raised an eyebrow and scrubbed a little harder.

Kate squirmed in the chair, trying to keep her mind off the sensation of her feet. At least it took her mind away from Jake and Charlotte. "It was right when we got to the restaurant."

"You and Alec," Elizabeth clarified.

Kate chewed her lip, suddenly feeling the need to slow down this conversation. "Yes, I had just met Alec. We were standing outside the restaurant when I saw him."

"And what did you do?"

Something completely crazy, she thought.

"I left," Kate said. *After I all but grabbed the best man's lapel and brought his mouth to mine.* Her stomach flipped at the memory of his lips on hers. Smooth but firm and oh... She set a hand to her belly.

"You just left?"

Eventually. "I didn't want to see Charlotte. I'm just not ready. I've gotten comfortable with not having her around."

That wasn't true, though, and from the look on Elizabeth's face, she knew it, too. Charlotte's absence was obvious. If it wasn't, she wouldn't be giving her so much thought.

Elizabeth laughed. "I can't imagine that went over well with Alec. I doubt he's used to anyone running off on him like that."

"Probably not." Kate eased her foot back into the water, trading it for the next one, bracing herself as the woman lifted the pumice stone. Alec hadn't called, and she hadn't, either. She supposed an apology was in order, or at least an explanation, but what was she to even say? She'd humiliated herself, soliciting a kiss like that, and worse was that she enjoyed it.

"So you didn't get to see his best man speech then," Elizabeth said.

Kate felt a flicker of panic. "I'll handle it," she assured her friend. And she would.

"So anything else eventful happen last night that I should know about?" Elizabeth winked. She always had a way of easing away from tense topics, but this time, she'd touched on something.

"Nothing at all," Kate replied, but she was wrestling with the secret she was keeping, the knowledge that something quite eventful had happened last night.

There was no sense in mentioning that kiss. Or even thinking about it.

And there definitely wasn't any sense in wishing it might happen again.

* * *

Alec was still trying to clear that kiss from his mind when he joined William for a late lunch at a dockside café. The smell of salt air and the breeze from the ocean gave a relaxed feeling to the casual place, but Alec still felt tense and restless. He shifted in the wicker chair, unable to find a comfortable position. He skimmed the menu with forced concentration, determined to pull his mind from the taste of Kate's lips ... and the way she'd run off after their kiss.

"I can't believe it's already Thursday." William stirred some milk into his coffee. "This wedding preparation stuff has been more work than I expected."

A week ago Alec wanted one thing and one thing only: to have his brother back in Boston, rebuilding the Montgomery Group together. Now ... He opened the menu and stared hard at it. Now he almost dreaded the thought of going back to Boston at all.

"All ready for Saturday?" he asked, wondering if any jitters had set in.

"I think at this point all I have to do is show up," William said with a shrug. "Elizabeth's got this whole thing pretty much planned. And Kate's amazing."

That she is. Alec drew a slow breath and leaned back into his chair, resting his elbows on the armrests.

"Elizabeth mentioned you were having dinner with Kate last night," William said. His eyes glinted with mischief. "Was that about the rehearsal dinner or just ... fun?"

"We had a change of plans," Alec said, not wanting to give anything away. "She had to leave before we could sit down."

"Oh?" William chided.

"Come on, William," Alec said through a faint smile. "I told you—"

William held up his palms. "I know, I know. The great Alec Montgomery has no room in his life for love."

"There are only so many hours in a day." Even to his own ears, the excuse felt lame. Sure, if he'd spotted Kate across a crowded room he'd want to go over and say hello, maybe buy her a glass of wine. Maybe even take her home for a night. But then he'd spent some time with her, and he realized he wanted to do a lot more things than just chat her up over an evening cocktail. *A lot more things, indeed.*

"She'll be at the party tonight."

Alec frowned in confusion. "The party?"

"Elizabeth and I are having the wedding party out to our place for a barbecue tonight. Something a little more casual than the rehearsal dinner tomorrow." William paused. "You didn't know?"

He supposed it was on the itinerary Kate had given him. The one he'd never looked at. He mentally ran through the many envelopes and invitations related to the wedding that he had received in recent months. Something about a lawn party came to mind... "Is this the lawn party?"

William shook his head. "Some fancy way of wording a barbecue."

"Let me guess. Kate's idea?" He could see her typing up the invitation now. He couldn't help but smile.

"None other. She and Elizabeth have been in cahoots about this for a while." William rolled his eyes, but Alec could tell he was secretly pleased. "Seems you and Kate are really hitting it off."

Alec shot him a warning look. "Come on, Will."

"What?" William's grin broadened and all at once, there it was. His little brother. That annoying, punk kid, goading him.

Alec frowned. God, he'd missed him.

"Kate and I spent some time together going over plans for the rehearsal dinner," he explained. His gut twisted with dread when he thought of the dinner he was technically supposed to be hosting. A dinner he might not even be in attendance for.

He looked out across the water to a boat slicing through the choppy waves. He should tell him now about the meeting with Mason. It was the perfect opportunity. He'd make him understand. And it might be the perfect way to explain how tough business had been all these months.

"In case I haven't mentioned it, thanks for planning that dinner." A frown creased William's brow. "God knows Dad couldn't be bothered."

"Sure," Alec said, looking back down at the menu.

The meeting was twenty-four hours away, and instead of feeling excited or relieved about its possibilities, he felt inexplicably empty. Deciding on a lobster roll he was no longer hungry for, he closed the menu and looked out onto the water, watching the boats in the distance bob on the waves.

If things went well with Mason tomorrow, that meeting could last hours. There was no predicting the time it could take. Was he really ready to risk upsetting his brother like this?

And Kate.

He highly doubted that Kate, as the wedding planner, would

have anything nice to say over a missing best man at the rehearsal dinner. Especially if it seemed her job was dependent on the wedding being catastrophe-free.

She'd done nothing to deserve this.

And neither, he thought, looking at his brother, had William.

"I can see why you like it here," he suddenly said, almost wishing he hadn't opened the door to the conversation. But he had, and a part of him wanted to share it, to bond with his brother in a way they hadn't in all their time together back in that office. "It reminds me of our summers when we were kids."

William looked out onto the water. "I think about Mom sometimes."

"I've thought about her more here, too," Alec admitted.

The brothers locked eyes for a beat, before William turned away. "Do you remember that time we stole that canoe from the dock and took it out onto the water when all the adults were having cocktails on the porch?"

"We were lucky we didn't get too far. We didn't even have the sense to put on life vests." Alec chuckled. "Those were good times."

"They were," William said pensively. "I hope to give my own kids the same types of memories someday. Minus the boat stealing, of course." He grinned.

Alec frowned as reality bore down on him once more. His brother was serious. About the marriage, about a cozy domestic future. All things that didn't fit in with his city lifestyle.

"You nervous at all?" Alec asked, cringing at the lilt of hope in his tone.

"Not really." William shrugged. "But ask me again on Saturday when I'm hyperventilating. And don't you dare try and hold it against me," he said with a wag of his finger.

Alec watched him with a steady eye across the table. There was still a chance. Still a chance that his brother would come to his senses and walk away from all of this. But the more he thought about it, the more slim it felt.

William was in love with Elizabeth. He was in love with the life she gave him. A life that Alec was starting to realize was a hell of a lot better than the one William had had in Boston.

His phone vibrated against the tabletop.

"Probably Dad. You should take it," William said.

Begrudgingly, Alec tapped his password into his phone and scanned the newest text message from his assistant. Mason Lambert had confirmed the meeting for three o'clock tomorrow. He stared at the phone for a long moment. Three o'clock. He knew from experience that a meeting like this could go on for hours, often extending into dinner or drinks.

Another text popped up before he had a chance to push the phone into his pocket, out of sight for a while. It was his assistant again, informing him that if things went well, Mason would like Alec and his father to join him for a meeting on Saturday afternoon with his son. To make things official.

He blinked at the screen, contemplating his decision as his pulse drummed steadily. Friday was one thing, but Saturday? Mason Lambert was too big of an opportunity to pass up. But Mason knew William was getting married that day.

"William—" Alec halted. If he opened his mouth now, he would spoil the moment.

"Yeah?" William said casually, unsuspecting.

Alec hesitated. "Nothing. Just wondering . . . what time's the party again?"

"Six," William said. "It will mean a lot to have you there."

"Wouldn't miss it," he said as he shoved the phone into his pocket without replying to his assistant. He couldn't think about this today. Today he just wanted to enjoy talking with his brother again. Like old times.

Chapter Eighteen

⊗⊗⊗⊗

Bree was already unloading the flowers when Kate approached Elizabeth's house a few hours later. She stopped at the car's open trunk and reached for a box of centerpieces—a vibrant mix built around sunflowers.

"Thanks for the help!" Bree expertly maneuvered the box she was holding to one hand so she could slam the door closed.

Kate contemplated what she might say as she followed her cousin up the stone pathway and through the open fence gate. The tables had been delivered earlier and were neatly stacked against the back deck. The girls deposited the boxes of flowers onto the patio table and began dragging the folding tables across the lawn, deciding that it would be best to break things into stations for dessert, drinks, and food. The rest of the yard would be filled with the smaller bistro tables.

"Is Simon coming tonight?" Kate asked, as they unfolded the linens she'd brought to cover the tables.

"Oh...I'm not sure. I'm waiting to hear back on my latest text."

It wasn't the first time Bree was waiting to hear back on a text from Simon. Perhaps reading her thoughts, Bree added, "He might have to work late. He has an important job, you know."

Of course. Simon was an attorney. A quality that Bree often brought up when she was feeling defensive of him.

"So . . ." Kate smoothed down one of her favorite tablecloths with her palm. It was French country, vintage, and something she'd picked up at an antique sale two summers ago. As soon as Charlotte had seen it, she'd asked if she could borrow it sometime. Kate thinned her lips, feeling oddly possessive of the object. "Jake's back in town."

She looked up, searching her cousin's expression for something that might tell her that her cousin knew more, but Bree cringed instead. "So he came back this summer then? Here I thought he might stay in Boston. Forever, if possible."

So she didn't know then. Not about Jake. Presumably not about Charlotte, either.

For some reason Kate felt strangely disappointed by this.

"I guess it was inevitable," she said.

"Did you talk to him?" Bree asked carefully.

Kate walked over to the next table and began unfolding another tablecloth. "No. I don't even know if he saw me. He was alone," she added, glancing back at Bree.

Her cousin nodded, and then turned to fetch her arrangements from the boxes on the deck.

Kate sighed. So much for getting any more information. She was still no closer to knowing for certain if Charlotte was in town. Or why she'd been calling.

Or, come to think of it, why she'd stopped . . .

★ ★ ★

Kate was placing the last jelly jar votive on a picnic table when she saw Alec stroll into William and Elizabeth's backyard, his hands casually placed in the pockets of his khakis. With a shaking hand, she managed to light the candle before stealing another glance, wondering if he'd spotted her just yet. Wondering what she would say to him. How she would explain her behavior. That kiss!

See, this was why she liked planning. When you planned things, you didn't have to worry about unpredictable—and awkward—outcomes like this.

From the corner of her eye she caught Alec taking a glass of wine from a tray at the buffet table. He glanced her way, holding up an arm in hello, and Kate spared him a watery smile before he thankfully fell into conversation with William.

She glanced quickly at Elizabeth, who was standing near the patio, chatting with one of her cousins, but her back was to the lawn. She hadn't seen anything pass between them, and Kate was relieved for it. She didn't want to explain what was going on between herself and Alec. Not when she couldn't wrap her head around it just yet.

Kate busied herself with centering the flower arrangement, happy for the diversion of her maid of honor and wedding planning duties, even if Bree had made sure the flowers were perfectly in place.

One eye still on Alec's whereabouts, Kate walked over to the buffet table—a long, rustic table she'd had delivered from the Bride by Design prop "room," which was more of a warehouse—and checked that each of the labels she'd made were in front of the proper food tray, before turning her attention to the slices of crusty baguette and wheel of imported cheese at the far end of the station, where she rearranged the dried fruits and clusters of grapes.

"You've outdone yourself," Elizabeth announced, crossing the lawn with a big smile. Her pale yellow sundress swung at her knees.

"I enjoy this type of thing," Kate said, brushing aside the compliment. She skimmed her eyes over the buffet once more, loving how the colorful flower arrangements her cousin had made added a burst of color to each end of the table. Even though Bree claimed she'd just inherited Rose in Bloom, her grandmother had certainly taught her the ways of the business.

"Well, don't spend all night working. It's all set up and the party has started. Let's get a drink." Elizabeth looped her arm through Kate's and they walked over to the second food station of three, where tucked under draping eaves of a river birch tree were glass dispensers of fresh lemonade, in three flavors.

Kate took a sip of her strawberry lemonade and looked out onto the party. Elizabeth was right; it was in full swing, and it did look pretty, stepping back and admiring it from a distance. At the back patio, Kate had draped fairy lights from posts, and the tables they'd sprinkled randomly over the yard were illuminated by the candles in the low afternoon sun. Kate looked up. The only thing that could make this night complete was a perfect sunset.

"Great." Elizabeth stepped close behind her, her tone laced with dread as she touched her elbow. "He's here."

Kate didn't need to ask to know that Elizabeth was referring to Alec. She refilled her glass of lemonade, hoping it would cool the heat that had sprung in her face, and looked back over at the party.

"Looks like he's in a good mood," Kate said, shooting a cursory glance in his direction where he was talking with William. She detected the hopeful lilt in her voice. It was the wedding planner in her, she supposed. One less potential crisis. The best man had a strained enough relationship with the bride—any chance of reconciliation was one less issue to worry about.

Or so she told herself. Deep down she knew that if Alec could be on better terms with Elizabeth, it would open the door for her to pursue her feelings for him. *Feelings.* Did it extend that far? No, she told herself firmly. This wasn't about feelings. This was about attraction. He was a good-looking man. Many men were.

"I suppose," Elizabeth admitted with a sigh. "I keep hoping maybe he'll surprise us and show some genuine happiness over our wedding." She shrugged. "I suppose I should just be happy for William that he's here at all. Alec doesn't usually miss a day of work for anyone."

"Who are we talking about?" Colleen asked, coming over to grab a glass of raspberry lemonade. She had her wavy strawberry-blond hair down today, instead of in its usual bun, and a touch more makeup than she typically wore.

Kate surveyed the guests, noticing her cousin Matt at the far edge of the lawn near the rose trellis. She smiled to herself. Of course.

"You look pretty tonight," she commented, but Colleen just shot her a rueful look.

"Don't let my mother hear you say that." Not that she was there. "You know how she never ceases to remind me that I should never leave the house without a tube of lipstick in case I find the one." She rolled her eyes. "I told her that I didn't like to wear heels when I was transporting one of my cakes, but..." She kicked up her foot, revealing a four-inch wedge sandal. "She wore me down."

Kate looked over to the dessert table, where a strawberries and cream cake at least five layers high sat front and center.

"Oh my goodness, give me a spoon and forgo the plate," she laughed as the girls marveled at it.

"I was worried it would be too warm outside for the whipped cream, but we're having surprisingly nice weather all week!"

"Well, aside from Monday's rain shower," Elizabeth said, shooting Kate a worried look.

"It's supposed to be a beautiful weekend," Kate reminded them all. She looked up, happy at what she saw. "Not a cloud in the sky."

"Maybe not in the sky..." Elizabeth frowned over Kate's shoulder.

"Okay, I'm lost." Colleen set her hands on her hips. "Are we talking about the best man?"

Unfortunately, it seemed they were. Kate looked around for something to do to keep busy, an excuse to leave so she didn't have to be reminded of that kiss, or the guilt she felt over hiding it from her friend.

"Is he here? Point him out to me. I want a look." Colleen's sharp blue eyes darted with interest over the yard, until Elizabeth discreetly pointed him out. "Well, I'll be," Colleen breathed. She winked at Kate. "Maybe it was worth getting a little dolled up tonight, after all. But don't—"

"Tell your mother. I know." Kate smiled, but deep down she felt a flicker of... was it jealousy? Well, that was just ridiculous. Alec was single. Colleen was single. Why should she care? Colleen was just pointing out the obvious. The man was attractive. Tall, well built, and that smile... She grabbed a drink—a proper drink—from a waiter passing a tray and took a long sip of the cool, sweet Champagne.

"I thought you only had eyes for Matt," she said.

Colleen flushed. "What? Oh, no. I mean, you know... that's an old crush. But this best man... He might give me a reason to get over it once and for all."

Kate sipped from her glass, angry at herself for feeling so agitated by Colleen's reaction. It wasn't like Alec was special to her or anything. It wasn't like they had a connection...

She thought back to the night he'd helped her find the lace. And the way his mouth had felt on hers yesterday.

Nope, no connection at all, she thought, looking over to where Alec stood, laughing casually at something William was saying. He had a nice laugh. He didn't show it enough.

"Believe me, you don't want him," Elizabeth was saying to Colleen.

Colleen just laughed. "You sound like Bree. Can't I choose who I'm interested in?"

"Fine, but don't say I didn't warn you," Elizabeth said, raising her eyebrows. "As far as I know, he has never dated anyone consistently for even two weeks. If you're looking for some fancy dinners and a guy who doesn't make time for you, he's your man."

Kate stared at the drink in her hand, watching as the bubbles popped and fizzed.

"The man is married to his work. His family's company. It trumps everything," Elizabeth finished.

Everything her friend was saying sounded familiar. If she'd just stumbled upon the conversation, Kate might have just as easily assumed they were all discussing Jake, not Alec.

"Oh no," Elizabeth sighed, following Kate's gaze. "He's coming over here."

Before Kate could speak, Alec was already making his way across the lawn, his proximity growing at an alarming rate, leaving her breathless with possibilities. She brought her glass to her lips. The drink went down quickly.

She was happy to see that William had quickly caught up with his brother. With a nervous smile, she said, "Hi, guys!" and leaned in to give William a casual hug hello. The heat of Alec's stare bored through her as she pulled away from William, and she hesitated, wondering if she should greet him the same way, but that seemed too friendly, even for someone who had kissed her like that last night. Softly, she added to Alec, "Hi."

"Hi." He spared her a lopsided grin, but the knowing look in his eyes wasn't lost on her.

"Well, I wouldn't miss it," Alec said, but Kate noticed the way his jaw pulsed at the statement. She narrowed her eyes, studying his body language. He seemed nervous and slightly anxious, raking his hands through his hair before thrusting them into his pockets.

She looked over at Elizabeth to see if she noticed anything pass between them, but her friend just smiled politely and thanked Alec for coming to the party. Kate felt her stiffen beside her.

Kate felt a wash of shame creep over her.

What kind of friend was she to be warming up to Alec? To think that she'd had him into her home, given him a beer, let him hold Henry.

Henry.

She hadn't even thought about it. She hadn't even considered... She glanced down at her feet to her sweet little dog, who was now lying on his back, rolling in the grass, waving his paws in the air, all in a hopeful attempt to gain his new friend Alec's attention.

* * *

Two hours later, Kate watched in silent dismay as Henry hopped around Alec's feet, his tail wagging happily, making it obvious to anyone around that he was no stranger to the man. But her heart warmed as she watched Alec casually bend down and lift the little dog up, not even breaking his stride in conversation as Henry licked at his face and squirmed in his arms. They said children and animals were a good judge of character, didn't they?

"Look at that traitorous little dog," Elizabeth clucked.

"You know Henry," Kate said mildly. "He's friendly with anyone who's willing to pay him attention." And Alec was certainly happy to do just that, she thought, smiling.

"Just like Charlotte," Elizabeth said, and then immediately flushed. "Oh, Kate. I don't know why I said that. It's the Champagne, and the stress."

Kate set a hand on her friend's shoulder. "Don't apologize. Besides, you're right." Charlotte would light up around anyone who gave her attention. It was part of her charm. And her downfall.

"This wedding." Elizabeth shook her head. "Is it awful to say that I'm almost looking forward to it being over?"

Kate laughed. "It's something pretty much every one of my clients says at some point in time."

"I'm just tired. And well...there's still William's father to think about."

Of course. Kate made a mental note to worry about that tomorrow, when he was scheduled to arrive. Tonight she still had to get through the evening on good footing with the best man.

"Just two more nights to go as Elizabeth Jones," Kate chided.

Elizabeth gave a wistful smile. "So much can change in a year."

Kate couldn't agree more. She pushed aside the dark thoughts that threatened to ruin her evening and grabbed two glasses of Champagne from a tray, even though she wouldn't finish hers. She needed to keep a clear head, especially since she was still somewhat on duty. "A toast," she said. "To a perfect wedding day."

Elizabeth clinked her glass with Kate's. She shook her head in disbelief, but her eyes shone with joy, even in the moonlight.

It was a look Kate knew all too well. One she had seen in her own eyes once.

"Well, I suppose I should go make the rounds with William." Elizabeth leaned in and gave her a hug before wandering off to find her fiancé.

The party was dwindling, and Kate noticed that only a few friends lingered, all sleepily chatting, swatting at the mosquitoes that persisted despite the citronella candles Kate had scattered along the lawn. She watched as Elizabeth said good night to a group of people and disappeared into her house with William.

Kate knew she couldn't stand here forever—whether conscious or not, Alec had a firm grip on Henry, and there was no sneaking out without speaking to him. With a gulp of cool, fresh air for courage, Kate set her glass down on the nearest table and walked over to Alec. As he turned to her, the groomsman he had been chatting with nodded his goodbye, leaving the two of them alone.

"I came to steal him back," Kate said with an apologetic smile as she gestured to Henry. She reached out and scooped the dog into her arms, unable to ignore the tingle that coursed down her spine as her hand grazed Alec's bare forearm.

"I think Henry could have partied all night."

Kate grinned. "I should be getting home. It's late and I need to rest up for tomorrow. The day before the wedding is always the busiest. It's the final opportunity to take care of those last-minute details."

Alec's lips twitched. "You and those little details."

"Well, there are a lot of them." Good grief. She could have sworn her eyelashes fluttered.

Okay, this had to stop. She was lingering, flirting even. And she didn't flirt. Charlotte had tried to give her lessons on it once, when she was sixteen and Charlotte was fourteen. They'd role-played, per Charlotte's instruction. She'd play the girl; Kate got to be the boy. All Kate had to do was sit there and watch as Charlotte turned on her charm, batted her eyes, set a hand on her wrist as she paid a compliment, and then giggled sweetly at whatever Kate, still playing the guy, said.

Kate felt a pang in her chest. She didn't like thinking of those times with her sister. Not anymore.

Chapter Nineteen

⸻⸻

"M ind if I walk you out?" Alec asked, hoping to drag out the night a little longer. It beat going back to that lonely hotel room with only his work and his guilt to keep him company—and the memory of that kiss.

His eyes roamed her face, coming to rest on her mouth, before Henry barked, breaking the silence—and the underlying tension, he realized—as he and Kate both seemed to laugh in mutual relief.

Kate glanced around before nodding. "I think my duties for the evening are over, so . . . sure." She shrugged and shyly tilted her head toward the gate.

They fell into stride, cutting across the cool grass and past the wall of hedges that separated Kate's yard from William and Elizabeth's. "Where's your car?" Kate asked as they reached the front of her house.

"I took a cab," Alec explained. "I don't exactly know my way around town, and I figured I'd be having a few drinks."

"And we all know how well you hold your alcohol," Kate joked.

"I'm perfectly sober and clearheaded right now," he said, which made it even more troublesome that he couldn't resist the urge to touch her, to put his arms around her waist and finish what they'd started last night.

"So you need another cab to bring you back, I assume."

"Unless you care to have a nightcap." He shoved his hands in his pockets and rolled back on his heels, hoping she wouldn't have an excuse.

Kate seemed to consider this and then shrugged. "My wedding planning duties are over for the night. What's one more?"

He followed her to the front door and waited in the living room while Kate went into the kitchen to get a bottle of wine. Henry was eager to play, bringing over a squeaky toy in the shape of a frog and dropping it at his feet. Alec laughed and tossed it across the room for him, then pulled his phone out of his pocket. The thing had been vibrating all night long, but he hadn't wanted to deal with it.

The latest text from his father informed him that he'd rearranged his schedule to arrive earlier than planned tomorrow so he could attend the afternoon meeting with Mason. Of course, he hadn't shown the same urgency to be in town when it was over something as trivial as the rehearsal dinner.

Alec tossed the toy for Henry again, his stomach tightening with unease. Had his brother meant it when he'd hinted at them working together again? And could he really do it? Give up his life, everything he'd worked for, and turn his back on his father the way William had done, however unintentionally?

Only with Alec, it would be intentional, wouldn't it? About as intentional as missing his own brother's wedding for a business meeting.

"Everything okay?" Kate had removed her shoes and now padded barefoot into the living room, a bottle of wine in one hand, two glasses and a corkscrew in the other.

"Just looking for a number for the cab company." Alec shoved the phone back in his pocket and motioned for her to pass him the corkscrew.

"Eager to get away so quickly?" She smiled, but he detected a hint of disappointment in her tone.

"Didn't want to overstay my welcome." He waited until he'd uncorked the bottle and given them each a generous pour before adding, "I wasn't sure you'd want to see me again. After last night."

Kate's cheeks flushed. "I'm sorry about that."

"Which part? Running off or—"

Now her face was almost on fire. "I don't know what to say for myself. It was out of character. I'm not usually so...forward."

"You mean you usually schedule a kiss on your calendar first?" Alec cocked an eyebrow. He was pressing the issue, when what he should be doing was backing off. Letting it go.

"I saw someone I knew and...I guess you can say I wanted to make him jealous."

So that was it then. He'd been a convenient prop. No wonder she'd been so quick to run off. "Happy to be at your service."

Kate's eyes crinkled as she reached out and wrapped her fingers around his arm. Her touch was light, feminine, and soft. He tried to ignore the stir of pleasure the small gesture sparked. "It wasn't like that, Alec. I mean, it was, but then, after..." She trailed off and pulled a throw pillow onto her lap, hugging it tightly.

Daring to be curious, Alec asked, "Was it an old boyfriend?"

"An old fiancé," Kate clarified.

Wow. He hadn't seen that coming. William hadn't mentioned it. Not that he'd pressed for her romantic history. "I take it things didn't end well?"

"Is there such a possibility with a broken engagement?" Kate cocked an eyebrow. "Things didn't end well at all. He was cheating on me."

Alec frowned. He couldn't imagine any guy wanting to cheat on a woman like Kate. "Then he didn't deserve you," he said, his tone angrier than he'd expected.

"He was cheating on me with my sister." Kate's expression was neutral; her voice was almost unfittingly matter-of-fact. Clearly, she'd had some time to get used to this shocking outcome.

"Your sister? Now that's low." Alec thought back to the photos he'd seen in her parents' hallway. The way the room had fallen silent when Elizabeth's mother had mentioned that everyone was together. Clearly, someone was missing. "How did you find out?"

"They weren't shy about telling me. First Jake did, and then she confirmed it." She shook her head, closing her eyes to the memory.

Silence descended for a moment, but Alec suspected she still wanted to discuss the matter. "Are they still together?"

Kate shrugged and reached for her glass of wine. "I have no idea. Last I heard, they ran off to Boston together."

"When was this?"

"Last summer," she said.

Enough time to get over a broken heart, maybe. But enough

time to get over a sister's betrayal? "And you've had no contact with her? Your sister?"

She shook her head. "I don't need to know the details. And I have nothing to say to her."

"Holidays?"

"She didn't come back for Christmas. She hasn't come back to Misty Point since she left. She doesn't talk to my parents, either. The few times she has, they haven't involved me."

"How awful to be caught in the middle." In a strange sort of way, he felt their pain.

"Well, it's pretty black and white to me. But...they love her." She frowned, and something in her expression told him that Kate still loved her sister, too. It was strange, what you could forgive, when it came to family.

"Charlotte—that's my sister—has always sort of bounced around in life. She always had a boyfriend. She's very pretty. Men like her." Kate's lips turned down and she knitted her brow, studying the contents of her wineglass.

"I'm sure plenty of men like you, too." He wasn't just saying it to make her feel better. He was saying it because it was the truth, damn it, and this Jake fellow was a fool not to see it.

She blushed at the compliment. Clearly, it had been too long since she'd received one.

Kate curled her long legs up under her, inching closer to him as she shifted on the couch. Her long, bare calves were so close, he could skim them if he wanted to. And he did. Badly.

He reached for his wineglass instead, hoping it would chase away this feeling that was growing and wouldn't go away.

"The funny thing is that when we were younger, I could tell she always looked up to me and wanted to be like me. I'm two years older than her, and I guess that seemed like a big difference back then. But then as we got older, it felt more like she was competing with me or something. Like she was trying to prove something. I never understood why. Charlotte... Well, she's fun. She just hadn't figured her life out yet."

"Whereas you had a great job and a fiancé and everything going for you," Alec finished. "It sounds like she really looked up to you."

Kate gave a sad smile. "Or maybe she just wanted what I had. I thought Charlotte was happy for me. I mean, I would have been happy for her. I even asked her to be my maid of honor..."

At this her eyes welled, and Alec reached over and placed a sturdy hand on her wrist. She didn't flinch or move away, as he half expected her to do, and the desire to trace his hand farther up her bare arm grew with each passing second.

Kate managed an embarrassed laugh and wiped away a single tear. She sniffed loudly and with too-bright eyes said, "I know I should be over it by now. They deserve each other, after all."

"Are you... still in love with him?" Alec wasn't sure why the thought of it bothered him so much. Was it because this Jake person clearly didn't deserve Kate, or because he didn't like the thought of her having feelings for someone else?

Kate shook her head firmly. "No. Definitely not. Last night confirmed it. But that doesn't mean I don't still feel the sting of what he did to me. Or my sister. If it had been any other woman, I don't think it would have hit me so hard. But when it's your family..."

Alec nodded. He knew. No matter what they did or how

much they hurt you or let you down, family mattered. And they won out every time.

"I took a leave of absence from work to sort through my feelings. Then I got Henry. And I bought this house. Everyone's been really nice about it, considering the entire town knows my sordid story. In fact, I'm surprised you haven't heard it yet."

"Well, the only person in Misty Point I've really talked to is you and William."

"He and Elizabeth have been really wonderful. Without them..." She blew out a breath. "It's why it means so much to me to give them the wedding of their dreams. Repaying the favor, so to speak."

Alec nodded slowly as a flicker of shame wormed its way through his gut. Kate was pretty, sweet, smart, and good. Too good for him.

"Do you ever think you'll move past it?"

"Find love again, you mean?" Kate asked. With a shrug she sighed. "There was a time when I would have said no. But now that some time has passed, I've just realized I was with the wrong person from the start. I just didn't want to see it. I'd...like to believe I can find love." She looked at him. "But doesn't everyone?"

Not me, Alec almost said and then stopped himself. He had never been open to it before—never wanted it. His life had been so planned for him—he'd had no chance to think of anything other than staying the course. But the more he followed the path he had set out on, the more he wanted to break free from it and see what other possibilities the world held.

★ ★ ★

"Look at me blubbering on like this," Kate said through a watery smile. She couldn't believe what had come over her. The stress of this wedding must really be getting to her. And she had certainly chugged that glass of wine early in the evening. "You're probably wishing you had called a cab right after the party ended."

"Not at all." Alec's voice was smooth and sincere, and Kate became all too aware of the way his thumb was tracing circles on her wrist, sending shots of heat twisting and turning through her.

Kate shifted her gaze to the wineglass in her hands, not sure what she would do if she kept looking into those soft brown eyes. The silence was a heavy weight in the room, making the air feel thick and sticky. She should open another window for a cross breeze. Or turn on the fan. But both of those things would require standing up and leaving the room, and right now, the only place she wanted to be was right here next to Alec.

His thumb was still caressing her skin, softly, slowly, and maybe even a little suggestively. Unable to take it, she pushed up to a standing position. "I think I'll just turn on the fan," she said, only to remember she didn't have one in this room. There was no overhead lighting. Just the soft subtle glow from the tableside lamps and the moon shining in through the windows. "I mean, open a window."

Smooth, Kate. She closed her eyes once her back was to him and walked over to the front door, letting the air flow in through the screen. It was cool and refreshing and sobering.

Crickets chirped in the distance as she slowly turned back

to the living room, where Alec was still seated on her couch, Henry happily curled up on the armchair, watching them like a scene in a movie, as if he couldn't wait to see what happened next.

That makes two of us, buddy, she thought as she crept back toward the couch.

"I'm sorry you went through such a bad time," Alec said as he refilled her glass. "But it seems like you've handled it well, all things considered."

Had she? Her relationship with her parents had grown a little distant. And then there was the hiccup with her job, of course.

But yeah, maybe she had handled it pretty well. If you didn't count the five pounds she'd put on through ice cream consumption. Okay, ten. Or the investment in the Spanx...

"Well. It's all in the past now." Kate didn't want to dwell on things anymore tonight. She'd shared enough, but she was happy that she had. Alec hadn't judged, or given her head tilt, or winced about her current status. He saw it for what it was. And he seemed to understand it, too.

He handed her back her glass and they both took a sip. "I don't know if William has ever told you about our mother."

Kate knew very little of William's past. Like his brother, he was close-lipped about his childhood. But she did know the basic facts, and she was sorry for it. After a slight hesitation, she said, "He mentioned that she died when he was still a child."

Alec nodded his head. "She...she struggled a bit. She and my father never had the best marriage—he worked all the time and never really made time for her. Or us. The company was everything to him." He lowered his eyes. "I think she was lonely."

Alec's lips thinned. "When I was about ten, things really

changed for the worse. She'd always been a bit melancholic, looking back. Except for our days on the Cape. She was so happy then," he added, giving a wistful smile. "But then things really took a dramatic turn. I can't really explain it, but it was like everything shifted. I was so young, but I could still sense it. Something was just really, really wrong."

Kate held her breath. "What happened?"

"I remember she stopped picking me up from school. Our housekeeper started doing it. Then she stopped coming out of her room." His brow furrowed. "Sometimes days would pass before I would see her, and then I felt like she was looking right through me."

"How confusing," Kate thought aloud.

"One day she went into her room and closed the door. I knew better than to interrupt her, but I had made a card for her at school to cheer her up and I really wanted to show it to her. She was lying there. So still..." He looked her square in the eye. "She was dead."

Surely he couldn't be saying what she thought he was. She said nothing, waiting for him to continue, wondering how Elizabeth had never shared this with her, or if she even knew. "She didn't..."

Alec nodded and met her horror-stricken gaze. His eyes looked dark and lost—like a man haunted by the image. "She committed suicide. After that, my father became even more distant than ever. He hired live-in nannies. He'd disappear for months on end. He sold that beach house she'd loved so much. It was like I lost both my parents in one fell swoop."

Kate looked away, around the room, trying to imagine a young boy walking in on something like that. "And William?"

she asked, turning back to face Alec. "William never said anything."

"William was still young enough that he didn't understand, and my father and I tried to keep it that way. But once he did...He doesn't discuss it. Neither do I."

"So you don't ever talk about it, to each other?" Kate asked.

"Nope." Alec shrugged. "Sometimes it's easier not to go there. Not to retrace those bad feelings."

Kate understood. "I'm so sorry. I can't even imagine."

"I'm sure William has told you how our father can be." He slid her a rueful grin and Kate smiled, feeling relieved that they were finally tearing down this wall.

"He's told me a few things," she said, not wanting to make things worse.

Alec shifted in his seat and he faced her head-on, his eyes searching hers. "The thing is that I pity the man almost as much as I blame him. It's complicated with family." He looked at her for a moment. "Do you think you'll ever forgive your sister?"

Kate's chest tightened just like it did every time she thought of Charlotte. She avoided the question by posing another. "You don't think it will ever get better between you and your dad?"

"I don't know. He's always been distant. My mother brought out the softer side of him, but even then, it wasn't enough." He paused. "He cheated on her. A lot. She loved him in spite of it. She never got over it."

Kate stiffened. "So that's why you blame him."

Alec nodded.

"Can I ask you something?" Kate knew she couldn't let this go, and since they were being so honest, she may as well come right out and ask. "Why do you disapprove of Elizabeth so much?"

Alec eyed her. "I wondered when this would come up."

"So, it's true then."

"Look. Elizabeth seems like a nice person. I don't even know her. This is more about my brother than her."

"Let me guess, you think he could do better? Someone from a better family?"

Alec looked at her with such confusion that Kate immediately realized just how wrong she was. "I'm sorry. I'm... projecting I guess. And going off what Elizabeth has said."

She should have listened to her gut. Gone with her instinct. Trusted herself. Deep down she knew Alec was a decent guy, and the hurt in his eyes proved it.

"Is that what she thinks?" He stared at her, looking for an explanation. "That I don't think she's good enough, rich enough, something like that?" He cursed under his breath as he studied the drink in his hands. "Damn. No. God no."

"It's an easy assumption around here," Kate explained. "There are the townies, like us, and then all the wealthy vacationers."

"So she just assumed...Wow." He looked at her sharply. "And you thought that, too?"

Kate shrugged. "To a degree. But I had firsthand experience. Jake, my ex...his family thought he should find someone within their circle. They came to dinner at my parents' house exactly once, and let's just say it was awkward."

"At your parents' house? And here I was thinking that was about as close to a perfect night as I could get."

Kate blinked at him. "Seriously?"

He gave a boyish grin. "The last time I had a family dinner

was before my mom died. And even then, it wasn't like that. And your house...it was so warm and lived in. Like this place. It felt...like a home."

She laughed. "Well, that's what it is."

"Guess I wouldn't know. For me, where I've lived has been just that. Except when William's around." His brow pinched and he took another sip of his wine. "So you want to know why I haven't embraced Elizabeth with open arms. I guess I don't see why he had to throw it all away—the family business. Boston. Why couldn't he have stayed and had both? Because Elizabeth made him choose?"

"It was William who insisted on moving here," Kate corrected him. "He wanted a more balanced life. And I think, from what he's hinted at...I think he was afraid if he had stayed he would have turned into his father." There, she'd said it.

"Or me." A shadow crept over Alec's rugged features. He released a little laugh as he pushed his hair back from his brow.

"You love your job, though."

"I did. I do. I don't know...Sometimes I wonder if it's really everything I once thought it was." Alec's voice was thick with regret, and Kate knew then and there that there was more to all of this than Elizabeth knew and no matter how badly she wanted to stand by her friend and dislike this man sitting beside her, she couldn't. "It just seemed to make sense to take over my father's company. Maybe I was hoping it would bring him closer to us."

"What would you rather be doing with your life?"

Alec smiled his first real smile since they'd started this conversation. "That's actually the first time anyone's asked me that question."

"Really?"

"I've never even thought about it before. Never dared to, really." He settled back against the couch, more relaxed. "But being here, away from the office and the stress... I've had time to see how different it could all be."

Kate smiled and reached out to pat his knee, but the moment she did his hand clasped hers. Her breath caught as she lifted her eyes to his. "You know, I don't usually open up to people like this."

"Oh?" Despite the question in the one syllable she could manage, she couldn't pull her mind from the feel of his thumb tracing circles in her palm.

"I know we got off on the wrong foot, but I really like you, Kate."

Oh God. Oh no.

She thought of something to say, some excuse to give, to leave the room or downplay their connection, but then his mouth was on hers. Just like last night. Only better. This time the kiss was slow, deliberate. Wonderful, really.

"That's twice in two nights," he said, his voice husky as he pulled away.

She could have said twice was enough, thank you very much. When she thought of the fact that on Sunday he was leaving, she should say just that. But she didn't want to worry about the future anymore. Not when she could enjoy the present.

She grinned. "Don't they say that the third time's the charm?"

Chapter Twenty

⸺∞∞∞⸺

Charlotte was awake before Audrey's first cry, but for the first time in months, she felt perfectly rested. She looked over at the clock on her nightstand. A little past six, and normally Audrey was testing her lungs before the sun had come up.

She smiled down at the bassinet her mother had set up for her in her old bedroom. Clearly, Misty Point was agreeing with Audrey, too.

Flopping back on her pillow, Charlotte stared at the ceiling as anxiety began to knot her stomach again. She'd actually done it. She'd taken the first step and called her parents. Given them the surprise of their lives by telling them about Audrey and everything that had led up to her birth. She'd planned to take the bus back to town, if they'd be open to her coming home, but they'd insisted on driving and picking her up. She didn't think she would ever forget the glisten in her dad's eye when he first held his granddaughter. For a moment, it was as if the clouds had parted and the struggle was over and everything felt right again.

But there was still Kate to deal with, and something told her that she wouldn't be nearly as understanding as her parents had been.

When the first hint of brewing coffee could be detected, Charlotte grabbed her robe and tiptoed down the stairs, happy to see her mother in the kitchen. Her hair was pulled back with a clip, and her favorite coffee mug was already clutched in her hands. Charlotte was struck by how little had changed in Misty Point...but how much had transpired for her while she'd been away.

"The baby's still asleep?" her mother asked, surprised. "My, you're lucky. You used to have me up at three on the dot, every morning until you were six months old."

"Believe me, this is a first. I can't remember the last time I didn't start my day in the dark." Charlotte opened a cabinet and took out her mug, her heart pulling when she realized it was still there, waiting for her.

"I know I said it yesterday, but I only wish you had told us sooner." Maura shook her head. "When I think of you doing this all on your own..."

Charlotte set a hand on her mother's shoulder and looked her square in the eye. "Mom, it's fine. Audrey is fine. And, well, I'm going to be fine. I just needed some time to figure things out." She dropped her hand and reached for the coffee, disappointment landing squarely in her chest when she thought of everything she'd been through, only to end up back in her childhood bedroom, without a dime to her name. "So much for that."

"What do you mean by that?" her mother asked sharply.

Charlotte splashed some milk into her coffee and leaned

against the counter. "Look at me, Mom. I tried to do it on my own and I failed. I had to call you and Dad to come save me. Some role model for my daughter that makes me."

"Quite the opposite," her mother scolded. "You went through all these months on your own, and you finally had the good sense to ask for help when you needed it."

"But that's just it, Mom. I didn't want to have to ask for help. I wanted to show . . . I guess I wanted to show that I've changed."

"You have changed," Maura insisted, taking her by the hand and leading her over to the table. She waited until she was settled into a chair to continue. "You could have called us months ago asking for money, or help, but you didn't. You chose to struggle. To pick up the pieces and try to put your life back together. That takes courage, Charlotte. And I'm proud of you."

Proud of her? Charlotte wondered just how proud her mother would be if she knew about the credit card debt and the fact that she hadn't paid her last month of rent on that month-to-month in Boston.

Well, there was the security deposit. Yes, that would cover it.

Still, not exactly a pinnacle of women's independence. Not a poster child for a successful single mother.

But still. She was doing the best she could. Maybe to her mother, that was enough.

But it wasn't enough for Charlotte. Yet.

"I should get Audrey's bottle ready," she said, sighing, as she set down her coffee and reached for the baby supplies she'd piled onto her parents' counter last night. "She'll be up any minute, hungry for it."

Her mother looked up at the clock that hung above the old rotary telephone. Charlotte could still remember stretching that cord to capacity so she could huddle in the corner of the adjacent dining room, whispering to boys or talking about them with her friends. Kate would also be in the kitchen, usually helping her mother with dinner prep when Charlotte reappeared. She'd never offered to help, and no one had ever expected her to. There was Kate for that.

Back then Kate was boring. Eventually Kate became safe.

Then Kate became the person Charlotte wished she could be. Someone who had it together. Someone whose life was going places. Someone who knew who they were.

"It's Elizabeth's wedding tomorrow," her mother added. "You met William, right?"

A few times. Handsome. Rich. Charlotte felt a twinge of remorse when she thought about the way she'd tried to engage him in conversation the one time she'd tagged along to dinner with everyone last summer. Elizabeth had gone to the bathroom, and William was making an effort to keep the single girl at the table engaged. In a brotherly way.

Kate had been too busy talking with Jake to notice, and William's eyes had narrowed a bit when he realized what was happening.

God. What an idiot she'd been! Now...now the last thing she wanted was attention from anyone. Except from her daughter.

"Elizabeth will make a beautiful bride," her mother was saying.

Charlotte stopped rinsing out the bottle and set it to the side. She refrained from saying anything. Kate had always clicked more with Elizabeth than with her—her own sister. Sure, it made sense at first given that she was two years younger, but now she was twenty-eight and Kate was thirty. Thirty! Other people she knew were inseparable with their sisters by the second half of their twenties. Not their best friends.

But then, maybe she was to blame for that. She picked up her coffee mug and stared blearily into it. She hesitated before asking the question that had plagued her for months, afraid to know the answer. "Do you think Kate will ever forgive me?"

Her mother nodded firmly. "I think once your sister hears you out, she'll come around."

"But what if she won't speak to me? What if I can't make her understand?" Charlotte chewed on her nail, worrying.

Maura sighed. "I don't know. But I can only hope that someday our family will be whole again."

Charlotte looked her mother straight in the eye. "It will be, Mom. If it's up to me, it will be."

★ ★ ★

Charlotte waited until Audrey went down for her afternoon nap before daring to venture into town. She had given up all hope that Kate would ever take one of her calls, and as much as she hated the thought of what Kate's reaction might be if she ambushed her at home or work, she supposed there might be little harm if she were to, say, just . . . stumble upon her?

According to their mother, Kate now lived in a cute little house right next door to Elizabeth and William. And she had a dog. A funny, rambunctious little puppy that Charlotte suddenly longed to meet. She could just imagine Audrey playing with the little guy.

Maybe she'd get Audrey a puppy of her own one day. Well,

once she was completely back on her feet. For now, one baby was enough responsibility. No sense in overdoing it.

She laughed at herself as she noticed a parking spot up ahead and pulled in. What a difference a year made. And an unexpected pregnancy. This time last summer she was busy fantasizing about a new dress she wanted to wear to a party. Now she was thinking of how she might add even more mouths to feed to her plate.

It wasn't all about herself anymore. Thank God for that, she thought, sighing satisfyingly.

She climbed out of the car, grinning as the warm sunshine hit her face, and paid the meter, deciding on an optimistic whim to max out the time, just in case things went well and she and Kate decided to bond over a latte or something.

She frowned. Who was she kidding? She'd be lucky if her sister would even say hello to her.

But she just needed to make her hear her out.

She swept her eyes over the street, all the way up to Bride by Design, where Kate worked with that pill Meredith Smith. She knew Kate loved her job and that, like Bob, bosses could be difficult, but Meredith was far from a peach. If anyone asked her, she'd say Kate was better off on her own. But then, there was no sense in trying to tell Kate that. Charlotte was hardly in a position to be voicing her opinion on what Kate should be doing with her life.

Sisters did that. And she'd sort of lost that right, hadn't she?

She squared her shoulders. Well, today she intended to get it back. Or die trying, she thought.

She crossed the street to the Harbor Street Café, knowing Kate often stopped in there throughout the day for coffee or lunch. It probably gave her an excuse to get away from her boss, she thought, laughing to herself, but all amusement stopped as she came closer to the door.

Kate could be inside, right this minute, just a matter of feet away. She could open the door and see her. Walk over and speak to her. Tap her on the shoulder, say her name, and watch her sister turn and look at her, first in surprise ... and then? She'd hardly greet her with open arms. Would she storm off, yell? Charlotte didn't know.

She suddenly felt as if she could be sick.

She swallowed hard, staring at the big brass door handle as if it were on fire, and nearly jumped out of her skin when the door pushed open on her, locking eyes with a confused middle-aged woman who clearly thought Charlotte was a little odd.

Maybe she was odd. She was scared of her own sister, after all. How normal was that?

Heaving a sigh of annoyance with herself, she grabbed the handle before the door had closed all the way and marched into the overly air-conditioned room. Her initial glance revealed nothing, and she felt her shoulders sink in relief. But as she swept her eyes more closely over the tables, an emotion closer to disappointment crept in.

What had she been thinking, hoping to run into Kate at random? She could spend all day in here, staring out the window, eyes trained on the intersection near Bride by Design like some stalker, or she could be the adult she was trying to become and deal with this head-on.

She played out that scenario as she walked back out onto the sidewalk, glancing nervously up the street. She'd tried to imagine herself in Kate's position over and over again all these months, and each time she'd reached the same horrible conclusion. If the situation were reversed, and if she only knew what Kate knew, wouldn't she hate herself, too? And wouldn't she be the last person on earth—well, other than Jake, obviously—that she'd want to see or speak to ever again?

Showing up unannounced would be cruel. Kate was a planner. She'd never been one for surprises, especially bad ones. And hadn't she had enough of those for one year?

Deflated, Charlotte walked to her car. She'd been crazy thinking she could come back here and make things right. And no doubt her sister would find out she was home, soon enough. She was living at their parents' house after all. And Misty Point was small. Just standing out here on Harbor Street, she was exposed. For all she knew, Kate had already spotted her out a window.

She dug the keys to her mom's car from her bag as she approached it. So much for maxing out the meter; no doubt she was about to make someone's day when they pulled into her spot. She pressed the button on the key, unlocking the doors, but she couldn't bring herself to pull the handle. Now what? She'd go home, feed Audrey, fret some more about how she would handle things with Kate going forward, see that shadow in her mother's eye that she had put there? She could look for jobs, but would she look for them in Misty Point?

She looked down the street, once more eyeing Bride by Design. The front door was flanked by two black planters overflowing with blue hydrangeas. Charlotte perked up, suddenly having an idea.

She had to get through to Kate; that much was sure. And she suddenly had just the way to do it.

Rose in Bloom was just down Harbor Street, in the opposite direction of Bride by Design. With its black and white striped awning and boxwood hedges along the black-framed windows, it was a chic, inviting store that Charlotte had been coming to long before Bree took over the place.

Bree and Charlotte used to be close. Of course, Charlotte could only assume she was on her cousin's blacklist now. Yet another relationship she'd have to repair. Well, there was no time like the present.

The glass-paned door to the shop was open, allowing fresh air and sunlight to flow in almost as much as it allowed the containers of flowers to flow out. From across the street, Charlotte was able to see that the shop was empty, and she hurried across the road, not even bothering to wait for the light to change, hoping to make her purchase and get home. And then . . . wait.

She spotted the perfect selection as soon as she came into the shop. Apricot roses that reminded her of the wallpaper in Kate's bedroom at home. They were simple, and pretty, and she could just imagine the smile on her sister's face when she received them.

Until she thought of how her face might look when she read the card.

She suddenly pictured the beautiful bouquet of roses she was holding slammed down in the bottom of a trash can. She hesitated as she brought the petals to her nose and took in their scent.

It was worth a try. And she was quickly running out of ideas. Her parents had offered to explain everything to Kate, but this was her mess. And hers to set right.

Bree was on the phone in the back room; Charlotte could

make out the sound of her voice taking down an order as she approached the front desk to select a greeting card. She chose a plain white one, considering there were none that read anything along the lines of "Sorry for ruining your life," and grabbed a pen from the jar. Her hand hovered over the cardstock, and her handwriting came out stiff and shaky as she scribbled the message, keeping it as simple as she could and hoping that she was getting it right. There might not be another chance.

Bree was hanging up the phone as Charlotte was wedging the card into the small envelope. She licked the seal as Bree appeared, flush-faced and smiling and muttering her apologies for the delay, but as she locked eyes with Charlotte, her expression changed.

Charlotte felt her stomach knot. She'd known it wouldn't be easy to come back. But it wasn't easy to stay in Boston.

This is a step in the right direction, she reminded herself firmly. Even if not everyone knows that yet.

"Charlotte." Bree was all business as she came behind the desk. "This is a surprise. I didn't know you were back in town." She hesitated, her eyes turning knowing. "But Jake is back, so I suppose that makes sense."

It was summer. Of course Jake was back. For some reason she hadn't factored that into her plans, though. If you could call her last-minute decision to finally face her family a plan.

She didn't have a plan at all, she realized with panic. Not for what she would say to Kate. Or how she would say it. Not for what she was going to do with the next two weeks, much less the rest of her life.

She almost snorted to herself. What else was new?

Misty Point was small. So small that it was a damn miracle

she hadn't run into Kate so far today, and she probably could, if she hovered around town much longer. Her eyes darted out the window, wondering if Jake was about to pop into the café or if he'd been in there when she'd stopped in, and she just hadn't seen him because she was too busy looking for Kate.

He hadn't even met his daughter yet. Would he have a change of heart when he saw her?

Suddenly, she wasn't so sure she liked that idea. As much as it broke her heart to think that Audrey's father didn't want her, the other part of her knew that he didn't deserve her.

"I...I didn't come with Jake," Charlotte said. She'd given up on Jake, on the possibility of the idyllic family life she'd desperately hoped could come of this mess. In Boston, she could hope, but she could also be free. In Misty Point, there was nowhere to hide. From Jake. From her sister. From the judgment in everyone's eyes.

But now Bree's eyes had softened, she noticed. She looked confused, even a little distressed.

Charlotte decided to spare her further confusion. "Jake and I aren't together."

They were never together. Not unless you counted one night. But oh, so much could change from one single night.

Her hands were shaking as she set the bouquet on the table along with the card. She pulled her wallet from her bag, trying to remember how much was left on her credit card and deciding she may as well just max it out. She was close anyway. What did another thirty bucks matter when you were in this deep?

"Can you deliver these to Kate for me?" She locked Bree's gaze, knowing a protest was on the tip of her cousin's tongue, and before she had a chance to refuse, pleaded, "Please. I don't know what else to do."

After a long pause, Bree gave one nod of her head. "I'll give them to her."

"Thank you," Charlotte said quietly. She watched in silence as the transaction went through, realizing she had been holding her breath as the card was processed.

"I'm not trying to get you involved," she said as she slid the card back into her wallet, even though she should probably just ask to borrow Bree's garden sheers and snip the thing in half. It was maxed out, just like her others. And without a job, she had no hope of paying it off.

"I'm already involved," Bree said, and the coldness in her tone made Charlotte flinch.

"Of course. You always loved Kate."

"I thought you did, too." Bree's gaze had turned stony, and it took everything in Charlotte not to become defensive. After all, from the way everyone saw it, she had willingly betrayed her sister, stolen something precious from her. She could have set them straight at the beginning. But she was in denial then. Still hoping that things might work out with Jake after all. That the man her sister had loved would stand by her, and his child.

She shook her head. What a mess.

"It's complicated," she said, but her words fell flat. "I want more than anything to have things back to the way they were." She paused. Was this true? Did she really want to go back to being the girl who spent Monday through Friday planning her weekend outfits, and every Thursday through Saturday night partying in town? Some role model for Audrey that would make her. And the energy! Just the thought of going out past eight o'clock felt like a new form of torture.

"A lot of damage has been done." Bree eyed her sternly. "Don't go upsetting Kate. Promise me that."

Is that what Bree thought she intended? She nodded softly and walked to the door, her heart pounding as her eyes scanned the road that led back to her car, in case her sister was coming around the corner. But she paused as she reached the door.

"Can I ask one more favor?" She was hardly in the position to be asking for anything, given what she'd taken, but this was one request she needed to fulfill. "Don't tell Kate that Jake and I aren't together. There's a lot she doesn't know, and it would be better if I told her myself. If she'll let me."

Bree frowned, but finally nodded. "I won't tell her."

"Thank you," Charlotte said, giving a watery smile.

"And, Charlotte?" Bree called, startling Charlotte as she stepped onto the sidewalk.

She turned back, wondering what lecture she was going to hear, if Bree had been boiling with anger for what Charlotte had done to Kate the way half the town probably would, if she had a message to deliver to Charlotte, if she was going to have her peace once and for all.

But Bree just said gently, "Take care of yourself, Charlotte. And for what it's worth, all I want is for things to go back to the way they were, too."

Charlotte felt the tears spring to her eyes as she swallowed back the emotions that were building inside her. She turned away and hurried down the street, happy that she'd worn sunglasses so no one could see that she was crying.

It wasn't much, but it was enough. She had hope again. Hope that people could forgive. And that maybe her sister was one of them.

Chapter Twenty-One

⸺ ∘∞∞∘ ⸺

The first stop after lunch was Rose in Bloom. Kate knew Bree was a stickler for spotting even the slightest hint of a wilted petal, but she couldn't cross the item off her list without checking, and besides, she looked forward to a visit with her cousin.

The flower shop was only a few blocks from her office, but Kate still felt on edge as she walked down the sidewalk. If Charlotte was back, what did that mean? And if Jake was here, then wouldn't Charlotte be, too?

A phone call to her parents would confirm her suspicion. Had they seen their youngest daughter? What had they said? Deep down Kate knew that they obviously loved Charlotte. But how could they love her and forgive what Charlotte had done?

She was frowning by the time she arrived at the shop, but she had arrived, without altercation or an unfortunate run-in. That was a small victory.

In a town as small as Misty Point, she wouldn't always be so lucky.

She'd have to prepare herself for the inevitable. But first, she needed to get through this wedding. The door to the shop was open, as Bree tended to keep it, even on stormy days, claiming she liked the smell of rain and that she had no business being a florist if she didn't embrace nature to its fullest.

Kate breathed in the fragrant air, nearly tasting its sweetness, and wandered up to the big workbench at the back of the room, where Bree was assembling a colorful arrangement. She paused to smell a bunch of peonies and then kept walking, trying her best not to get caught up in the beauty of her surroundings. She wasn't here to ooh and aah, as easy as it would be. She had a job to do, and the sooner she approved the flowers for Elizabeth's bouquets, the sooner she could move on to the next item on her list, which was to pick up the dresses from the bridal boutique.

"These are gorgeous," she murmured, resisting the urge to touch one of the cherry red dahlias that sprung from a galvanized pot.

Bree looked up in greeting and said through a sigh, "Give me just thirty seconds to tuck in the last of these stems and I'm yours. You know how it is; you have to fulfill the vision when it is still clear! Or else it slips and is gone forever."

Bree tucked the last stem into the vase and stepped back to study it with fine scrutiny. "Perfect!" She flashed a big smile and turned the arrangement toward Kate. "What do you think?"

It was exquisite work. The colors were vivid and unexpected, the arrangement tight and modern. Bree's grandmother had come up with lovely designs, but Bree was born to do this. "Gorgeous." Kate smiled. "How are the arrangements for tonight?"

For the rehearsal dinner, they'd decided to stick with a green and white theme, opting for creamy white roses. Simple and clean and just elegant enough to underscore such a special occasion.

"They're in the back room and all ready to go. I'll bring them over an hour early as we discussed. And look what I picked up first thing this morning. Straight from the flower market." Bree lifted a finger to signal Kate to wait and quickly returned from the back room with a big bucket of vibrant pink dahlias.

"Oh my goodness," Kate gasped, stunned at how fresh and full the blooms were, even though Bree only selected the best. "Elizabeth is going to be thrilled."

"The wedding bouquets will be beautiful. As well as the centerpieces." Bree winked. "I'll be getting an early start on them tomorrow. Don't worry, I've asked one of my summer part-time girls to help out with the table arrangements in the afternoon so I can attend to my bridesmaid duties." Before Kate had a chance to say anything, she added, "Don't fret. She's perfectly capable of making sure the centerpieces are exactly centered and all accounted for."

Kate winced. "Is it that obvious I was worried?"

"Let's just say I'm not sure who is more nervous about this wedding, you or the bride." Bree reached over and patted Kate's hand. "Relax, Kate. Don't let that awful Meredith get to you so much."

"I wish it were that easy," Kate sighed. She looked around the shop longingly, imagining a different path. "It must be nice to control your own fate. To not have to worry about losing your job."

"Oh, I worry," Bree chuckled. "Gran may not be with me in

the physical sense anymore, but I hate the thought of letting her down."

"Have you given more thought to the house?" Kate asked casually.

"No. Simon said something about taking me on a trip to Nantucket one weekend before the end of summer." Bree's eyes danced.

Kate stifled a groan. If that trip ever materialized, she would toss a hundred bucks into her Future jar, in lieu of lunches out for a month.

"Besides, I'm too tired to think about that house most days. Working in the shop with Gran was different than running it on my own. I feel like I could fall asleep on my feet most days. I may not have a boss, but I have clients. And they are not always easy to please. But it is nice to do things my way without someone breathing down my neck or threatening to fire me, not that Gran ever did that. Why, are you thinking of going out on your own?"

"More like dreaming." Kate sighed.

"I'd love to see nothing more than for you to stick it to that woman. She's bitter, that's what she is. Planning weddings. Never having one of her own." Bree's eyes grew wide in alarm at her misstep.

Kate held up a hand before the apology came. "She is bitter. That's it exactly." And it was a scary reminder of where her own path could lead, if she let it. "Well, no sense in thinking of quitting when I should be thinking about this wedding tomorrow." Kate lifted her bag onto her shoulder. A long day was ahead and as much as she might like to hang out with her cousin, that would have to wait.

"I'll see you tonight, then. For the rehearsal dinner." She paused when she noticed a small card next to a bouquet of apricot roses, her stomach flipping when she saw her name. Her mind ran through the possibilities.

Alec. He didn't seem like the type to make sweeping romantic gestures. No, only one person she knew was the type to go overboard with things like that, in the end overlooking what really mattered. Jake.

He was back in town. Was he seeking her out? Had he come back to apologize?

God, I hope not.

She stared at the roses, licking her lips, wondering if she should just pretend she hadn't seen them, wait for Bree to say something instead. But curiosity was growing about as quickly as the hope that they were from Alec.

"Are these...for me?" She gave Bree a quizzical glance, at once feeling embarrassed for asking at all. Kate was a common name, after all.

Bree sighed as a guilty flush crept up her neck. She glanced down, and at once Kate was filled with dread. So her hunch was right. "Who are they from?" she asked, almost not wanting to know. From the look on Bree's face, they weren't from someone Bree thought she'd want to see.

"Don't tell me they're from Jake," she said flatly.

Bree looked at her with surprise. "No. Why? Are you... Have you spoken with him?"

Kate relaxed. "No. And I don't intend to. But if I must... well, I have nothing to say." She chewed her lip, eyeing the flowers. "Are they from Alec?"

"Alec?" Bree showed more surprise by that scenario than she

had when Kate's ex-fiancé was mentioned. "You mean the best man?"

Kate nodded, hoping the disappointment she felt didn't show on her face. Of course they weren't from Alec. Why would he have sent her flowers? They'd had a nice few days together, and a kiss. Well, several kisses, technically.

And by Sunday morning he'd be back in Boston. Back to his busy life that had no room for anything personal in it.

It was a little fact that she had managed to not think about too much these past few days. And from the way her heart sank, she should have.

"Why would you think they were from him?" Bree asked, leaning forward with sudden interest.

She and Alec had kissed last night, for real this time, and there was no way she could tell Elizabeth. But Bree...Bree could keep things to herself. She had to, in her line of work. She was probably the only person in all of Misty Point who knew the identity of everyone's secret admirers. But her lips were always sealed.

Kate brushed a hand through the air, feeling ridiculous. "I thought he might have sent them as a thank-you gift," she lied. "For helping him out so much this week."

Bree seemed to take this an answer, but her eyes glimmered a little when she looked back at Kate. "Here I was thinking that something might have happened between you two. I saw the way he was looking at you last night. Seemed like he really liked talking to you. And he's really cute."

That he was. "He's also really not Elizabeth's biggest fan," Kate pointed out, feeling that familiar stir of guilt every time she thought of her friend. "It's hard to overlook that."

Bree didn't seem concerned. "Oh, that will settle itself out in time, I think. But I guess it's best not to stir anything up before tomorrow."

No. It wasn't. And Kate didn't intend to, either. Besides, come Sunday, there might be nothing to tell.

"So, who are they from? Elizabeth?" She didn't know why the thought hadn't occurred to her sooner. It was just the type of gesture her friend would make to thank her for planning the wedding.

"Elizabeth already scheduled her delivery for you for Monday morning," Bree confided. Her mouth thinned and she held Kate's eyes a second longer than usual. "They're from Charlotte."

"Charlotte?" Kate repeated, knowing she had visibly blanched. So she was back.

"She was in here this morning. It was very important to her that you read the card. I...I didn't know what to say." Bree shook her head.

Kate's eyes darted to the window, and she suddenly had a desire to run back to her office and hide there for the rest of the day. Or maybe the rest of her life.

It was bad enough that her sister and Jake had run off to Boston together. But having them back in Misty Point...that was a hundred times worse.

"Charlotte didn't seem herself," Bree continued, watching Kate carefully. "She seemed a bit tired. She wasn't wearing any makeup or anything, and her hair...Well, you know how Charlotte is."

Yes, Kate knew. Charlotte was vain, always had been. And Charlotte never left the house without makeup...on her face or in her bag.

The pungent aroma of the flowers was becoming stifling, and she felt dizzy from the smell—or maybe from the newest information. She stepped back from the counter.

"Well, I should really go. You know how it is, the day before the wedding and all."

Bree smiled and gave a quick nod. "Do you want to take the card?"

Kate hesitated. Upon closer examination, she could make out Charlotte's loopy scroll, the very same since she'd learned cursive back in third grade. "No," she said decisively.

Bree nodded. "I understand." She slid the card into a drawer, out of sight, and then looked Kate square in the eye, huffing out a breath. "Look, I promised your sister I wouldn't say anything, but when I mentioned that Jake was back she said...she said they weren't together anymore."

Kate could only raise her eyebrows. Technically such news should have brought her pleasure, or at least satisfaction. But instead all she felt was disappointment. Charlotte flitted from one man to the next, and this was just her pattern repeating itself. Something that had meant nothing had ruined a lifetime of relationships, broken their family.

She shook her head. All for nothing.

"Something tells me there's more going on than we know," Bree went on.

"More like Jake broke up with her, and she came running after him," Kate said, turning to go. Just thinking about Charlotte and Jake made her heart race, and not in a good way. "I have to go pick up those dresses."

"I'm sorry I said anything." Bree looked miserable.

"Don't worry about telling me," Kate reassured her. "I'm glad you did." And if it hadn't been Bree, it would be her mother, who she'd be seeing tomorrow at the wedding anyway.

"I'll see you tonight?" Bree asked hopefully.

"See you tonight," Kate said, managing a smile. She gave a vague wave and dodged her way through the pots of flowers until she was out on the sidewalk, exposed. She didn't look around, but bent her head, put one foot in front of the other, and hurried all the way back to Bride by Design, for once finding relief in pulling open the blue door and slipping inside.

★ ★ ★

Alec paced the length of his hotel suite, playing out every scenario a second time. By the time he reached the far wall, he stopped and drew his attention to the window, hoping the view of the ocean would ease his anxiety.

A tapping at the door caused him to inhale sharply, and without further hesitation he crossed the room and opened the door, giving his father a tight smile by way of greeting.

"What time did you arrive?" Alec asked as his father walked over to the bar cart and began mixing a gin and tonic. George held up an empty glass by way of invitation, but Alec shook his head. He'd need a clear head to get through the conversation he was about to have.

"Just got in about ten minutes ago. What time's this meeting with Mason Lambert?"

"Three." Alec stared levelly at his father, but George was too busy mixing his drink to notice. "We need to talk, Dad."

His father took a sip of his drink. Alec could hear the ice clinking in the glass.

"We need to push back on another meeting tomorrow afternoon."

George's brow pinched. "We're hardly in a position to be making demands, Alec."

It was true, but Alec had already thought this through. "We don't want to look desperate, either. Mason is a smart man. Maybe he's testing us. He knows William is getting married tomorrow."

"So we have the meeting and then we go to the ceremony." George shrugged and took another swig from his glass.

"I just don't see it being that easy," Alec said. Today's schedule was tight enough. Tomorrow was impossible.

His father's jaw was tight. "We don't even know if we'll get to that meeting tomorrow. Let's see how today goes and take it from there."

"And if it goes well today and he wants to extend it to dinner?" He wouldn't put anything past Mason Lambert, from what he'd seen and read.

George walked over to the bar cart and made himself another drink. "William walked away from the company," he eventually said.

"So what? He turned his back on the family, and now we can turn our back on him?" Alec cursed under his breath. "I'm not so sure it's really like that."

"Then explain it to me," his father said.

"William is happy here, Dad. He's . . . different. In a good way. I think you'll see that for yourself tonight."

His father narrowed his eyes. "Are you telling me you no longer care if he stays in Misty Point?"

"Of course I care." Just maybe not in the way his father could ever understand. He shook his head. It was no use trying to reason with the old man. They were two different people.

"Then you should care about how this meeting with Mason goes," his father said. "Let's review our notes."

Alec walked over to the dining table and rummaged through his papers for the file. He handed it to his father and took a seat on an armchair. He'd meet with Mason today, but only until five. As for tomorrow . . . He'd have a choice to make. A choice that went much deeper than the fate of the business.

Chapter Twenty-Two

⤐⥁⥀⥂

"So the old man actually showed up." William arched a brow at Alec as he came to lean against the terrace rail, and despite himself, Alec laughed. It was a tight, uneasy sound. A guilty sound, he thought, thinking of how close they'd come to not making it to this rehearsal dinner after all.

The meeting with Mason had, predictably, lasted longer than originally planned, and Alec could see that his father was all too eager to keep it going, extend it into the evening with a round of drinks. It had been Alec who had cleared his throat, made his apologies, and explained that they had somewhere to be. He hadn't dared to meet his father's eye, but he could feel the glare burning from across the table.

Now he looked across the large deck to where his father sat, nodding his head politely at something Elizabeth's father was saying. The Joneses were doing a damn good job of making him feel welcome, and Alec was relieved for that. He hadn't spoken to his father since they'd left the meeting with Mason. Hadn't wanted to engage. He'd had his say, made it clear where he stood.

But it wasn't out of anger that he couldn't look at his dad. Not completely. It was out of something worse, maybe. Sadness, loss. Maybe even a little pity. That company was all his father had. All he'd chosen to have. And Alec could have helped him save it today.

Well, he told himself, scraping the last of the potatoes from his plate, it wasn't over yet. They'd made a good case for themselves, proven they were trustworthy and successful advisors. There was still a chance that Mason would want to work with them, and a big one.

And it was a risk that Alec was comfortable taking, he thought, shifting his gaze to his brother as he leaned back on the rail.

"Have you talked with him yet?" he asked, almost not wanting to bring it up. William and their father barely spoke anymore, and when they did it was stiff and tense. Both were hurt and offended. Alec frowned. In time maybe things would work themselves out. For now, he wouldn't hold his breath.

"Briefly," William said, reaching for his glass of wine. "He was perfectly polite in that wonderfully cold and sterile way of his."

"Then I would say the day was a success!" Alec laughed a little easier. He wanted to believe his own words, but the weekend felt long and looming and there was entirely too much room for something to go wrong.

William grew silent. The sounds of the party filled the air. The piano music was subtle in the background, the candlelight flickering, but in this corner of the terrace, it was dark and shadowed. "You know earlier, at the rehearsal, I...I couldn't stop thinking that it would have been nice if Mom were here."

Alec looked at him sharply. His pulse drummed. They didn't talk about her. They didn't say they missed her. Didn't imagine how life might have been.

At least he hadn't. Wouldn't. Couldn't.

Until now.

He shifted to turn toward the ocean, his back to the party, his arms draping over the rail. "Do you remember that time she let us stay up late to catch fireflies? She showed us how to cup them in our hands, just tight enough that they wouldn't get out, but just loose enough that we could see their light shining through." He gave a sad smile. "She was gentle like that."

"I wish I could remember." William's voice was filled with regret.

"You were little," Alec said. Hell, he'd been young himself, not more than six or seven. But he could still hear the sound of her laugh if he closed his eyes. See the light shining in her eyes. "That was a long time ago."

"He never talked about her," William said bitterly. "He never told us stories. Never kept her alive for us."

"It was easier for Dad that way," Alec explained. Easier for him, too. Now he knew he'd been wrong. "It was his way of coping with it."

"It doesn't make him right," William said.

"No," Alec agreed. It didn't make any of them right. Across the deck he noticed his father stand, shake Jeff Jones's hand, and start walking toward them. His jaw was squared, tense, the usual all-business stance he'd maintained over the years, but there was something different about him, Alec noticed, as he came closer. Something in his eyes.

From behind him, Elizabeth was waving, motioning William over. "Hate to leave you like this..."

Wouldn't be the first time, Alec thought. But the anger he'd felt had shifted these past few days. "Go. Have fun. I can handle Dad."

He took a long sip of his drink as his brother disappeared into the crowd and his father came to a stop in front of him.

"That lead we've had has panned out," George said, lifting a bushy eyebrow. "He wants to move forward with our meeting with him and his son."

Alec felt his mouth go dry. "This isn't the time to discuss business." He lifted his wineglass again, only to realize that it was empty.

It was going to happen. The meeting. Tomorrow. The day of his brother's wedding. His father knew as well as he did that they couldn't be in two places at once.

"Any chance of rescheduling?" Alec said.

His father shot him a look. Or maybe, Alec thought, a warning.

"Sounds like business is going well," William cut in, back at his side to reach for his cell phone, which he'd left on the deck rail.

"Not as good as yours, I'm sure." Their father's gaze turned hooded. "Should have had you sign a no-solicitation clause. But then, I never thought one of my sons would leave the family business and take a book of clients with him."

"I didn't take them. They came on their own." William's expression remained completely neutral as he tapped on the screen of his phone and then thrust the device back into his pocket.

"I'm where I need to be, Dad. It would mean a lot if you could be happy for me."

Father and son stared at each other until George tapped the railing twice and gave a curt nod. "I've had a long day and I'm turning in. I want nothing but the best for you, William. And you, Alec. With that, good night."

The brothers watched him go, until he disappeared inside the lobby. "Well, that could have gone worse," William declared.

It could have gone a lot worse, Alec thought. And it still sadly might.

"I should get back to Elizabeth," William said, but he stopped as he turned to go. "What I said the other day still stands, Alec."

Alec knew what his brother was referring to, but as with the first time the topic was broached, he didn't know how to respond. "It's complicated," he said, even though he couldn't ignore the lightness in his chest, the rare feeling of possibility.

William nodded. "I understand. But...do me a favor and think about it, will you? And, Alec," he said, lifting a finger. "Don't do it for me. Whatever happens...do what's best for you."

"Like you did?" Alec replied, catching the edge in his voice.

William gave him a long look. "It's what Mom would have wanted."

Alec didn't reply. His brother was right. Their mother had had a few glimpses of happiness in her life, ones he still remembered, when he allowed himself to. She would have wanted a different ending for them. Her boys. That's what she always called them. *Her boys.* Even then, when they were so little, she'd lumped them together, made them part of a team.

Somewhere along the way he'd almost lost that. And he'd been blaming the wrong person.

He watched as William approached Elizabeth, set an arm around her waist, laughed at something she whispered in his ear. He suddenly felt a yearning for something he'd almost lost but might still be able to have, if he was careful.

His gaze wandered to the left, catching Kate's eye. She gave him a small smile, and he held his hand up, grinning as he crossed the deck and grabbed two glasses of Champagne from a waiter passing a tray. He'd been eyeing Kate all through the wedding rehearsal and the immediately following dinner, but he had yet to steal a few minutes alone with her. She'd been in wedding planner mode, doing her job, making sure every detail was in order, that every guest and wedding participant was accounted for. Even their walk down the aisle had been interrupted by Kate's need to take the flower girl's hand and make sure she didn't drop down to play with the rose petals, as she had tried to. Twice.

She turned to give him her full attention as he approached the corner of the veranda where she was overseeing the setup of an elaborate dessert buffet.

"When I agreed to the pie, I didn't realize it would look like this," he said, raising his eyebrows at the individual-sized desserts topped with a perfect scoop of ice cream and drizzled with caramel sauce.

"Well, it's a rehearsal dinner. I didn't want it to be too casual."

"I should have known to listen to you. Sushi for the main course would not have worked." He laughed, and so did she.

"That's what I'm here for," she said. "But I have to admit, I'm looking forward to getting off work soon. My feet are killing me."

He traced the curves of her body to the hem of her pale purple cocktail dress and over her bare legs, finally resting on the
strappy sandals she wore.

"Here," he said, shaking the fog clear. "I figured you could
use this."

She accepted the Champagne flute with a grateful smile. "I've
been running around so much, I barely stopped to eat." She
glanced around, before shrugging her shoulders. "Everything is
pretty much wrapped up on my end, so...why not?"

Alec clinked her glass and gestured to the stairs. "I wouldn't
mind getting some air."

"I don't have anything left to do here," Kate said, adjusting
her shawl over her shoulders. "Lead the way."

Alec didn't know where he was leading her any more than
he knew which direction to take for himself. He was ambling,
searching for clarity, for an easy way out of this mess that
wouldn't require letting anyone down, or hurting anyone.

The meeting with Mason Lambert today had gone well. Too
well. In a perfect world he'd be celebrating tonight, but how
could he when everyone expected him to be in attendance tomorrow afternoon, just a few hours before his only brother's
wedding?

Everyone but his father, that is.

"Something wrong?"

Alec hesitated. "Do you ever worry about letting someone
down?"

Kate stopped when she reached the last step. "All I do is
worry these days."

She set her glass on the post at the end of the railing, bent
down, and began fumbling with her shoes. She lost her balance,

laughing as he reached out to steady her, and he didn't let go until she'd eased the last shoe from her heel, smiling into a sigh.

"Ah. Much better," she said as she righted herself.

His hand was still on her wrist, and as he watched her eyes sparkle in the moonlight, he couldn't resist. He set his glass next to hers, and without waiting, he leaned in, brought his mouth to hers, felt her lips part to his touch. He kissed her deeply, slowly, wanting to savor this moment. Wanting to make it last.

His hands were in her hair, pushing the strands from her face as quickly as the wind blew them forward. She brought her hands to his chest as he pulled her close, exploring her mouth, enjoying this heat, until a cheer from the deck above made him stop.

"Wow." Kate brought her fingers to her lips, covering her shy smile. Her gaze skirted from him to the terrace, where the band had picked up and people had started dancing. She slid her eyes back to his. "The party's just getting started."

He could suggest they go back, and maybe he should. Instead he jutted his chin toward the beach. The party could wait.

★ ★ ★

"Is that the famous lighthouse everyone was talking about the other night?" Alec asked, gesturing to the red and white striped structure at the end of the pier.

"The very one." Kate dipped her toe in the water, which bubbled and foamed on the wet sand. "Pretty, isn't it?"

"Let's check it out," Alec said, to her surprise. Pleased, Kate turned down the wooden pier with him.

"This is one of my favorite spots in town," Kate said.

Alec looked at her quizzically. "But as I seem to recall, you were in favor of changing it."

"Not changing it," Kate said. "More like...improving it. It's old, and it needs some maintenance. I hate to think of it being let go. I'd like it to last until..." She stopped herself. Until when? Once her future had been so certain. Now it was a gray fog.

"Come on," Alec said, walking over to the lighthouse. He paused at the doors, but only briefly. "It's unlocked!" He marveled over this discovery, his smile as broad as a little boy on Christmas morning, and Kate laughed.

She didn't have the heart to tell him that of course it wasn't locked. This was Misty Point, not the big city. She knew people who didn't bother to lock their house at night, not that she was one of them. You could never be too careful, after all...

She held back as she watched Alec disappear into the building and then poke his head back out. "Aren't you coming?"

"We're not supposed to be in there," Kate said nervously.

Alec shot her a look of amusement. "Do you always follow the rules?"

Kate couldn't deny it. "Always." At least until now. Until him.

"Come on. Take a risk. Live a little." He extended his hand. "What do you say?"

She looked at his palm, and knowing she might live to regret this, set her hand in his.

"Where are you leading me?" she asked, starting to enjoy herself. It was dark and dusty, but through the open windows the moon shone down, casting a spotlight on the space as they moved through it.

Alec motioned to the staircase. "There. Unless you're scared?"

"When we were little, we used to think it was haunted. I remember one time Elizabeth snuck inside and began howling. I've never seen Charlotte move so fast. Her face went ghostly pale, and then she was off. She didn't stop until she was halfway to town." Kate laughed. "She never forgave me for that."

Kate frowned, her heart suddenly feeling tight. She hadn't thought of that night in a long time. They used to joke about it every now and again. She walked to the stairs, forcing one leg in front of the other.

"You miss your sister," Alec observed, his voice low and husky behind her.

There was a slight echo when Kate cleared her throat. She'd slipped into the past again, when all she wanted to do was move forward. She climbed higher, eager to keep going. "If you go to the top, there's an amazing view of the town."

He laughed in triumph. "So you *have* been in here before!"

She felt her cheeks flush with guilt, but she was laughing, too. "I didn't say I'd never been inside. I just said you're not supposed to..."

Her breath caught as his hands caught her hips and held them there. She stopped at the landing as his chest came close to her back, his mouth so close to her ear that the heat of his breath sent a shiver down her spine. "I knew there was more to you than first met the eye."

"Still making assumptions about me then?" She closed her eyes as he traced his mouth down her neck, so gently she couldn't be sure if it was the breeze or his breath on her skin.

His arms wrapped around her waist, stirring up heat in her

stomach, and she turned to face him, aware of how close his face was to hers, that his gaze was on her mouth.

Kate smiled up at him, refusing to overthink the moment. Refusing to acknowledge the fact that she was dangerously close to losing her heart again, if she hadn't already.

Chapter Twenty-Three

⁓⊗⊗⊗⁓

Well. Now she'd done it. She'd officially gotten caught up in the moment. And slept with Alec.

It was something Charlotte would do, not her. Kate had rules about this type of thing, after all. She didn't kiss until the third date, didn't invite a guy over until the sixth, didn't sleep with him until—Well, no use thinking about that right now. Where had her rules gotten her before?

Kate pulled the car around to the front of the hotel and shifted the gear into park. She would have liked nothing better than to turn off the ignition and go inside with Alec. But today was wedding day, and even if it wasn't her own, it was the closest thing to it. Today was going to be perfect.

It was already off to a perfect start, she thought, sliding Alec a smile.

"What do you have going on before the ceremony today?" Alec asked, and Kate almost burst out laughing.

More like what *didn't* she have going on? It was wedding day. Meaning she would spend the day going over her checklist, making sure that every last detail was accounted for. Every last bobby pin secured, every boutonniere straightened. She'd be overseeing the tent and the caterers and counting the exact number of chairs at the ceremony. There were at least one hundred things to tick off her list, right down to making sure she had safety pins—in a variety of sizes, to boot.

But why bore Alec with the details?

"Oh, I just have a few things to tie up before I meet up with the girls to have lunch and get ready. Though I doubt Elizabeth will be able to eat anything," she said, imagining how her friend must be feeling this morning. Given the tension that still existed between the bride and best man, she quickly changed the topic to safer ground. "How about you? Plans with William before the big moment?"

"I've got some business to attend to before I meet up with him."

"Business?" Her heart sank as the words brought her straight back to reality. Despite the bliss of last night, there was no denying reality, and the fact was that Alec was very much married to his job. His job in Boston.

"It's always business with my father." Alec's jaw tensed, but when he looked at her again, his features relaxed. "I had a really nice time last night." His voice was low and gravelly and entirely too sexy for this time of morning.

"So did I," she admitted. Maybe too good of a time considering how quickly this wedding week was passing.

He hesitated. "I'm starting to dread the thought of going back to Boston in the morning."

Kate perked up. Once Elizabeth and William left for their

honeymoon tonight, she had every intention of kicking back tomorrow. She certainly wouldn't mind the company. "Maybe you can stick around a few days—" She stopped when she saw the way his eyes had gone flat.

He shook his head. "Impossible."

Of course. Silly her.

Her cheeks burned with the rejection, and she hastily turned to look out the window, noticing the tourists that were beginning to fill the sidewalks, getting an early start on the summer weekend. It was late and, like Alec, she needed to get to work. She shouldn't be sitting here in this car, lingering outside the hotel and wishing their time together didn't have to end. She would see him tonight, but it wouldn't be the same. Tonight was about Elizabeth.

"I should get to work," she said. "Wedding day."

Her mind raced with all the last-minute details she had to go over.

"Wait." Kate blinked in panic. How could she have forgotten the main reason she had agreed to spend so much time with this man? "The best man speech. Did you still want my help?"

Alec hesitated and then said, "I started something for it, but I'm not sure it's any good, honestly. I'm not really the best at expressing my emotions." His smile was so bashful that Kate refrained from telling him she'd like to meet a man who was.

"I'm happy to take a look."

"It's in my room. I'll run up and grab it. Unless you want to come up for a bit?"

Kate bit her lip, wishing she could park the car and run upstairs with him, but she shook her head firmly. "I have to get to work."

"Touché," he said, giving her a rueful grin as he stepped out of the car.

"Guilty as charged."

Only today she was guiltier of a lot more than putting work before romance.

She'd put her heart before her head, too.

★ ★ ★

Kate was still replaying last night as she walked into her office, sipping a coffee she'd bought on the way. She gave a more cheerful hello than usual to the receptionist, feeling the bounce in her step as she turned down the hall. But her pulse skipped a beat at the sight of Meredith standing in her doorway.

"There you are," Meredith commented, her undertone laced with disappointment.

Kate knew she was late, but only by two minutes, and she wouldn't have been if she hadn't gotten stuck behind a woman who insisted on writing a check to Harbor Street Café to pay for her latte and scone...

"Good morning!" With more determination than she felt, she bared a smile at Meredith and walked over to her desk. With any luck, today's wedding would be so stunning, Meredith could drop the micromanagement act for good. She squinted into the contents of her handbag as she retrieved the files she had taken home with her and the folder containing Alec's best man speech. The heat of Meredith's gaze burned a hole in the back of her head.

There was no avoiding it. "Can I help you with something, Meredith?"

"Let's go down the list and make sure everything is on track for today's event." Meredith crossed the room and sat down in a velvet tufted guest chair. She spread a notebook on Kate's desk and poised her pen, locking Kate's eyes expectantly.

Kate stifled a sigh and resigned herself for a long interrogation where Meredith was no doubt looking for holes in her story. "No problem."

Even if it was a very big problem. This was wedding day. Wedding day—and Meredith knew what that meant. She'd barely have enough time to gulp down this much-needed coffee, so how exactly did this conversation fit into her plans?

"All the men have their suits?"

"I've arranged to have them delivered." Quick, to the point. If she kept it up, Meredith could be on her merry way.

"Bridesmaids dresses?"

Though they'd already discussed this, Kate humored her. "I picked them up personally yesterday. Along with the bride's gown. And the veil," she added, knowing she would be asked.

Meredith pursed her lips and scratched the items off her notepad. "Caterers are confirmed. Final head count?"

"Yep." Kate shifted in her chair with agitation. "I'm going to call the photographer this morning to be sure he's clear on the key moments we want to capture. I'll also confirm the play list with the band."

"Good." Meredith studied her list. "Tell me again who will be handing out the programs?"

"We're actually leaving them under a seashell on each chair." As Meredith's eyes narrowed, Kate quickly explained, "It was Elizabeth's choice. She didn't want to assign the task to anyone."

"Let's just hope the wind doesn't pick up, then." Meredith's lips thinned but she scratched the item off the list just the same. "The favors are in?"

Kate's stomach overturned. The favors had arrived days ago, but she hadn't counted them out, meaning there was no guarantee they were all accounted for.

Averting her boss's gaze, she managed to say, "Yep!" and made a silent promise to herself that the moment Meredith left her office, she would open that box and confirm the shipment. Her pulse began to speed up as the questioning continued, and she bit back the urge to ask just how long this inquisition would continue and when the past could finally be put in the past, where it belonged. She was finally moving on. Couldn't everyone else?

"The wedding party has all arrived? No last-minute issues there?"

The only last-minute issue is this trial by fire, Meredith.

Instead, Kate let her mind drift to Alec, and she smiled her first real smile since she'd seen him this morning. "No issues. William's father arrived yesterday in time for the rehearsal dinner." She didn't bother mentioning that he had seemed bored and disinterested throughout the course of the meal. "Only ten more out-of-town guests are yet to arrive, and they're scheduled to check in by eleven."

"Everyone knows their role? No glitches at the rehearsal?" When Kate stopped bobbing her head in response, Meredith continued. "The toasts and speeches are all confirmed? No unforeseen disasters there?"

Kate gave a mild smile. "I'm sure Elizabeth's family will give a lovely toast. And William's brother has asked me to look over his best man speech." As she spoke, she retrieved the folder Alec had handed her that morning from the stack on her desk and opened it, noticing in confusion that the papers in front of her didn't look anything like a speech. In her hands was a stack of financial papers.

He'd handed her the wrong papers. She mentally shrugged it off as an unfortunate inconvenience—she could swing by the hotel after she called the photographer. She brightened at the thought of seeing him again when a handwritten note on the bottom of a spreadsheet caught her eye.

Lambert. Her breath stilled as she felt the blood drain from her face. She glanced closer at the writing and then skimmed the page, air locking tight in her chest. With trembling hands she thumbed through the rest of the pages until her mounting fears grew to a point of panic.

Mason Lambert. Jake's father.

She scanned the rest of the page, barely taking it in. A business meeting. Today. Something about Saturday...a meeting with Mason and his son. She blinked, trying to understand what she was looking at.

Business. He was in town for business. He had said it so many times. When had she stopped listening?

She ran her gaze over the papers once more, trying to understand their meaning. She didn't know exactly what he was planning or what she was specifically looking for as she scanned each page, barely taking in a word as she dismissed one section after another until she found it.

There it was. Black and white. Typed out neatly. It couldn't have been clearer.

A meeting with Mason. And his *son*. At the same time as the wedding.

Elizabeth had been right about him. He was exactly the man Kate had been warned about, the man she had refused to accept. She hadn't wanted to see it. She had wanted to believe he was someone else. Someone better. Someone different from Jake.

But from the looks of it, they were just one and the same.

Chapter Twenty-Four

Kate didn't know how she managed to get through the next fifteen minutes without showing her panic. It wasn't until Meredith finally gave her a tight smile and briskly exited her office that Kate slumped back against her chair and closed her eyes. Her mind replayed the events of the past week, trying to make sense of it all, but no matter how many times she went over it, there was no denying the cold, harsh truth.

Alec had been lying to her. He'd had an agenda the entire time, one that involved anything but celebrating William and Elizabeth's wedding.

She'd said all along that she'd be damned if Jake ruined two weddings. From the looks of things, he and Alec were about to do just that.

Her heart ached when she thought of the smile Alec had given her that morning. The way his hand had lingered on hers. The way his lips had skimmed her mouth so tenderly. It seemed impossible to think that he had been planning this all along, behind her back, knowing what it would cost her. What it would do to his brother.

Was it revenge, for William leaving the family company? An eye for an eye? What was this, the Dark Ages? Kate shook her head, trying to make sense of it all.

Heaving a sigh, she leaned over and popped the tape on the box that had arrived earlier in the week. Inside were hundreds of silver tins labeled with vintage-inspired scroll with William and Elizabeth's wedding date. She twisted the top of one of the lids and managed to smile at the creamy pale pink candle molded inside. So much thought had gone into this wedding. So many little details…and it was all about to come crashing down.

With a sniff, she popped the top back onto the tin and set the candle in the box. She would load them into her car later and personally set them on each place today before heading over to Elizabeth's house with the dresses.

Elizabeth. Kate's stomach rolled over at the thought of her friend, who was probably jittery and nervous and overwhelmed with excitement at this very minute. How could she not say something to William?

She shook her head. Shame on her for following her heart instead of heeding the opinion of the person she trusted most in the world. If she had, surely she would have kept her distance from Alec all along.

She had a couple hours before she had to meet the girls. She'd hoped to use this time to go over the seating chart one last time and check on the status of the tent, but those were things she'd just have to trust were in place.

Alec Montgomery was about to ruin William and Elizabeth's

wedding, and that was one not-so-small detail she had somehow managed to overlook.

★ ★ ★

Fifteen minutes later, Kate stood on the steps of the Beacon Inn, sweeping her gaze from one end of the porch to the other. Several attempts to reach Alec via phone had resulted in nothing but voice mail, and with the wedding only hours away, there was nothing left to do other than try to find him at the best place she knew to reach him.

He'd known. And maybe he was trying to warn her. Hadn't everyone warned her, after all? And despite her closest friend's opinions, she hadn't heeded her advice. She'd trusted her heart instead. Her broken heart.

Deciding she couldn't waste any more time hovering outside, she walked into the lobby, and not seeing him there, decided to check out the restaurant, where just a few days ago they'd had breakfast together...before he'd run off for a meeting. Kate closed her eyes, silently cursing to herself. Now she was sure that meeting had been with Mason.

Had he known the connection all along? Did he care? She couldn't be sure, but she intended to find out.

She was just about to go to the front desk and call up to his room when a hand grabbed her arm, forcing her to turn around.

"Jake," she gasped. She stood completely still, her chest rising and falling from the pounding of her heart, until she finally shook away the shock and jerked her arm out of his grip.

Jake's familiar smile was gone. His lips were thin and his typically bright green eyes were flat, the way they were the last time they'd spoken, the day he'd told her there wouldn't be a cake tasting, wouldn't be a wedding at all. It had been almost a year since she had seen him this close, and she couldn't help noticing how much he had changed in that time. He was still handsome, objectively speaking, but the spark that had captured her heart had fizzled. In a strange sort of way it was sad, she registered. This person had meant more than anything at one point in time. Now he meant nothing at all.

"What are you doing here?" she asked, breaking the silence, even if she already knew the answer. He was here to meet with Alec and George Montgomery.

"I have a meeting." His eyes locked hers as if he were looking for something in her expression. An answer. A question. Something.

Charlotte.

The phone calls. Bree's strange insinuation. Now this shiftiness, this strange suspicion she'd never seen in him before, even when he was lying to her, even when he was cheating.

Something was wrong. His jaw flinched as he studied her face, gauging her reaction. She knew that look—it was the same look he had when the truth of his deceit had finally come to light that terrible day all those months ago, the day the handsome man she had loved so much had turned into a stranger. And it was that man who was standing before her right now. Hard, unapproachable, cold.

What had she ever seen in this person?

"I heard you were back in town," she said evenly, not bothering to mention that she had noticed him on the street the other night. She half-heartedly wondered if he had seen her kissing Alec and decided it didn't matter. She didn't care what Jake thought of her. And she realized, he probably didn't think of her often. Her happiness, her heartbreak...none of it had mattered.

"Don't believe everything you hear, Kate." His mossy-green eyes never left hers. The weight of his stare made Kate shift uncomfortably in her heels.

"What's that supposed to mean?" she replied, narrowing her gaze on him.

"I'm just saying, there are two sides to every story."

"Like how there were two sides to your cheating on me with my sister?" She shook her head in disgust. What had happened to this person? When had he changed?

Or why hadn't I noticed, she thought, pursing her lips. Her mind floated to Alec. She sure knew how to pick 'em.

"I have nothing to say about your sister or her allegations," Jake replied stonily.

Now that had her attention. Kate frowned at her ex, giving him her full attention. "*Allegations?*"

"Misty Point is still a small town. I don't need Charlotte making trouble."

"Any more trouble than you've already made? Please, Jake. If you're trying to pass blame, it's far too late."

He hesitated. "I take it you haven't spoken to your sister."

Kate frowned. The phone calls. There must have been ten, maybe more. Charlotte had been reaching out, trying to tell her something. Something Jake didn't want her to know.

What was it?

* * *

Alec stepped off the elevator feeling better than he had since that first night at Kate's house. His entire future suddenly seemed wide open with opportunity. The world was his. He would never again spend a weekend in his corner office, staring at a computer screen, breathing stale air and wearing yesterday's shirt. The days of meandering through life like a robot, acting on autopilot, doing anything and everything to reach the end goal were over. He had been in survival mode for so long, he hadn't known what it felt like to stop and take a look around, to ask himself what he wanted, what mattered. But not anymore. Today was the start of a new life. What he would do with tomorrow, he wasn't yet sure. But he knew it would be better than the life he had been living. It had to be.

Alec did a quick scan of the hotel restaurant and checked his watch. Mason Lambert would be here any moment, and Alec was eager to see the man's reaction when he heard what Alec had come to say. Until this week, he had been dangerously close to following in his father's footsteps. It was a road that would lead to nothing in the end. A life without family, friends, or love.

A life he didn't want anymore.

He *was* his father's son. And that, for once, would have to be enough.

Alec thrust his hands into his pockets and wandered into the lobby, his pulse quickening at the surprising sight of Kate at the far end of the room. No doubt busy preparing for the wedding. He could see the papers she clutched to her chest. Yep, the endless to-do list.

On a closer look he noticed the tension in her posture, the lack of color in her normally rosy cheeks. Alec turned his attention to the man who was talking to her and decided he didn't like the aggression in his expression one bit.

"Kate." His voice cut across the lobby as he approached. It might not be his place to interrupt what was clearly a personal conversation, but Kate was personal to him, and that made her his business.

Kate stopped talking at the sight of him, and her wide eyes shifted from the man to him and back again. "Alec. I was looking for you," she said, but her voice lacked any warmth that could convince him her words were true. "You handed me the wrong file, it seems."

As soon as she thrust the manila folder at him, he realized his error. In his rush that morning, he had handed her his notes for the meeting with Mason. The notes he hadn't needed to refer to again. The notes that proved he was exactly the man everyone thought he was. The man he didn't want to be.

"Kate, you don't understand—"

"Oh, I understand." Her laugh was bitter, and his chest burned at the sound. "I understand all too well." She swept her hand over the man next to her. "Alec, this is Jake. Jake *Lambert*," she added meaningfully.

Alec frowned. Jake. It was the same Jake. Jake Lambert. Mason's son. Kate's ex.

Jake kept his eyes trained on Kate. Any doubt that those two didn't share a history was erased as quickly as the hope of ever making things right with her again. "Remember what I said, Kate. Every story has two sides."

With a hard glance at Alec, he stormed off.

Kate folded her arms across her chest and narrowed her eyes on Alec. "Is that true, Alec? Every story has two sides?"

Alec held up a hand. "Kate, you've misunderstood."

"That's what everyone keeps telling me. What were the papers then, Alec? Was this all planned? Did you know that I was engaged to Jake? You sure seem to do your homework—after all, you had all this planned when you came to Misty Point. Were you looking for inside tips, something to help you land the business?"

Alec heaved a sigh. There was no hiding it. "I didn't know about your connection to Mason's son."

"But you still had this planned all week? Knowing what it meant to your brother? To me?" Her voice cracked on the last word, and he closed his eyes at the sound. "I have to go," she said, turning to leave.

"Kate." He took a step toward her. "If you'll just let me explain."

But there was no excuse. The notes she had found were real. There was no denying his plans. He had chosen not to go through with them, but it was simply too late. The intention had been there, and that was incriminating enough.

"There's nothing to explain, Alec. It was all explained to me right there in that file. You're *exactly* the person Elizabeth said you were. The person she warned me about. And I didn't listen. I didn't listen," she said quietly, shaking her head.

"Then listen to me now." He raised his hand to grab her arm and then thought better of it. "I never meant to hurt you."

"But you did, Alec. And I'm not the only person you hurt." She searched his face. "Why bother coming to town at all? Why couldn't you have just said you couldn't make it? Why put us all through this?"

"It wasn't meant to go this far. This meeting today, it didn't come about until the other day, I promise." He waited, and seeing the way her stance softened a bit, continued. "I came to town to meet with Mason on Monday. Then I stayed around to see if there was any way William might rejoin the firm. The business is in trouble—"

She closed her eyes. Held up a hand. "I've heard enough. I have to go."

"Kate."

"Goodbye, Alec." She backed away toward the door, the distance between them growing one step at a time before he knew it was too late to stop her. "I hope it was worth it to you. And I hope that you find what you're looking for," she said before she was gone.

* * *

Kate was already out the door before he could catch up with her. He stood on the porch where just a week ago he'd sat on a wicker chair, watching her march out on him over something stupid he'd said. But that time it was still lighthearted. Maybe even a little fun. And that time all he'd had to do was call her name and she'd come back.

He knew it would take a lot more than that to get her back again.

Alec ran a hand through his hair, cursing to himself as he glanced at his watch. He'd see her at the wedding, but he didn't want to wait until then. He needed to explain, to her, and to William.

William. No doubt that's where she was going. To warn him. She'd never let him explain, never let him tell her that he'd spoken to his father this morning. That he wouldn't be attending the meeting. That he'd made his choice.

In the distance he could see that the tents were already being set up near the shoreline, a reminder of the events that were under way, the plan that was in motion. Had he ruined it? Had he been too late?

There was only one way to find out.

Turning to go back inside to get his car keys from his hotel suite, he came face-to-face with Jake Lambert, who stared stonily at him from the entrance to the lobby.

"I hadn't realized when we met that you're Alec Montgomery." His gaze was cool.

"My father will be handling the meeting today," Alec said, still moving toward the elevator bank. "I'll be attending my brother's wedding."

"I didn't realize you knew Kate. How'd that come about?"

Alec thought back on the dinner he'd spent with Elizabeth and her family at Kate's parents' home and felt his defenses grow. Here was a man who could have been a part of that, a loving, warm, bustling family, and instead he'd turned his nose up, broken promises, and broken hearts.

He stopped. Nailed the jackass with a hard look. "My brother's marrying Kate's best friend. We're practically family." Family. He liked the sound of that.

Jake cocked an eyebrow. "Then I'm going to tell you what I told Kate. Whatever you hear from Charlotte, you have to consider the source."

Alec frowned, not understanding where the guy was going with this but not liking it either. "You made your choices with Charlotte," he said.

Jake took a step forward. "That's right, I did. But it doesn't mean I'm that baby's father. With a girl like Charlotte... well, I think she's shown what she's all about."

Alec fought the urge to punch the guy in the nose. God knew he deserved it. "I don't know about that, but I do know that I can see what you're all about. And I don't like it."

He brushed past the man, trying to digest what he'd just heard and wondering just how much Kate had learned before he'd interrupted their conversation. From what he could tell, she didn't know what he knew.

All the more reason to find her and set things right. For everyone.

Chapter Twenty-Five

Kate knew she should have checked on the tent setup, but if there was a problem, she was reachable by phone. Instead she took a detour, stopped at Harbor Street Café, slowly sipped a latte, gathering up the courage to talk to William. To warn him, and probably, she knew, break his heart.

She'd taken the long way home, each mile closer filling her with dread, until she couldn't stall any longer. It was time to stop hiding.

She blinked back tears as she pulled the car to a stop in her driveway and stared at the house across the hedge. She should have known that it was all too good to be true, that Elizabeth knew what she was talking about, that she wouldn't misjudge someone the way Kate had so many times.

She hesitated, unable to get out of the car and cross the lawn, even though she knew she should, even though she knew she had to. Not just as the wedding planner, but as...a friend.

She closed her eyes, pushing aside that little part of herself that still wanted to believe Alec could be different, trying to ignore the urgency in his voice, the pleading look in his eyes. He'd been caught in the act, scrambling to find a way out of his mess without looking like a complete jerk. That's all it was.

Or was it?

Enough. The man was a jerk. A big one, at that. And she of all people should know how to spot one.

She pushed open the car door, just in time to see her mother's silver sedan pull in. Well, great. She didn't want to have a conversation about Charlotte. Not now.

"Hi there." She smiled, hoping to mask her feelings as she walked over to greet her mother, but it was no use. Maura took one look at her and frowned.

"What's wrong?"

What wasn't?

Kate smiled a little bigger, but she could feel the tears shining in her eyes. "Nothing. Just busy. Wedding day and all!"

"Oh, honey." There was the dreaded head tilt. Here it came. "It's hard, I know. But your turn *will* come."

Kate could only nod. She struggled to swallow against the lump in her throat. Would her time come? And did she even want it to? She wasn't so sure anymore. If anything, she was less sure now than she'd been a year ago.

Maura reached out and gave Kate's hand a squeeze. "Just think of how much this means to Elizabeth."

"Oh, I know how much this means to her all right, and that's why . . . " She shook her head and furiously brushed at a hot tear that escaped.

"Honey." Maura's voice lilted with concern and she squinted

at Kate. "Is this really because Elizabeth and William are getting married?"

Or is it because Charlotte was back in town? That's what she was really implying.

"It's because they might not be getting married, Mom. Or because if they do, the day might be ruined. And it's my fault. I should have known. I should have listened!" If she'd heeded her best friend's advice, kept an eye on Alec instead of falling for his charm, then maybe all this could have been avoided, or at least detected sooner.

"Okay, you're going to have to fill me in." Maura led Kate over to the small garden bench tucked under the tree near her garage. They were hidden, out of view of William and Elizabeth's house, and Kate was grateful for it. Just seeing it was a reminder of how much excitement had gone into this single day, and how much everyone stood to lose.

"You know William's brother?" It felt good to admit this, to tell someone the truth, even if it was to her mom, someone she had pushed away this past year, because she didn't know what else to do. Now, sitting side by side, her mother's familiar hand in hers, she realized how much she missed these talks.

"Alec. Of course. Such a polite young man." Her mother's smile was wistful.

Kate pinched her lips at that. "Elizabeth warned me about him. She was worried he would do something to ruin their wedding. I thought she was being silly, that it was wedding jitters and all that. But she was right, Mom. And I didn't listen."

"But you spent all that time with him this week!" Maura cut in, but then her expression took on a knowing look. "Oh. I see."

"I liked him, Mom. I . . . felt excited at the thought of seeing him. He made me start to believe that there are better men than Jake out there. Men that won't lie to me. Betray me." Her voice broke, and she closed her eyes again. Fool. What a fool she'd been.

"But there are men like that, Kate," Maura said softly.

"Well, not Alec," Kate said firmly. "He wasn't the person I thought he was. He's the person Elizabeth has always insisted he is."

Kate had expected her mother to be outraged, to demand to know why she felt this way, but instead her brows pinched and she turned thoughtful. "Are you sure about that?"

"Yes, I'm sure! I couldn't be more sure!" She had an entire file folder to prove it. "He was planning on skipping the wedding, Mom, in favor of a business meeting. With the Lamberts."

"The Lamberts?" Maura paled. "You mean Mason and—"

"Jake," Kate finished for her.

Kate followed her gaze, thinking of what Jake had said, his cryptic words, but decided now wasn't the time to discuss Charlotte. Kate just needed her mom right now. No history. No family problems. Just mother and daughter. The way it used to be.

"Sometimes there's more to the story than meets the eye." Maura sighed. "Talk to him, Kate."

"Mom, no offense, but you don't know the whole story!"

"I do," her mother said firmly. "Talk to him. For me."

Maura jutted her head to the road, where Alec was standing, his hands thrust in his pockets, his frown visible even from this distance.

Her mother released her hand, but not before saying, "You always had a good sense of people, when you listened to that little voice. Listen to it now. And...believe in second chances."

Kate knew her mother was referring to Charlotte as much as she was implying she should forgive Alec, but she wasn't ready to do either of those things right now. She had to focus on the facts, and the fact was that her best friend's wedding was about to be ruined, just like her own had been.

★ ★ ★

Kate stood, but she didn't make any motion to walk closer to him. "Unless you're here to tell me there is no meeting and you will be attending the wedding, I have nothing to say to you."

"I'm here to tell you that I am attending the wedding," Alec replied, and Kate's eyes turned sharply on his. "You wouldn't let me explain."

She hesitated at the edge of the path, glancing from William's house back to him. "But...the file."

Alec sighed. "I'm not going to lie to you, Kate. And I wasn't trying to."

"Then what do you call what you were doing?"

"Figuring things out," he replied. And he had. It just might be too late. He motioned to the bench. "Can we sit?"

Kate seemed to waver, but after a long pause, nodded. Noticing the firm set of her mouth, he made sure to sit as close to the edge as the space allowed, even though he wanted nothing more than to reach over, take her hand, kiss her mouth, and bring them right back to last night.

"This week...I came to town to see if I could convince my brother to come back, rejoin the firm."

Her brow pinched. "And what about the wedding?"

He wasn't proud, but he also knew there was no way to move forward unless he was completely honest. Kate deserved to know the truth.

"Whether or not he got married wasn't my concern. If he got married, but came to Boston, great. But if he couldn't have both...I wanted him back, Kate. My dad...my dad needed him back. That's the difference."

"I don't follow," Kate said. Her eyes were flat and hooded, and Alec shifted forward, eager to close this distance that had grown between them.

"The business is in trouble. When William left, big clients followed. They liked working with him. I don't blame them." He gave a low chuckle, even though it wasn't funny. "The way we saw it, the Montgomery Group had less than a year unless our revenue increased. We needed the old clients back or some big new ones to replace them."

"Like Mason Lambert," Kate said.

Alec nodded. "The thing is, though, for me...it was more than just the business. I missed my brother, Kate. I missed having him at the office. Maybe that makes me sound selfish. Maybe I am. But...he's all I have."

Her expression softened at this, and she met his eye, looking away quickly when she did. "And now? What's changed? Why did you cancel the meeting?"

"Oh, the meeting's still on. My dad's attending it without me," Alec added, seeing the confusion in her eyes. He pulled in a breath, releasing it slowly. "You asked me the other day what

I wanted. I never knew. I never stopped to think about it. I was too busy hiding, too focused on trying to make the best of what I had, rather than finding something more."

He reached out and set a hand on hers. He hated the way she flinched at his touch. "This is what I want, Kate. I want laughter, and a dog, and a home to come back to at the end of the day. I want to put myself out there, not live behind walls. I want you."

★ ★ ★

His hand was warm, sturdy and strong, and he didn't release it, even when she didn't hold it back. She tried to listen to her heart, to search for that little voice that might tell her to shake him off, stand up, walk away. But it didn't.

"Can't we start over, Kate?"

Kate frowned and stood up. Forcing physical space between them would make it easier to think clearly, to remember what he'd done... until she considered his reasons for it. Until now this house had been her haven. Her safe place. Her fresh start.

And she'd invited him into it.

"Stop hiding." His voice was clear, firm, and gentle enough to stop her in her tracks.

"What's that supposed to mean?" But even as she said it, she knew he was right. She had spent the past year of her life hiding. Hiding from anyone and anything that caused her distress. Jake. Charlotte. Her parents.

"It means there are some things in life you have to face and not try to deny. I did it for too long, Kate. I don't want you to make the same mistake."

"And what is it I am trying to deny exactly?"

He stood and walked forward until he was standing right in front of her, forcing her to look up into his eyes. He brushed a strand of hair from her cheek, grazing his thumb over her skin. She closed her eyes to the touch, hating just how good it felt almost as much as she relished it. "Me. You and me. Us."

Kate stilled. This was it. A turning point. She could move forward, dare to try, or she could go into her house, shut the door, stay in her safe place. She swallowed hard. "There is no us," she said with more determination than she felt.

His mouth curved into a half smile. "There could be."

"No," she chuckled softly, thinking of how close he'd come to breaking her heart and deceiving her. "No, there can't."

"Why not? Give me one good answer why, and then I'll go and leave you alone forever."

Alone forever. Elizabeth's words echoed in her head. Was that really what she wanted? She drew a shaky breath. It didn't matter what she wanted anymore. It mattered what made sense. And opening her heart didn't make any sense at all. She had done it twice now, and look how it had ended.

Only this time it didn't have to end.

"Love doesn't last," she said simply, forcing herself to stay strong.

A shadow passed over Alec's face before he challenged, "I used to think that, too. But this week I saw that it can. I want to believe it might for us."

She wanted to believe that, too. More than she wanted to admit. To herself. To him. She shook her head. She knew how it ended. She'd been there before.

"You're just saying that because you've been hurt, but don't you see, I'm not here to hurt you, Kate. I'm here because for the first time in my life I am standing where I want to be. This is what I want. This. Right here. You and me."

God, he was good. But not good enough. She took a step backward. She really needed to get away from him. She needed to get inside, with sweet little Henry, curl up on the bed with a good book, and shut him out. Shut the world out.

"I know you, Kate, and I know that you love what you do because it's a part of you. You're a hopeless romantic." He grinned.

"Hopeless," Kate snorted. That was the word all right.

"Fine." Alec straightened his back. "If you're not going to be the romantic in this relationship, I will."

"What?" Kate faltered. This wasn't something he was supposed to say. He was supposed to...give up. Walk away. Go back to Boston. His business.

But he didn't want those things anymore, did he? No. He wanted her.

"I want you, Kate," he murmured as he grazed a hand over her hip, the other reaching around the curve of her waist. His face was so close, she could smell the musk of his skin and see the gold flecks in his deep brown eyes. "I never wanted anything in my life more, and I took a chance—a big chance—and left everything else behind to try and have the life I want to have. I have no idea how it will turn out, but I know it has to be better than what it was. Take a chance on me, too. Take a chance on this."

He lifted his hand to brush the back of his fingers against her cheek, and she felt herself melt under the heat of his touch. He bent down and grazed his lips to hers, slowly at first, until she felt her resistance weaken and she opened her mouth to his. She combed her fingers through the hair at the nape of his neck, not caring that Elizabeth or William could drive by at any point, or that if Meredith found out about this, she would be fired for good. All that mattered was that Alec was in her arms. That he had found her. And that he had made her believe in love again.

Chapter Twenty-Six

⸻

Kate checked her watch with a start. It was later than she'd expected, and if she had any hope of checking on the tents, she'd have to leave now. "I have to check on some things before I meet the girls," she explained.

Alec reached down and took both of her hands in his. "There's something you should know. I didn't come here alone."

Kate straightened in alarm. "There's someone in the car, you mean?" Only then did she realize the engine was still running, the soft purr of it noticeable on the quiet street.

"When you left the hotel, I went looking for you. I tried your parents' house first." He blew out a breath as Kate's heart began to hammer, trying to make sense of what he was telling her. "It's Charlotte, Kate. I think you should talk to your sister."

"What?" She pulled back, feeling the heat spread to her face as she stared at him, and then glanced at the car. The windows were tinted, and she had no way of seeing in, but her sister... Her sister was watching her. Sitting there. Waiting.

Those phone calls...

"Don't be mad, Kate. It was something Jake said. Something I thought he might have told you. I thought you might have gone to your parents' house, and when I didn't find you, I talked to your sister." He stepped forward, took her hand again, gave it a firm, tight squeeze and didn't let go, even when she wanted him to, even when a part of her wanted to turn and run into the house nearly as much as she wanted to walk to that car.

She blinked back tears, looking up at him. "You know what she did."

"And you know what kind of man Jake Lambert is," he replied. He arched an eyebrow, silencing anything else she might have said. "This week I learned what family is all about. It's about moving forward, accepting people for who they are even if you don't like some things they've done. The past can't be undone. But it can be...put in its place."

Kate nodded, knowing he was right. She looked at the car again, thinking of those calls, knowing it must have taken courage for Charlotte to reach out, and knowing that she was sitting there right now, waiting. And hoping.

"Thank you," Kate whispered. She let his hand go and walked slowly to the car, her heart pounding as she thought of what she might say, how she might react, but everything she came up with disappeared when the door opened before she was even halfway down the path, and out came her sister. Holding a baby.

★ ★ ★

Charlotte stood pale faced with wide eyes, her auburn hair pulled back in a disheveled ponytail, staring back at her. The baby was small. An infant. It was wrapped in a light pink blanket, its tiny hands curled into small fists below its chin.

"This is Audrey," Charlotte said quietly, her large green eyes filling with tears. "Your niece."

"My..." Kate blinked, trying to understand. This was Charlotte's baby. Charlotte and... Jake's.

There are two sides to the story. I don't need Charlotte making trouble.

She looked at her sister. Gone were the sparkling eyes and the big smile and that laugh, that infectious laugh. Her sister looked like she hadn't slept in months. She probably hadn't.

"It's Jake's," Charlotte confirmed, without having to be asked. She pinched her lips, shifting the baby in her arms. She struggled to make eye contact. "Not that he'll admit it."

Kate frowned deeply. Of course not. Jake wasn't the kind of man to honor promises or responsibilities. And Charlotte. Flirty, fun-loving Charlotte... Maybe Charlotte wasn't the kind of person she'd started to think she was, either. She'd changed. And not just in physical appearance. She had grown up. It was there, in her eyes, when she looked down at her daughter, when she tucked the blanket a little higher.

The Charlotte from last summer probably wouldn't have been chosen to babysit the neighborhood kids. But the woman standing before her was a mother. Her little sister. A mother. It didn't seem possible.

Charlotte looked up, her big eyes searching. "I didn't do it on purpose, Kate. It's not how it looks. I promise. Jake—he saw me at a bar one night, told me you'd broken up with him, gave me this sob story about the wedding being called off..."

The lying cad. Why had she believed his story, when he was

capable of admitting to cheating on her? Why hadn't she cut her sister some slack, assumed there must be more, that her own sister wouldn't deliberately hurt her?

Because she'd been too hurt. Too blindsided. Because she'd trusted Jake and he'd broken that trust. Not just for him, but for everyone else.

Kate sucked in a breath. All this time... "And you believed him. Just like I did." The lies... all lies.

Charlotte shrugged. "I shouldn't have believed him. Or I should have called you, checked the facts, checked to see how you were. Instead I fell for his line. His charm. I didn't know he was using me as some pawn for a clear-cut break with you. It was that or be cut off by his family, you know. That's why he did it. By the time I knew the truth, you believed something else. I didn't blame you for hating me. What I did was unforgiveable."

Everything was so clear now. So... obvious. His family had never been supportive, but she'd never considered they'd take it this far. "He should have just told me. Ended it. He didn't need to break us apart."

"I don't think he was thinking of anything but himself." Charlotte sighed. "For what it's worth, Kate, I think he did love you. Maybe he didn't think he'd have the guts to end it decently. I think he used me to be sure there was no going back. That it was over."

Maybe there was some truth in that, but she didn't care anymore if Jake had ever loved her. She had been jilted, but Charlotte had fared much worse. Charlotte, and this sweet little baby who was her niece, had been abandoned. Looking at the little baby now, Kate knew she'd go through all of it again. The same, she could tell by the way her sister looked at her little daughter, could be said for Charlotte.

"I guess I got what I deserved in the end." Charlotte sniffed.

"Don't say that," Kate said firmly. "We were both betrayed by that man."

"But I shouldn't have gone along with him that night. And then afterwards...how could I not? For the sake of my baby I wanted to try and make it work. I followed him to Boston. I know it probably looked like we ran off together." Charlotte frowned. "Can you ever forgive me?"

I already have. Just seeing the remorse in her sister's eyes was all the relief Kate needed to wash away the pain she had felt for so long. She just wished that her sister wasn't suffering as a result. "Can you ever forgive me for not being there when you needed me the most?" she asked, leaning down to touch the hand of the baby girl resting peacefully in Charlotte's arms. Her skin was soft as silk; she had never felt anything like it.

"I've managed," Charlotte sighed. "Mom and Dad have helped a lot since I called them."

Kate almost didn't dare broach what she suspected to be true. "And Jake?"

Charlotte shook her head. "He won't take my calls. He's never met his daughter."

The bastard. Well, this was it. The end. Kate had given that man enough of her time. Today was the day she let go of the past. Today was the day she didn't just move forward, forcing one foot in front of the other. Today was the day she looked forward.

"I can't tell you how much it means to me to see you." Charlotte reached out and touched her arm. "I thought you would never speak to me again."

"I'm sorry you felt that way. I'm sorry…for a lot of things. I should have answered the phone when you called. I just wasn't ready for what I might hear."

Her phone started ringing in her bag, alerting her that it was time to leave for the hotel, to go over a last-minute walk-through with the hotel liaison.

Kate shook her head in regret. "I wish I could stay. But Elizabeth's getting married today."

"Mom told me." Charlotte smiled. "I'm happy for her. William seems like a good guy from the few times I met him last summer. And his brother is pretty great, too."

Kate stiffened, wondering if she should be worried, if Charlotte was going to make a play for him. But then she saw the way Charlotte was gazing down at her baby and she knew she didn't need to worry about that anymore. Charlotte had learned her lesson. The hard way. But more than that, she'd changed.

"He is pretty great." Kate grinned. "How about tomorrow morning? Want to come over?"

"Wouldn't miss it," Charlotte said, reaching in for a hug.

Kate kissed her sleeping niece on the forehead, wishing she could scoop her into her arms and snuggle her, but knowing it wouldn't be fair to wake her. "Tomorrow then," she said quietly, realizing she could barely wait for the day to come.

She walked slowly up the path to where Alec was sitting on the bench, waiting for her. "Oh, Alec, I should have answered the phone. I should have known something was wrong. I was so busy thinking of how angry I was, how much I had been hurt—"

"Don't blame yourself," Alec said, pulling her down to sit beside him. "It's all going to be fine now, right?"

Kate thought of spending an entire day with her sister and niece, catching up, laughing, healing wounds she'd thought could never be mended. "You know, I think it is."

Silence stretched and Alec finally spoke. "She's on her own, I take it."

Kate shook her head. "Not anymore. Not after today. Thanks to you."

Beside her, she heard Alec release a long, angry sigh. "That fellow of yours is a real jerk."

Kate nodded. That much could never be argued. "There's just one part of your assessment that I have to disagree with."

Alec looked at her sharply. "What's that?"

"Jake's not my fellow."

"Oh." Alec's lips tugged into a slow grin, and Kate reached out to hold his hand. This might end in disaster, but she'd never know unless she tried. And she knew that there was only way to live life without regret now. And that was to take a chance when your heart told you it was the right thing to do.

"I was sort of hoping that maybe you could be my fellow."

Alec's smile broadened. "I'd like that. If you don't mind seeing me every day."

Her pulse quickened at what he was implying. "So you're staying in Misty Point, then?"

He nodded. "Joining William's practice. I told him so this morning." He grinned.

"And your dad?"

Alec pulled in a breath and released it heavily. "My dad is who he is. William realized that long before I did. Maybe the family business wasn't meant to last forever. Maybe it's going to have another chance, here, with us running it."

Kate licked her lips. She wasn't one for impulsive decisions. But she was one for leaps of faith. "I've decided to make some career changes, too. I'm going out on my own. I'll give my notice on Monday."

Alec looked at her thoughtfully. "I was wondering when you would come to your senses."

"The future's looking bright," Kate said, admiring the man in front of her.

And full of possibility.

Epilogue

⬥⬥⬥

Kate smoothed her pink bridesmaid dress and shifted her bouquet to her left hand, so she could pull open the curtain of the tent where the bridal party was gathered, waiting for their cue from the string quartet. The sun was shining; the music from the instruments was mixing with the call of the seagulls that swooped overhead and out to the sea beyond. Kate did a quick scan of the guests, just in case there were a few stragglers, but she stopped counting when she saw her sister sitting in the fourth row, beside her parents.

Well, crap. She hadn't seen this coming.

"Elizabeth." She licked her lips, trying to figure out how to word this to her friend and wondering if she should even bother. The bride might not even notice the extra guest sitting in the audience. Her eyes would be on the groom, after all.

Still. "There's something you should know."

Elizabeth's eyes burst open in panic. "Oh my God. Is my dress ripped? Do I have a stain?" She craned her neck to inspect the back, and Kate held out a hand to settle her arm, letting the curtain fall behind them, shielding her once more from the view.

"No. Your dress is fine. It's . . . my sister. It seems she's crashed the wedding."

Because that's something that Charlotte would do. She closed her eyes, feeling the disappointment land heavy in her chest. She'd dared to think something had changed. Now, everything felt uncertain again.

"She didn't crash the wedding." Elizabeth gave a small laugh. "I meant to tell you, but . . . well, I had other things on my mind." She gestured to her veil.

"You mean, you knew?"

Elizabeth nodded. "Our moms talked. When I heard what happened . . . Well, it didn't seem right not to invite her. I figured it might be a nice way for you guys to spend a little time together."

Kate felt her eyes brim with tears. "You did this for me? But . . . I know how you feel about Charlotte."

"Look, it's you I care about. I'm on your side, always. And if you want to welcome Charlotte back into your life, then I support that." Elizabeth grinned. "However, I'm not really sure how this is going to impact those seating arrangements."

The seating arrangements. A few days ago something like this would have sent her into a panic, but today, Kate didn't care. All she cared was that her best friend was going to have the best day she could.

And if possible, she might just try to do the same.

A shiver of excitement chased its way down Kate's spine as the string quartet gained momentum. Kate glanced over at Elizabeth, who gave her a nervous smile from behind her veil.

"Are you ready?" Her voice caught in her throat and came

out in a hushed whisper. She clutched her best friend's hand, willing herself not to tear up at how radiant Elizabeth looked in her wedding gown.

She'd seen hundreds of brides on their wedding day, after all, but this one was different, she knew. This time, it was extra special.

"More than I thought I would be," Elizabeth admitted, but her smile shone in her eyes.

Kate marveled at how calm Elizabeth was—of all the brides she had ever worked with, Elizabeth stood, waiting for her cue, with more poise and composure than she had seen before.

It was a good sign, Kate thought. It meant she was marrying her true love.

Kate poked her head out of the curtain to make sure everyone was in place and felt Elizabeth wiggle beside her. "He's actually there," her friend breathed. A month ago this type of comment would have made Kate's breath catch, would have brought back the horrible reminder that her own groom hadn't stuck around to see the wedding, but there was none of that now; those days were over.

"Alec looks handsome today," Elizabeth observed, and Kate pulled back, turning in surprise.

"I thought you didn't like him!"

Elizabeth shrugged. "What can I say? He's grown on me this week."

Kate's stomach turned over as a smile took over her face. "It's almost wedding time."

Elizabeth stood quietly clutching her flowers, her cheeks naturally flushed, her eyes bright and shiny, and Kate knew that this was what it all came down to in the end. This moment. She had wanted so much to give her dearest friend the wedding of her dreams, but despite all her efforts, she wasn't the person to offer that gift. There was only one person who could make today everything it was meant to be, and that person was already standing at the altar. Waiting for his bride.

Her family members had begun chatting in hushed and excited voices around her, and Colleen and Bree were smoothing her veil and adjusting the train of her dress. Kate had never seen her friend so happy, and she knew that no matter what happened today, the wedding was going to be perfect. It wasn't about the favors or the food or even the cake. It was about the beginning of her life with the man she loved.

The music shifted and Kate changed from maid of honor to wedding planner, checking on the flower girl and ring bearer one last time to make sure the rings were still on the pillow and that the basket of flower petals hadn't already been tipped.

The procession was starting, and Kate instructed the first bridesmaid to begin her march. She watched as each of the women before her disappeared through the curtain and onto the pathway along the sand, only daring to give one last glance behind her at Elizabeth before she clutched her bouquet tightly in two hands, waiting for her turn.

It wasn't the walk she'd imagined she'd be taking a year ago, and the bouquet wasn't the one she'd chosen for herself, and the man who came to take her arm wasn't the one she'd envisioned . . . He was so much better.

"You're more nervous than the bride," Alec whispered in her ear.

"I just want it to be perfect for her," she said, emotions making her voice thick.

"It already is. Look," Alec murmured, and Kate followed his gaze to look at Elizabeth, who stood at the back of the aisle, her hand hooked through her father's arm, her joy obvious to everyone in attendance.

"Maybe the next time we're walking down the aisle, it will be at our own wedding," Alec whispered as the children started their walk down the aisle, the flower girl scattering petals in the sand. The *aww* from the crowd always made her smile, every time.

"Aren't you getting a little ahead of yourself?" she replied, even though her pulse skipped a beat at the thought of it.

"I've learned a lot of things the hard way, but there's one thing I always stick to," Alec whispered.

"What's that?"

"When something good comes along, don't let it pass you by."

"At any cost?" Kate asked, thinking back to how far Alec had been willing to go time and again for something he wanted.

She felt his eyes on her and turned to meet his eyes. "Some things are worth the sacrifice, Kate. And you are the best thing to come along in a long time. Probably ever."

Kate beamed and looked away, knowing she still had a job to do. Not as a wedding planner. But as Elizabeth's maid of honor. She would stand at the altar and watch her best friend walk down the aisle. She would stand at her side as she pledged her love to the man who had stolen her heart and would now promise to treasure it.

Arm in arm, Kate and Alec finished their walk down the aisle, smiling faces guiding their way. For years she had stood at the back of the room, watching as bride after bride strode down the aisle, hope swelling her heart each time as she thought that maybe, just maybe, her turn would someday come. She may not be wearing a white dress or veil today, and the man who had her heart might be standing beside her rather than in front of her, but she felt every bit as special as she hoped she would feel when her turn came. It was a feeling of hope, and excitement, and perfect contentment.

And she had a feeling this was just a practice run.

Single mom Charlotte Daniels is slowly winning back her sister Kate's trust. But when a relationship with their high-profile client turns personal, Charlotte fears her latest indiscretion will cost her more than just the business.

A preview of
The Winter Wedding Plan
follows.

Chapter One

Charlotte Daniels knew that it was customary for resolutions to take place on New Year's Eve, but considering the current state of her affairs, she wasn't exactly in a position to wait that long this year, and so, in one of those strange bursts of optimism that border slightly on denial and usually only come about when things are particularly dire, she decided that Thanksgiving would just have to do.

First up: she'd organize her apartment. Get the closets in order and make the bed every morning before work—in other words, customary adult responsibilities that she just didn't seem to have time for these days but would make time for, starting today! Next (and this was a big one), she'd get her finances together and pay back that loan her parents had so generously given her for a security deposit on an apartment when she'd moved back to Misty Point this past summer. And third, she'd focus on the future, not the past with all its icky mistakes, and start building the life that her daughter deserved.

It started today. About a month before Christmas. Baby's first Christmas, she thought with a smile as she walked into her parents' dining room and tucked Audrey into the nicked wooden high chair that had been passed down from her sister, Kate, to her and now to her seven-month-old daughter. Charlotte felt her eyes begin to mist when she thought of how her family had opened their arms to her surprise baby girl. It was more than Audrey's father had ever done... Not that any of them would be discussing him today. Or any other day for that matter. No, he was part of her past. Not her future. And she wasn't going to be dwelling on her past anymore, was she?

Nope. It was on the list. A resolution. One she was sticking to.

"Doesn't Audrey look sweet in her new Thanksgiving dress!" Charlotte's father grinned as he carried two bottles of wine into the room and set them on the table her mother had covered in an orange linen cloth, just for the occasion. The moment his hands were free, he reached for the camera that was within arm's reach at all times, and began snapping some candids of Audrey, who was happily chewing on her fingers, a habit she'd picked up when she started teething. Charlotte stifled a sigh and leaned in close, smiling into the lens and hoping that the dark circles under her eyes from lack of sleep weren't accentuated by the overhead lighting.

"It fits perfectly," Charlotte commented once Frank had reluctantly turned off the camera and positioned it close to his place setting. There was no denying that Audrey was the best-dressed baby in their small Rhode Island town, not that she could take any of the credit. Any money she had went to the necessities, but soon that would all change. Soon she hoped to give her only child all that she deserved. She'd already started by giving her the gift of family. Next it would be a nice home. And after that... Well, some might say that a father figure would benefit Audrey, but Charlotte wasn't taking any risks in that department any time soon. If ever.

Charlotte's mother came into the room with a bowl of roasted squash. "Before you leave tonight, remind me that I have a few more things to give you."

"Mom." Charlotte felt her face flush. She darted her eyes to the doorway, happy that the friends and family who had gathered for the day were still in the kitchen, snacking on appetizers. Her mother was forever buying gifts lately, and while the clothes and toys were understandable, things like paper towels or laundry detergent made her always feel a strange mix of gratitude and humiliation.

Maura winked. "Just a few little things I couldn't pass up. On sale for a steal. I couldn't resist!"

Charlotte inwardly cringed. It wouldn't be exactly easy to ask for yet another favor tonight when her parents were already offering up so much.

She wrapped a bib around Audrey's neck—another gift, this one from her sister, Kate, and her fiancé, Alec—and snapped it closed. Her stomach felt funny as she mentally rehearsed the speech she would give. It had all seemed so much easier when she'd practiced in the shower this morning while Audrey took a brief nap.

"Turkey coming through!" Kate cried out now as Uncle Bill carried the large bird into the room and set it down on the center of the table.

Her cousin Bree, a strict vegetarian, hovered in the doorway, her top lip curling slightly. "Please tell me I will be eating more than mashed potatoes today."

"There's bread." Bree's mother, Charlotte's aunt Ellen, handed Bree a basket of rolls and disappeared back into the kitchen.

"Yum. Bread." Bree's older but considerably less mature brother, Matt, snatched one and took a large bite, causing Bree to swat him on the arm.

"It's a good thing I had the sense to bring a salad," Bree muttered.

"Out of curiosity," Alec said as he came into the room. "Would you ever date a carnivore, Bree?"

Bree's cheeks turned pink at the question. "Why? Did you have someone specific in mind?"

Now it was Alec's turn to look uncomfortable. "Just curious is all." He pulled out a chair and quickly settled himself into it.

Bree pinched her lips as she dropped the basket onto the table. "Good. The last thing I need right now is to be set up."

Charlotte quietly seconded that sentiment as everyone took their seats, which wasn't an easy feat this year with so many people tucked around the table. This year Alec's brother, William, and his wife, also Kate's best friend, Elizabeth, had joined with Elizabeth's parents and brother. The two families were merging in a way, expanding the holiday cheer, and Charlotte was happy for it. She liked William. And she'd always liked Elizabeth. Even if she did make her feel a little uncomfortable these days.

She slid into the chair next to Elizabeth, feeling out the situation. Sure enough, Elizabeth's smile was a little strained. Well, who could blame her? She was a loyal friend. And Charlotte...well, Charlotte hadn't exactly been the most loyal sister in the recent past. And rectifying that was her top resolution.

"I think we're ready to eat!" Frank said, his eyes shining as he practically licked his lips.

"The potatoes!" Maura suddenly cried as she started to push back her chair.

Charlotte, who had bent to pick up the spoon Audrey had dropped, stood and set her hand on her mother's shoulders. "Allow me."

It was the least she could do, considering the pumpkin cheesecake she'd baked that morning had inexplicably curdled in the oven while the graham cracker crust had burnt to a crisp, causing the smoke alarms in her apartment to go off until she'd been forced to open the front door for thirty straight minutes and sit with Audrey in the car to stay warm. The one thing she was asked to contribute, and she'd managed to ruin it. She'd brought a bottle of wine instead. Nice. Traditional. Perfectly acceptable once she'd wiped off the dust and checked the label, hoping that the age of it was a good thing, since it had been sitting in the back of her pantry for months and *might* have belonged to the former tenants.

She walked into the kitchen, her eyes coming to rest on her sister Kate's magazine-cover-worthy apple tart, complete with a perfect lattice crust and no doubt homemade vanilla bean ice cream to accompany it. Something Kate had whipped up when it was announced that Charlotte wouldn't be bringing the dessert after all.

Charlotte grumbled under her breath. Then, because she couldn't resist, flung open the freezer door and narrowed her eyes on the simple white carton that rested primly on the second shelf. Suspicion confirmed.

"I forgot the cranberries, too!" Her mother sighed as she came up behind her, but she paused when she noticed Charlotte's frown. "Honey, what's wrong?"

Charlotte closed the freezer with a guilty shrug. "Nothing." Yet so much all at once. "I just feel bad about my cheesecake." It was the first thing that came to mind, but she was horrified to realize a single hot tear had slipped down her cheek.

"Honey!" Maura's laugh was good-natured as she brushed the tear away with the pad of her thumb. "It's the thought that counts. Besides, we have this apple tart to enjoy. It looks beautiful, doesn't it?"

"Hmm." Charlotte felt her lips thin. She had spent Audrey's entire morning nap carefully following the recipe she had printed from the office yesterday. She'd even made a special trip to the grocery store for the ingredients last night, which had cost a pretty penny. By the time she'd pulled the mess from the oven and stared at it in complete bewilderment, wondering where exactly she had gone wrong, Audrey had started crying again, needing to be changed and fed. And then the smoke alarm started to blare...

Now Charlotte set a hand to her forehead. She was just tired, that was all. Running on interrupted sleep for months on end could do that to anyone. She was crying over a cheesecake, of all things. A curdled, inedible, burnt-to-the-edges cheesecake.

But she knew from the ache in her chest that it really was about so much more.

"I guess I just wonder if I'll ever get anything right," she said as she spooned the mashed potatoes from the pot that was warming on the stovetop into one of her mother's best serving bowls.

"We all make mistakes, Charlotte. Don't let them define you." Her mother's hand on her shoulder was kind, but her words were firm, and ones that Charlotte knew she should heed.

She finished filling the bowl slowly, wondering if now was the time to ask about moving back home for a while, just until she'd landed on steadier ground. No need to admit the extent of it. But even though she knew she had to ask—today—she couldn't bring her mouth to form the words. To admit that she'd tried. And failed. Again.

"I have the cranberries," Maura announced. "All set with the potatoes?"

The moment now lost, Charlotte nodded briskly and took a deep breath before following her mother back into the dining room, where everyone was clutching their forks, eager for the meal to begin.

As they did every Thanksgiving, each person went around the table and said what they were thankful for as her father carved the massive bird, which was a bit larger than usual this year.

"I'm thankful for the new additions to our Thanksgiving table," Maura said, giving Audrey a little kiss on the head. "We don't just have this precious little baby with us this year; we also have a fine young man. Alec, we're so happy to welcome you to the family."

Charlotte raised her glass to toast the happy couple on cue, but she couldn't help but feel a little uneasy at the turn of events. Her sister was engaged (for the second time, but no need to harp on those details just now), and Charlotte was sitting pretty all alone. No man was waiting for her at home tonight. No man had gotten down on one knee and popped the question.

Jake Lambert hadn't even met his daughter, much less acknowledged that she was his. Not that Charlotte would be admitting that to anyone. They all assumed he was contributing something, and she let them all think so. It was easier that way.

Alec's turn was next. "I'm grateful for a short engagement," he said with a mischievous grin.

"Oh, isn't that sweet," Maura said, tilting her head as she smiled wistfully.

"It's not for the reason you think, Mom," Kate corrected. She held out her plate as their father piled turkey onto it. "It's not that he can't wait to be married. It's that he knows he only has to tolerate all my wedding planning for another six weeks."

Alec held up his palms. "Guilty as charged. Who knew there were so many varieties of roses?"

From beside her, Bree raised her hand, eliciting a laugh from the table. "Alec, I could tell you just how many varieties of roses there are, but I don't think we have enough wine to keep you from panicking. Besides, I am happy to let you know that Kate has already been into my shop, and she has narrowed down her choices to two different looks. Two very different looks, I might add, but all the same, two."

Really? Charlotte frowned, wondering why she hadn't been let it on this earlier. So Kate had gone to Bree's flower shop, chatted about colors and arrangements and all that fun stuff, while Charlotte was either filing paperwork at the office they shared or sitting in her apartment with Audrey. Either way, she hadn't been invited.

She glanced at Elizabeth, who was nodding along casually. Sure enough.

"Well, if it were up to me, we'd have gone to city hall last month when I proposed," Alec said ruefully.

"That's what Frank and I did, and I've always regretted it," Maura said.

"That's what I try telling Alec." Kate shook her head. "But he's too practical."

"Aw, now..." Alec roped an arm over Kate's shoulders and gave her a peck on the cheek. "You know I want you to have the wedding of your dreams. I just don't want you losing sleep over it while you're planning it!"

Kate gave a resigned smile. "It's true that I have been losing some sleep. There are just so many hours in the day, and with client weddings to plan and Christmas parties, too, there's always something to take my attention away from our big day." She sighed as she poked at her plate. "Maybe we should have planned for something for spring. But I had my heart set on a winter wedding."

"January is a wonderful month to get married," Maura said. "A new year. A new beginning. And Misty Point is so pretty when it's covered with snow."

"I can help," Charlotte offered, eager to make herself useful, and not just because she wanted to preserve the good standing she had with her sister. She'd been working part-time in Kate's new event planning company since August, and every extra assignment would go that much further to bettering her circumstances and, from the sound of it, Kate's, too.

"I don't want to put too much pressure on you, with a new baby and all that..." Kate looked uncertain, and Charlotte had to clench her teeth from blurting out that the income from the event company was all she had in this world, now that she'd gone through the loan their parents had given her, at an alarming rate, mind you. That there were no monthly stipends from

Jake. That if anyone wanted to talk about pressure, it came in the form of the landlord breathing down her neck for November's rent check.

She forced a reassuring smile. "It's no pressure at all! I'm eager to build up my resume, and I really enjoy the work, Kate." Sure, it was a struggle to balance her schedule with Audrey at times. Her sitter wasn't always available, and she didn't have the funds for day care just yet, but she needed to work. And she wanted to work. To prove to herself that she could stick with something. And to prove to Kate—and everyone else at this table—that she wasn't the girl she'd once been.

"Well, next week is gearing up to be a tough one for me with two holiday parties and a fitting with my newest bridezilla. And I *had* hoped to finalize those floral arrangements..."

"Finally!" Bree blurted, shaking her head. She grabbed another roll from the basket and added it to her plate, which consisted solely of mashed potatoes and squash. The salad she had brought sat untouched at the far end of the table.

Kate eyed Charlotte, as if weighing her options. "All right, I'll bring you in full-time through the month, starting Monday."

Monday morning. Charlotte hoped the panic she felt didn't show in her face. She hadn't expected to go into the office until Tuesday afternoon, as usual, and she knew that her sitter was currently away for the holiday weekend in Connecticut. She supposed she could call her anyway, but Lisa hated short notice—always charged up for it, too, savvy opportunist that she was.

She squeezed the napkin in her lap, working through the logistics, and decided she had no alternative. Her mother still worked at the town library during the week. There was no one else to call on for a last-minute favor. And really, what choice did she have?

"Monday morning it is then," she said, feeling her spirits lift at the thought of a steadier paycheck.

"Wow, I feel like a load has been lifted from my shoulders already," Kate said through a smile, and Charlotte felt her heart warm as it did every time her sister paid her a compliment.

"Your turn, Kate," Frank said, steering the conversation back to the holiday tradition.

Kate reached over and slipped her hand onto Alec's. "I'm grateful for second chances," she said, and Charlotte found it hard to swallow the food she was chewing.

A second chance. That's what this was, all right. And she wasn't about to blow it. Last Thanksgiving Charlotte had been pregnant and alone, in a dark and musty basement apartment in Boston, twisted with anxiety, wondering if she would ever again be welcome in her childhood home. And now she was about to ask to move back into it. To admit that her second attempt to swing it on her own wasn't working out.

She reached for her wineglass and allowed herself a sip— only because she wouldn't be driving for a while. She'd stick around and help clean up after the rest of the family left. She'd explain to her parents that money was tight, and she wanted to build up her savings. She'd offer to pay a bit of rent, or help out around the house. Tidying up had never been her strong suit—that was more Kate's area—but she could learn. Or at least try.

She set her wineglass down, wondering if it would be that easy. Or if they'd ask how Jake's child support payments weren't enough, given what he was worth, and where she was spending the money. Even if they didn't say it, she knew they'd wonder if she was being irresponsible. The way she used to be.

"What about you, Charlotte?" her mother asked.

Her heart felt heavy as she considered her response. There were so many things she could say, but only one thing mattered, really. "I'm just grateful to be here."

No one said anything, but she knew that everyone at the table understood. It had been a rough year, for all of them in many ways, but this holiday, like Kate's upcoming wedding, sparked a new beginning.

She eyed her sister, thinking of the rough times they'd been through and how far they'd come. Everything had fallen into place . . . well, for Kate. As for herself, Charlotte was almost there. Soon she'd be finished paying for her mistakes. She'd move back in. Save some money. And then . . . And then things would be better.

"Since we're all gathered together, we have some news to share." Frank eyed Maura knowingly, and Charlotte shot her sister a look of alarm. No good news started with an announcement. Unless it was a marriage or a birth. And she very much doubted either of those were on the table for her parents.

"As you know, Grandma Daniels hasn't been doing well for a while," her father continued, and Charlotte murmured her sympathy, feeling all at once like a heel for panicking. Of course. Her grandmother had struggled with her health for a while now. It had been a source of stress for her father, who, as the only child, was forever hopping on a plane to tend to her or worrying about her from afar. Charlotte looked around the table, thinking it was a shame that Granny couldn't have joined them today.

She looked at her father, waiting for him to continue, wondering if he would announce that Granny was moving up to Rhode Island, to maybe live with them. She chewed her lip, selfishly wondering if that would impact her plans to move back in herself, but then decided that she and Audrey would just have to share her old bedroom while Granny took Kate's. Not ideal, but what was anymore?

"It's been a tough decision, but... Well, there's no easy way to say it. We've decided to move to Florida to be with her."

Leave Misty Point? Rhode Island had been their home forever.

Silence fell over the room, and all that Charlotte could hear was the pounding of her own heart. She looked at her mother, then Kate, who seemed almost more bewildered than she herself felt.

"The warm air is better for her, and she needs family right now."

But I need family right now! Charlotte wanted to cry. She reached for her water glass with a shaking hand and brought it to her lips. There was nothing she could say. Nothing that wouldn't sound completely selfish.

"When do you plan to go?" Kate finally asked, breaking the silence.

"Saturday," her mother replied, and Charlotte nearly choked on the water. She coughed, and her mother slid her a strange look. "We've been talking about it for a while, and there just never seemed to be a good time to bring it up. It won't be forever. We're keeping the house—"

Oh, sweet heaven. Thank goodness for small blessings. Charlotte closed her eyes, slumping back in her chair, feeling her panic subside.

"But we're renting it out."

"Will you be able to find a renter at this time of year?" Kate

asked. Everyone knew that Misty Point was a summer destina-
tion.

Her mother looked to Ellen, and Charlotte felt another
prickle of panic. Aunt Ellen was a Realtor. And she'd clearly
been let in on these plans long before everyone else had.
"Thanks to my sister's help, a couple came forward for a De-
cember first lease. We'd thought we'd go down south in January
after the wedding, but, well, we decided to move up our plans!"

The conversation seemed to go on and on but Charlotte
stopped listening. Her head felt murky and her heart was racing,
but despite all the questions she had and all the confusion, one
thing was very clear: she was in trouble. Again.

READING GROUP GUIDE

DISCUSSION QUESTIONS

1. As she plans Elizabeth's wedding, Kate works to hide her own heartbreak over Jake's betrayal. Talk about a time when you had to hide your feelings from a loved one. Why did you do it? Do you think it was the right decision?

2. Kate says about her dog Henry: "Henry deserved a life that was overflowing with love. Didn't everyone?" How does this belief illustrate Kate's general outlook? How do you think that outlook affects Kate's relationships? Do you think it made it easier for her to forgive Charlotte at the end of the book? Why or why not?

3. At one point, Kate notes that "thirty is a far cry from eighteen, when the world felt so full of promise." How does your outlook change as you grow older? Do the possibilities for your life really diminish, or does it just feel like they do? Have they for Kate? How does her journey throughout the book illustrate that?

4. Charlotte's "life hadn't taken such a traditional route, but was instead being taped and glued together piece

by piece." What's the value in living a glued-together life? What's the downside? Has your life followed a traditional route, or has it been more cobbled together?

5. When asked about whether or not he thinks that the town should undertake renovations on the Misty Point Lighthouse, Alec says yes, adding, "The only way for progress is to move forward, not stay rooted in the past." How does this apply to the way he lives his life? What about Kate? Do you believe that you can have progress without letting go of the past? Why or why not?

6. In the beginning of the book, Alec and Kate can't stand each other, and by the end they've fallen in love. How do you think they were able to overcome their initial bad first impressions? Has there been a time in your own life when you've realized that your first impression of someone was wrong? What made you realize that?

7. Both Alec and Kate struggle in their relationships with their siblings but ultimately find peace. How do the two very different sibling relationships illustrate the complicated ways that families interact emotionally?

8. At the end of the book, Kate forgives Charlotte, after hearing what really happened with Jake. Why do you think what seemed like an impossibility for Kate happened so easily in the end? Do you think that forgive-

ness lessens the pain caused by a betrayal or strengthens it? What makes forgiveness so hard?

A DISCUSSION WITH THE AUTHOR

1. This novel is a bit of a departure for you. What inspired you to write it?

Kate and Charlotte's conflict is such a big one that I wanted to explore their complicated relationship a bit more while still developing their individual story lines. A year had passed since they'd spoken, and yet they were both at a turning point in their lives that triggered mixed feelings. While this novel still has a romantic subplot, ultimately the center of the story is sisterhood.

2. Misty Point is such a lovely setting. Is it based on anywhere you've been in real life? Where did you get the idea for it?

Misty Point is loosely based on Newport, Rhode Island. I grew up in New England, and I will forever hold a fondness for it.

3. Kate is asked to forgive a major betrayal by her younger sister, Charlotte. Have you ever had to forgive someone when you didn't want to? How did that experience help shape the way you wrote about it here?

Every long-term relationship has its share of ups and downs—whether it's a marriage, a friendship, or, in this case, a family situation. I tried to be very careful with how I handled Kate's feelings toward Charlotte, because deep down, she loves her sister, but she also recognizes a side of her that she doesn't always like.

4. Two of the most important relationships in this book are sibling relationships: William and Alec, and Kate and Charlotte. Are either of these sibling relationships close to your own? What inspired the different conflicts these two sets of siblings experience? Do you think our siblings shape us as people?

In order for Kate to sympathize with Alec, I felt there was a need for commonality, which in this case was the complex relationship he had with his younger brother. For both Kate and Alec, they are the older sibling, the more responsible one, and they don't feel they have the same freedoms as their younger siblings do, which in time they start to resent a bit. It was through their sibling dynamics and conflicts that they were challenged to break away from their family roles and finally become the people they wanted to be.

5. One of the most fun parts about this novel is that it's centered around a wedding. Were there any similarities between your own wedding and Elizabeth and William's? Was it more fun to plan their wedding or your own? Tell us about your wedding.

I had a winter wedding, in a city, so there were very few similarities between my wedding and Elizabeth's. But I always love thinking of how my wedding day might have been in a different season or location, and by writing this book, I could do just that! And of course it's a little more fun to plan a fictional wedding, because you don't have to worry about actually organizing anything. You just get to sit back and enjoy your dream wedding, as a guest.